ABOUT

Thorne Moore lives in a north Pembrokeshire farm cottage on the site of a medieval manor, with an excellent view of the stars, but she grew up in Luton and studied history at Aberystwyth. Nine years later, after a spell working in a library, she returned to Wales, to run a restaurant with her sister, and a craft business making miniature furniture.

She took a law degree through the Open University, and occasionally taught genealogy, but these days, she writes, as she had always intended, after retiring from 40 years of craft work.

Besides her psychological crime and historical mysteries, including 'A Time for Silence' (finalist for the People's Book Prize and Bookseller Top Ten best seller), she also writes science fiction.

For some years she ran the Narberth Book Fair with fellow author Judith Barrow, and she is a member of Crime Cymru.

Published in Great Britain in 2022
By Diamond Crime

ISBN 978–1–7397448-1-6

Diamond Crime is an imprint of Diamond Books Ltd.

Thanks to

Judith Barrow for her help and encouragement

and

The Rhosygilwen writers' group
for the sailing jargon

Book design: jacksonbone.co.uk
Cover photograph: Dr Rebekah Moore, iStock
and image creation Lance Bellers

For information about Diamond Crime authors
and their books, visit:
www.diamondbooks.co.uk

To Becky, as always

FATAL
COLLISION

Thorne Moore

THORNE MOORE

PART ONE

1

She was out there, the woman, standing on the pavement, staring at my house. Staring with unmistakable hatred. The hood of her raincoat shielded most of her face, but I could feel that hatred coming at me in waves from eyes that burned out of the shadows.

I was convinced those eyes were pinning me in place, transfixed by my own inability to understand or get a grip on the situation. On any situation. What was I supposed to do? Challenge a woman for standing on a public pavement, doing nothing? She had the right to stand wherever she wanted.

But if she dared to move just a yard or two to the right, to the pavement at my gate, the one place on earth where no one had any right to stand, I would act. I would scream. I would erupt in a rage equal to her own. I could feel the scream building up, a sickness curdling within me. Was this going to go on all day?

Carla came striding through my gate and the spell was broken. Even the sight of a friend marching across that spot upset me, but she could have no idea. She nodded in an off-hand way at my sinister stalker, who hunched her shoulders and turned away, slouching down the road.

Only when I felt my breath burst out in an explosion of relief did I realise that I had been holding it. I hurried to open the door before Carla could knock.

"Nicki. How are you?" Carla wrapped care and sympathy round me.

I wasn't sure I could cope with it much longer. I had been swamped with kindness in the early days, so many people rallying round, and it had carried me through, saving me from a complete break-down. But now the love and compassion were beginning to have the reverse effect. Whenever I glimpsed possibilities beyond grief, sympathy reminded me of the thick black mud sucking me down.

"I'm okay," I said. *I'm fine* is what I would have said once, meaning nothing at all except *Hi, greeting's over so let's talk*. But these days, *fine* was so palpably untrue. "Coping. Come in, I'll make some coffee."

"How's Willow?"

Carla, my childless agent, had been playing affectionate aunt to my daughter from her birth, so she always asked after her. Usually meaning, how is Willow liking her new school, how did she do at the dentist, did she enjoy her birthday? Now it meant, is she managing to survive from day to day?

I swallowed and smiled. "Well, you know. We're getting through it."

"How did she cope with her exams?"

"They're finished. Last one a week ago, and how they went is anyone's guess. All I get is a shrug and 'Okay.' She's scarcely been out of her room since they began, but I don't know if she was in there revising or just... you know."

"Grieving."

"Yes. Anyway, they're done. I doubt if she'll get the results we were hoping for a year ago, but her Head says they make allowances for bereavement." I tasted bitter lemon, saying the word, an anodyne label, pigeonholing us with others in the same boat, identified and contained. But no one was in our boat. We were alone and adrift, Willow and me.

"I'm sure the universities will, too. She'll be fine." Carla put mugs ready as I fiddled with the cafetière.

"Maybe. We just have to wait." I braced myself on the draining board and looked out over the back garden, seeing nothing. "We'll both get an A star in that: waiting. We'll have practiced until we're perfect by the time this is all over. Not that it ever will be."

"It will be." Carla squeezed my arm. Perhaps she sensed that I'd reached saturation point with tender sympathy. She changed her tone, sounding cheerfully brisk as she carried the tray through to the living room. "I think it's time you stepped aside from that waiting game and started getting a bit more focused on ordinary life again."

"I tell myself that every day."

"So, I'm a shit for nagging, but you pay me to be a shit. I'm your business bitch. We cancelled last month's exhibition. No one expected you to cope with that. But do you really want me to cancel the November one as well? The gallery is very keen."

"I don't know. I haven't thought that far ahead. No, I suppose not. If I haven't kick-started myself again by then, I might as well give up. Go looking for a proper job."

She eyed me quickly. "You're not going to give up, are you? I want to know that, Nicki, before I head off across the pond. Say it. Say you're not going to give up."

3

"I'm not going to give up."

"Now say it as if you mean it."

"I am not going to give up."

"Good, because you have a proper job."

"If you say so. We both know that I've got by as an artist because Adam was willing to sacrifice his own dreams. Now I'm on my own…"

"You're not alone. Adam's sacrifice is your best reason to carry on. Not that it was a sacrifice. He was a brilliant teacher. Ask his students. And he hasn't left you stranded. I know it will take a while to get everything in order, but he arranged insurance and so on precisely so that, if anything happened to him, you could carry on."

"I know," I said, dully.

"So, now I'm going to be a heartless cow and start pushing you around. I've been looking after the crap for you. Now I'm going to look after you. From a purely business point of view, of course. You've got a market, Nicki. Your name is worth something, but people won't stay interested if you let yourself drift out of their line of vision. You must keep going." She sniffed as she poured our coffees. "Like I said, heartless cow. But I'm trying to think of your best interests."

"I know. You always do."

"Have you managed to start anything new?"

"Well…" I gave in. "No, not really. I can't – it's this place, I think. It's our home, it's where Adam still is, all I have left of him. But at the same time it's a nightmare. I go up to my studio and all I see is him standing there, head on one side, looking at my work. Or bringing me a coffee. Or massaging my shoulders. I'm paralysed. And his study… I can't open the door, because he'll be sitting there – no, that's the point. He won't be sitting there. He won't be anywhere. As for going out, some days…" I cradled my mug, preparing to say what I'd never said, even though my daughter had probably realised it. "Some days I can't bring myself to leave the house, because… The liaison officer, she's very efficient, assures me it's all cleaned up, they've even replaced the gate post, but all I see is It."

"I get it." Carla's knuckles were white around her mug. My agent was a purposeful, woman, always waving away objections, wonderfully bullish with shops and galleries and the press, but since my husband's death, I had discovered a different side to her. She'd been friend to both of us, from college, and she'd had her own grief for him to cope with, but she was strong enough to step back and be official crap-handler, while I reeled. My rock.

She looked around the room, summing up our home. Victorian semi, bought because the attic would make a studio for me and the back bedroom a study for Adam. Our creative Shangri-la. Perfect while we both shared it, but now…

"How about selling up, moving somewhere new?"

"Oh God." I groaned. "I don't know. Maybe one day. Half of me wants to run away from it all, but it would be like wiping it out. Wiping him out. I don't want to do that. Besides, I can't cope with anything that complicated just now."

"No, of course not. Okay, so how about just getting away, for a break. Somewhere with no memories, bad or good, to give you time to get your head straight."

"Maybe."

She stuck out her lower lip, swirling her coffee. "Would a tiny place do the two of you?"

"What do you mean?"

"Our weekender. Pembrokeshire. It's small, I mean seriously small, but it's got the essentials, even a bit of a summerhouse you could use as a studio, and it's away from all this. Totally away from just about everything, to be honest. Geoff and I won't be using it while we're Stateside, so if you fancied a complete change of scenery – it's on a clifftop, looking over Cardigan Bay."

"Sounds great, but – I don't know."

"It might be just what you need to jolt your inspiration back into life."

"Maybe. But it's not just me and my inspiration I have to think about."

"Discuss it with Willow. She'll want a summer holiday, won't she?"

* * *

Willow was of an age when she might well have had plans of her own, but not this year. We sat together at dinner time, contemplating a limp supermarket pizza. I'd lost the will to chop and mince and sizzle since Adam's death. All food had lost its flavour.

It didn't matter to Willow. She just pushed her food round her plate, no matter what I served. She was locked so tightly in herself I could no longer tell anything from her expression. I wanted to fight to get back the daughter I had known, but there were days when I couldn't drag myself out of my own pit, let alone tackle hers.

"How do you fancy going away for the summer?" I asked.

"Not Dorset," she said, flatly.

We'd had our favourite haunt in Dorset. Haunt was the word. Adam's ghost would be there, reminding us, every hour of every day. "No, not Dorset," I said. "Carla McDonald came to see me today. She suggested something."

"Yeah?" Willow started rolling a bit of melted cheese into a ball.

"You know she's off to America for a bit? She's got a holiday cottage in Wales, won't be needing it, so she offered it to us while she's away."

"A holiday cottage." No reaction.

"Pembrokeshire. By the sea. We could get away from here for a bit?"

"For how long?"

"As long as we want. All summer, until college starts – whatever you like. Carla will be gone for a whole year, so really whenever we want it."

Willow ripped up another piece of pizza and shrugged.

"I thought it would be good for us to have a break, a change of scenery. It was just a suggestion. Somewhere we've never been, so..."

A rattle at the front door made us turn towards the hall. Even now, I still expected to hear Adam's key in the lock. This wasn't a key though. It was the letterbox, and it was too late for the post. I got up and went to see. A folded sheet lay on the mat. I opened it. One word.

BITCH

Why? Everything inside me went tight, not with fear or anger or distress, but in a silent scream against everything in the whole bloody world. I flung the door open. My watcher was there, hurrying away, hood up. For a second she looked back, with a snarl of accusation.

How dare she! How dare she have crossed that spot, to do this!

"It's her again. That woman." Willow was at my shoulder. If I hadn't been blocking her way, she'd have been out, chasing my persecutor.

I pushed her back, shutting the door and crumpling the paper.

"What does it say?" demanded Willow.

"Nothing," I said, but she had the screwed-up ball out of my hand before I could stop her. "Bitch." Her shoulders shook with sobs.

I snatched the paper back and tore it into tiny pieces. Then I let the pieces fall and threw my arms round her. "Forget her, whoever she is, her and her stupid notes. Forget her."

Willow straightened, wiping the back of her hand across her nose. "How can we forget her when she's always there?" She sniffed again. "Let's go away. To this cottage thing. Anywhere. I don't want to be here anymore."

"All right then." My head was throbbing. I wanted air. Fresh air. Sea air. Ice-cold waves. "We'll go."

2

We stared in silence through the blurred windscreen at the cottage enveloped in pale mist, shifting in and out of focus as the fog drifted. It was low and squat, crouching into the grey-green turf, tiny windows cut deep into whitewashed walls, under a sea-grey, limed and sagging roof.

It was unreal.

Willow spoke at last. "Yeah."

"Yeah," I agreed.

"Looks like it might dissolve if we touch it."

"Let's see." I opened the car door and chill foggy air with a tang of salt flooded in. I got out. "Listen!" The clamminess of the mist couldn't disguise the ocean freshness that was welling up behind it, nor muffle the shivering, surging sough of waves on rocks, and the echoing cries of gulls. On a cliff top, Carla had said, and the ethereal sound told me it was true, even though I could barely see ten yards ahead.

Willow peered in through a window, while I dug out the key Carla had given me. "Ah. She said it gets stiff. Maybe we'll need a battering ram."

Willow applied her shoulder to the plank door and the warped wood finally agreed to budge. The interior felt chill and slightly damp, as any place would after standing empty for weeks, but other than that I had no complaints. If the cottage had been fitted out with tastefully contrived quaintness, Laura Ashley and willow pattern, I'd have felt an uncomfortable trespasser, but Carla had gone for casual comfort rather than style. There were open beams and deep slate windowsills with stoneware jugs, but this was just a holiday retreat for an active couple. A large sagging sofa, littered with random cushions, faced a woodburning stove in the inglenook, with logs piled ready. A dresser of bleached pine was loaded untidily with books. A thick rug in the centre left the flagstones bare around the edges to accommodate sodden boots and sou'westers and assorted nautical tackle. Geoff and Carla were keen sailors.

"Broadband." Willow brushed her fingers across the hub on a table in the corner. "Seems weird here. We ought to use owls."

"Not sure owls could cope with Carla's correspondence when she works here." I opened the door to the adjoining room. The bedroom with a big brass bed. Intended for two. A couple. Don't dwell on it.

The living room had open rafters, but there was a loft of sorts over the bedroom, a railed gallery. Reached by a sturdy ladder, it was a sleeping space rather than bedroom, low but sufficient to accommodate a futon and a three-drawer chest. Willow was already half-way up the ladder, something almost like a smile on her lips. "Great!"

"You really want to sleep up there? You won't even be able to stand up."

"Don't need to stand up." To demonstrate, she slithered over the top of the ladder and onto the futon.

"There's a sofa bed down here if you prefer."

"No way. This is cool."

"All right then." I returned to the bedroom. My private space, where I could be alone. There was a bleeding chunk of me that would always be alone now, even with Willow near. It hurt, but then being alone was all I wanted for now. I couldn't cope with people coming at me, not knowing what to say, or saying stupid things about nothing that mattered any more. I needed silence, to get to grips with who I was now.

There was a long spotted oval mirror on the door of the very retro wardrobe. I stared at my reflection, trying to connect with my own image. Was that really me? Who the hell was I?

Nicola Bryce.

Forty-four.

Artist. Used to be.

Daughter of Ron Bryce.

Mother of Willow.

Wife… widow of Adam Winters.

Woman who held her husband's head as he died in the gateway of our home.

Woman floundering in grief.

Woman waiting for closure, official and unofficial.

Woman who's going to have to move on, said Adam.

"But I'm not ready," I said aloud. "Don't push me, please."

He was a breath on my neck. *Not yet. When you are back in time and space, but not yet.*

Not yet because here, in this mysterious little hideaway lost in mist, separated from the rest of the world, time and reality were suspended. I peered out of the tiny window. Nothing but blurred shapes in the whiteness. The mist was an enchantment that would hold us safe for ever.

I returned to the living room and Willow looked down at me. "You okay?"

"Yes, I'm fine. We're quite lost here, aren't we?"

"Maybe we've crossed into another dimension. It's really weird this, in the fog. Might be anything out there. Dinosaurs."

"I hadn't thought of dinosaurs. There's a cliff, though. Carla didn't say how close it was."

"Let's go and see." She was down the ladder and flinging the front door open before I could object, letting the cold breath of fog pour in.

I wanted to be shut in, forever, but maybe the fog would do that, so I stepped out to join my daughter. The eerie sound of waves and gulls told us the cliff was somewhere behind the cottage.

"I'm not sure about this. We might go hurtling over the cliff before we even see it."

"It's not that bad," said Willow, and she was right, of course. I could see our car, twenty feet away. Just.

"We might have trouble finding our way back."

Willow was undeterred. She scooped up a handful of the gravel or grit that made up the parking space. "Breadcrumbs."

I laughed and followed her round the cottage, out across rough turf, dribbling a trail of grit at regular intervals.

"Keep talking," I said, "or I'll lose you."

"Yeah," said Willow, but we walked on in silence because talking seemed too intrusive. The mist was clustering diamonds on our hair, cold fingers on our faces. An advancing army loomed up before us and transformed into a hedge, wind-shorn and creaking. We followed it until a gap came in sight, barred by a crumbling grey stile. We looked out into nothingness. Just mist, a shifting illusion, a veil through which wafted booms of waves in deep caves and the incessant screeching of sea birds.

But nothing visible. Nothing real.

"It's so…" I stopped, the words draining out of me.

A shape was coming towards us out of the fog. Out of the sea. Out of the unreality. In the realm of ghosts, a ghost was there, a silhouette shrouded in silver grey, approaching in silence. My heart stopped. I put out my hand and Willow squeezed it so hard I thought my bones would break, but I welcomed the pain. Neither of us dared to breathe. Then the shape solidified. Not Adam, not a ghost, just a hiker, striding along, raising a hand in greeting as he passed.

"Afternoon."

I couldn't reply. I couldn't do anything. The apparition was gone. Willow's hand dropped from mine, but I could feel her shaking with silent sobs. I groped desperately in my pockets as we turned and walked blindly, in silence, the grit trail forgotten. Why was there never a tissue when I needed one?

The mist was breaking before us, the breeze whipping up, cutting through the fog. The cottage sprang into view, gaining in solidity with every step, a streak of blue opening above it. Hedges appeared around us.

"Come on, let's unpack. I need a coffee." If I concentrated on the utterly prosaic, would that help?

It didn't. Willow joined me in the narrow galley kitchen at the back of the cottage, ransacking cupboards for mismatched mugs and kettles and tins. It was a kitchen fitted out with the bare essentials but that was fine. The microwave would do for me.

"Where did I stash the coffee?"

"Under the passenger seat, so we'd find it easily."

Yes, I'd said that as we'd stowed our luggage into the boot as quietly as possible, five thirty that morning. A secret silent get-away. Our stalker had been known to be in position before seven and I wanted us gone before she could catch us escaping her clutches.

We'd done it. We'd fled and now we were free. Safe in a magical shield of mist that no one could penetrate. But the mist was dissipating, leaving us vulnerable to who knew what.

"I'll go and…"

A loud, authoritative knock on the front door froze us both. Ghosts don't knock so who? No. It wasn't possible. Who knew we were here? No-one except Carla who was in America. Our stalker couldn't have followed us. She wouldn't know. She couldn't know.

Willow was white-faced, staring at me, the same horrified thought reflecting in her eyes. Then she licked her lips, pulled herself together and gripped my arm to reinforce me.

"Yes. Stupid," I said, as the knock repeated. Bracing, I returned to the living room, Willow still gripping my arm, my heart pounding as I opened the door.

A man stood there. Big. Very big. Curly greying hair. Friendly features. Inquisitive eyes. He touched his brow in a casual salute. "Mrs Winters, is it? Harry Roberts. Mrs McDonald said you'd be coming. Asked me to see to the gas for you. Saw your car pass."

"Oh." A giant balloon of anxiety deflated inside me. Willow released my arm. I managed to say "Thank you. Yes. I hadn't even thought about gas."

"Runs the cooker, that's all. You'll be wanting to cook, I expect."

"Yes. I suppose." Eventually. One day I'd have to move on from ready meals. "Please. Show me what's what. Would you like a cup of tea while you're here?"

"Oh, well, that's a nice thought, but I'll just fix the gas and leave you to it for now. I expect you've got a lot of unpacking to do."

I followed him out into the mist. "You saw us pass? The fog was so thick I could barely see a thing. It took us an age to find the turning."

"Heard your car pass. Only one house along here, apart from the big one." We were rounding the side of the house and Harry Roberts rubbed his hands in readiness as he approached a pair of sinister red cylinders, standing to attention by the side wall, next to a couple of dustbins.

"You've got a full tank spare, so you shouldn't have to worry," he said, as he manhandled controls on the gas.

"Right. Thanks."

"There. Bit of a holiday, is it? Mrs McDonald said she didn't know how long you'd be here."

"Yes. I don't know either, to be honest. A couple of months maybe."

"You let me know if you need anything. Ask for Harry Roberts down at the quay. They'll know where to find me. Well, there you go then, Mrs Winters."

He held out a large hand. I hesitated. Despite a belated marriage certificate, I had always kept my maiden name, Bryce, my professional name, but now... Now I wanted Adam's name. Winters. All that I had left of him. Yes, I was Mrs Winters. I grasped the proffered hand and shook it. "Thank you. You're very kind."

I watched him stride off. The fog had lifted, leaving shreds of unattached spectres floating this way and that. There was a battered truck parked beyond our car. I heard the driver's door clunk shut, the engine cough into life and the truck rumbled off, its wheels bumping and grinding on the rough track.

A landscape lay bald and visible before me, scrubby woodland, the blue dip of a valley and distant hills. No more room for unreality, the magic was destroyed. I wandered back to the rear of the cottage, desperate to recapture the illusion of mist that must still lurk on the cliffs.

But even there, the mystery was shattered. The last of the mist disintegrated before my eyes... and where one illusion had bewitched me, another burst out in its place: the sea, under a cobalt sky, a dazzling expanse of ultramarine, sparkling and flashing with the light of a million suns and moons and stars. The light of a limitless universe, folding around me.

3

"It's fine." After a night testing it, Willow was perfectly relaxed about the futon.

"Did you really sleep okay?"

"Yeah. Better than you."

"Oh God, did I wake you?"

"No. Not really. It doesn't matter."

I had tossed and turned. Maybe I cried. I usually did. Maybe I should start taking the sleeping pills I'd been prescribed. And there was no point worrying about the futon. Willow was young. She'd managed on far worse at sleepovers without any ill effects.

She drained the last of the milk onto her cereal.

"Don't I get any for my coffee?"

She shook out a couple of drops into my mug. "You like it black sometimes."

"Just as well. But I suppose we'd better go shopping, get some basics in. Can't live on cup-a-soup alone."

"Right," said Willow. "Can I drive?"

She'd obtained her provisional licence as soon as she turned seventeen, and she'd got as far as failing her test for the first time, but her father's death had intervened and the second had been abandoned. She hadn't shown any desire to be back at the wheel until now, and I had no wish to encourage her. When you've witnessed a speeding car mow down your loved one, you become neurotically conscious that every vehicle was a murder weapon.

"We'll walk," I said. "Find this path that Carla told me about. She said the village was less than a mile away."

"A mile!"

"That's nothing. Come on."

Armed with carrier bags and cagoules, because the odd grey cloud persisted in challenging the sun, we strolled down to the old stile and surveyed the scene that had been hidden by fog on our arrival: a footpath, trodden into bare earth, fringed by swathes of gorse and burnet rose, campion and tall daisies. Beyond it was the true cliff edge, a hundred-foot drop and an eternity of blue. To our left the cliff thrust out in a craggy promontory, its crumbling walls peppered with white birds and fading clumps of flowers. To our right, the path curved round and down into the inlet of Tregelli, our nearest village.

Tregelli had been so completely engulfed in fog when we'd driven through it the day before that I hadn't really taken it in at all, just an impression of looming houses and unexpected jutting walls. In clear light it transformed into a little harbour settlement at the head of a narrow creek, where a curving seawall sheltered a couple of dozen yachts, motorboats and dinghies. As we clambered down a flight of muddy plank-edged steps past a row of cottage gardens to the harbour, I could see the whole village cupped in a valley.

No supermarket here, just a sprawling pub, café, gallery, and a modest village store that doubled as a post office. There were maybe a dozen old fishermen's cottages and a couple of boat sheds clustered around the stone quay at the head of the inlet. A stream seeped out under a bridge onto a pebbled beach and beyond it newer houses climbed up the gorse-speckled hillside.

I was quietly relieved that Tregelli was no bigger. If I had to start confronting the world, this was a stage I could probably manage. The shop had a reasonable selection of fresh fruit and vegetables, as well the normal dry goods, and there were packs of meat from a local farm in the freezer, among the oven chips, burgers and fishfingers, so we wouldn't starve.

With our laden bags, we glanced in the window of the little gallery.

"Is that one of yours?" asked Willow, critically eying a picture within, a study in greens and greys. "It looks like one of yours."

"It is. Of course it would be. It's Carla's local gallery, after all, and she never misses a trick, does she? I should pay more attention when she shows me the sales paperwork." I was always too much the artist to bother with the nitty gritty. Anything that Carla hadn't managed, Adam had dealt with. Accounts and rates and bank statements and bills. From now on, the dreary nitty gritty was going to descend on me. I wasn't ready for it, but I wasn't ready to return to my artistic zone either. I was at a crossroads. Dangling on a gibbet.

I turned away.

"Aren't we going in?" asked Willow. "Not going to introduce yourself?"

"I will, I suppose. Just, not now. Not the right time."

"Okay." She didn't push it.

We walked on, along the quay, to a pile of lobster pots around a bollard, against which a chalked sign was propped, advertising boat trips with the promise of seals and dolphins, Monday to Saturday. The boat in question, the Lotte Lenya, was tethered to the bollard, an unglamorous motorboat with a pervading whiff of fish.

"You fancy a boat trip?" I asked, thinking of it only as a distraction from painting. Or rather, from not painting.

"Don't mind."

"Is that a 'don't mind, I'd quite like it,' or a 'don't mind if I absolutely must?'"

"Whatever. Don't mind. Sounds okay."

"Right! Well…"

"I'll be going at midday," said a voice behind me. I turned to find Harry Roberts standing there, hands in his pockets, sturdy, weathered, tanned by sun and wind, the same navy sweater, grubby cords and rubber boots he'd worn the day before. It was obvious now that he was a fisherman. He just needed a cap and a Popeye pipe.

"You run the trips?" I asked.

"I do. You fancy joining me?"

"Maybe not today. I need to get this shopping home. There's frozen stuff. Sorry."

"You can leave that at the Bell," said Harry. "Chloe will put it in the freezer for you."

I glanced at the chalk sign again, with a frown. "Twenty pounds a head?"

Harry twitched a smile. "In your case, twenty for the both of you."

Willow was already heading for the pub, decision made, so why was I resisting? "If you think the landlady won't mind."

"Chloe? Oh no." Harry was guiding me firmly to the Bell.

I didn't like pubs. I wanted all drinkers lined up against a wall and shot – at least when I wasn't self-medicating on gin – and I wanted all pubs demolished, but it seemed I'd have to make an exception for this one. Under the swinging sign of a ship's bell bright against a stormy sky, the low door stood open, and a murmur of voices accompanied the aroma of beer, chips and shellfish emanating from the dark interior.

Still only mid-morning but there were already customers. A couple were studying a map by the massive-beamed fireplace over cups of coffee, and, at another table, a biker in leathers was tucking into a cooked breakfast. At the long gleaming bar, encrusted with ships' carvings, three men who looked like city gents on a yachting holiday were chatting to the landlady, a woman with apricot hair and hooped earrings. She waved the men aside in a familiar manner and smiled at us, brows raised. "Morning, Harry."

He leaned an elbow on the bar and planted one boot on the brass rail at the base as if it were his natural station. "Morning, Chloe. Got Mrs Winters here. Staying up at Carregwen, The McDonalds" place."

"Ah! So you're Carla's friend. The…"

I interrupted. "Her friend, yes. Nicki." What had she been about to say? The bereaved? The widow?

She beamed. "Heard all about you."

"Thought they'd come out with me in the boat," said Harry. "Any chance of keeping their shopping for them?"

"Oh sure."

"Some of it in the freezer?"

"Anything for you, Harry."

"That's my girl." He passed our carriers over the counter. "There you go. All sorted. Now, why don't you stay, have a drink, wait here until the boat's ready."

Willow was leaning over the bar, studying the range of alcopops and continental lagers. I wasn't having that. "Could we have coffee? Two Cappuccinos?"

"Coming right up." Chloe busied herself at an impressive coffee station. "So, are you staying long?"

"We haven't really decided. Carla's letting us have the cottage while they're in America."

"Lovely. Your first time in Tregelli, is it?"

"First time in Pembrokeshire."

"You've got it at the best time. Quiet. Wait till the school hols start and you won't be able to move." She loaded a tray with cups and the obligatory little biscuits. "Anything else?"

"No, thanks." I paid up and took the tray to a table by a window overlooking the quay.

"Coffee!" said Willow, following me.

"Yes, coffee. It's only eleven."

"I've seen you drinking gin in the morning."

I winced. "Not anymore, I promise."

"Not complaining. I mean, it's… you know."

"Yes. We both know, don't we." I squeezed her hand.

She stared for a moment at the dissolving heart on her coffee. "Do you ever talk to him?" She looked up at me.

23

"Dad. Do you? Sometimes I think he's there. Do you ever think you see him?"

"All the time." I reached around the table and hugged her.

"Not me being mad then?"

"We're probably both a bit mad. Not surprising, is it? Anyway, maybe we see him because he's here. A part of us. Always will be."

She nodded.

I gazed out of the window, blinking away the tears that blurred the sparkle of sunlight on the water in the harbour. "Adam would have loved it here."

"He would!" said Willow, fiercely, as if she'd just been waiting for permission to talk. It seemed to matter enormously to both of us that he would have approved of our retreat. "That's what I thought as soon as I saw Carregwen. Like he was there, waiting for us. In the mist."

I stroked her hair, not sure what to say.

"When I can't sleep, I talk to him," she said.

"Does he talk back?"

"Sometimes."

"It's part of the healing, maybe. Preparing us to move on."

"I don't want to move on, not away from him."

"It won't be away from him. He'll stay as long as you need him. Even when you go to college, Exeter or Newcastle, he'll be there."

She was silent for a moment, shifting away from me. "Don't know."

"He will."

"I mean, I don't know that I want to go any more."

"Why? Do you think you messed up your exams? You won't get your grades? I'm sure…"

"No, I mean I don't know that I want to go to University. It's sort of pointless, isn't it? What's it all for?"

"What's it for? You know what it's for."

"Oh yeah, sure, it would mean prospects and all that. You want me to get a good job, earn loads of money."

"That's not what it's about. When did I ever say that education was about getting a job or earning money? It's about stretching yourself, discovering who you are, what your own potential is."

"I don't need to go to college to do that. I could stay here, get a job."

"Do you seriously imagine there'd be jobs here? Doing what? Come on, Willow. You can't just give up now. You know your father would say…"

"Don't you dare use Dad! I'm not going to listen to you."

My heart lurched at her anger. "Listen to him then. Because you do, don't you?"

She was silent.

"I'm sorry," I said. "I don't want to force you to do anything. But don't make any hasty decisions, please." I wiped my cheeks hurriedly, and glanced around. Chloe, the landlady, pretending to polish the bar, was watching us, all ears. I whispered, "I think we've provided enough entertainment here, don't you?"

Willow forced a smile, and swigged back her coffee. "Yeah. Let's go."

"Enjoy the boat trip," said Chloe, raising a hand in farewell, as we headed for the door. "Lunches served all day!"

4

We sauntered back along the quay towards the fishing boat, where a trio of fellow trippers were waiting – a young couple and a solitary birdwatcher.

The couple smiled, ready to launch into the statutory conversational gambits.

"Let's hope we're lucky with the weather. You never know, do you. But fingers crossed."

I smiled and nodded and said yes and no. The birdwatcher said nothing, dismissing us while he made a fuss of unpacking his binoculars, camera and notebook. Then our captain arrived.

He nodded at us before addressing the other passengers. "Harry Roberts. And this 'ere's Rhys Hughes."

This 'ere was a young lad, fifteen at most, who had a deafening lack of interest in us, though he spared one slightly less dismissive glance at Willow. Harry pocketed twenty pounds apiece from the other passengers, and then mine, sizing us up with a calculating eye before doling out life jackets. Rhys, who had already dropped heavily into the boat, stuck out his arm as support while we scrambled on board, his eyes fixed on his feet.

"Right then," said Harry, once we were all safely stowed on the hard benches to his satisfaction, and the engine was chugging like a dog waiting patiently for walkies. He glanced at Rhys, who wasn't looking.

"Rhys!" He nodded at the rope tethering us to the quay and, with a great sigh, Rhys leaned over and cast off.

The Lotte Lenya steered a genteel course between buoys, through the centre of the harbour, anchored boats tilting and curtseying to either side of us. The swell was like a cradle gently rocking. Then we came to the sheltering sea wall, steered gracefully round it out onto the open ocean and into a brisk wind. Forget the cradle. The Lotte Lenya was rising and falling like a rollercoaster. My stomach lurched this way and that as waves smacked into us. The young woman shrieked at the shock of it, and her partner looked grave, his knuckles whitening as he gripped the side. The birdwatcher merely grunted annoyance that he couldn't focus clearly enough. I was clinging quietly to my seat, but Willow, to my surprise, was on her feet, against orders, standing with piratical abandon, swaying with the boat's motion and looking as if she'd been born to seafaring. Maybe the confidence in her stance transmitted to me. The shock subsided as I realised the swell wasn't disturbing me. The young woman continued to give an occasional fearful cry during the voyage, but I had discovered sea legs and my stomach stopped rebelling. I pulled up my jacket collar against the invigorating chill of the wind and the salt spray and smiled at Willow. We would be all right.

Fatal thought. The familiar anguish began to seethe inside me. All right? How could we ever be all right in a future that offered only emptiness, grief and pain? As the Lotte Lenya chugged away from land, I found myself urging it to keep going, out to that indefinite space where the sea melded into the haze of the sky and I would be nothing at all.

I dug my nails into my palms. I had to stop succumbing to these violent swings between determination and despair. I had my daughter to think about. A daughter so emotionally shaken by her father's death that she was thinking about giving up on her future. I couldn't let that happen. I had to be strong, for her. Determination would have to win. I watched the water surging past our boat, muscular mermaid tails refusing to halt their flow. I needed to drink in that refusal, let it flood my veins.

You hang on in there, said Adam.

"Right." I looked around, forcing a smile at my companions. Rhys was still glowering at his feet, and Harry, in the wheelhouse, glanced back at him as he steered, raising his eyes in silent exasperation. The young couple, still clinging on for dear life, were pointing out a flash in the far distance.

"Now that," said Harry, turning to address us, "that's Strumble Head lighthouse. Isn't that right, Rhys?"

"Yeah," said Rhys, lethargically fraying a bit of rope,

"And this here headland is Pendiawl. Devil's headland. Dangerous rocks under here. Rhys will tell you about them."

"There's rocks," Rhys grunted, with a shrug.

Harry rolled his eyes again. I smiled in sympathy and Harry flashed a quick grin, then proceeded to give us the tale of a ship that had run aground on the rocks in a long-ago storm. The villagers of Tregelli on the clifftop, could only watch as the crew and passengers perished, all except one dark figure who appeared to walk on the crashing waves and disappear into a cave, never to be seen again. But no creatures had ever entered that cave since.

He told a good story, did Harry, but it was obvious he would rather be looking to the boat, leaving the entertainment to his mate. His mate wasn't playing.

I decided Harry deserved a helping hand. The high cliffs, rearing up to our left as we chugged westward, were riddled with gaping black mouths, the waves booming deep within. "I bet all these caves have stories," I said, demanding Rhys's attention.

He gave another shrug and looked out to sea. "No. Not really."

"No pirates or smugglers?"

"No."

"But I bet there are seals."

Another shrug. "Sometimes."

I could tell by the shift of Harry's shoulders than he had decided to throw in the towel and leave the boy to his sulk. The paying customers still wanted their money's worth, though, so he steered and talked at the same time.

Tales of smugglers, probably inspired by my suggestion. Tales of Black Bart the pirate, of severed heads entertaining men for a hundred years, of lands lost beneath the waves and sunken forests and mystical islands, of submarines dragging unsuspecting fishing boats down into the deeps.

"What about that?" I asked, pointing to a short concrete quay in a narrow inlet, expecting it to be identified as a smuggler's retreat, with stories of battling excise men. Its silent shadows begged for such a story.

Harry peered at it, frowning, his powers of invention flagging at last. "Oh that. Just a private landing site."

The birdwatcher diverted him with a sudden surge of energy as a black spot hovered over the cliffs.

"Peregrine falcon," said Harry and the birdwatcher in one breath. It was all serious information from then on – geological, historical, economic and ornithological. Harry Roberts knew his own seas and all that dwelt therein. We didn't see seals, there'd be more later he said, but we saw a million razorbills, guillemots, oystercatchers and kittiwakes, all of which I would have called seagulls, and a couple of choughs that I would have called crows. I decided to search the dresser for bird books when I got home, to amend my ignorance.

Finally, we glimpsed something out at sea that Harry identified as a pod of dolphins, though all I saw was a hint of darkness on the waves. What delighted me far more was the sight of Willow, diligently listening, craning to see everything with binoculars that Harry had passed her, drinking it all up like a parched traveller at an oasis. My daughter, brought back to life by a boat trip.

At last, Harry steered the Lotte Lenya back into Tregelli harbour, and we slowed to a crawl, edging into position beside the quay.

The tide had ebbed while we were out. The quay loomed over us, accessible by iron rungs clamped to the stonework. Rhys was up and out, escaping from the boat as if the Devil of Pendiawl were after him. He stood, impatient and unhelpful, as we struggled out of our lifejackets and clambered up the ladder, Harry giving us a helping hand from behind. The birdwatcher hurried away. The young couple twittered thanks before heading for the Bell, thronging now with lunchtime customers, noisy even from a hundred yards away.

Harry climbed up after Willow, the last to leave the boat. "You two okay?"

"Yes," I said. "Thanks. It was therapeutic."

Harry smiled, his eye on Willow. "Reckon you took it all in?"

Willow shrugged, not dismissively but confidently. "More or less."

"A pity your helper wasn't quite so enthusiastic." I turned to see what had become of Rhys. He had loped off towards a woman who was waiting, arms folded, along the quay.

"My nephew." Harry shook his head. "I thought he'd like to earn a bit of pocket money, but he's not keen. Wants to be a rock star, not a sailor. Now you…" He stepped back to look Willow over. "I reckon you could do it."

I wasn't prepared for the speed at which Willow jumped in with "Sure. Okay. Tomorrow?"

Harry raised his hands. "Not tomorrow. Monday. See how we go, eh?"

Willow gave me a triumphant smile. No jobs here, I'd said, and she'd walked straight into one. For a few summer weeks, though, that was all. I hoped she appreciated that.

Harry was gazing along the quay at the waiting woman. She raised a hand in greeting. He raised his in reply.

"Your sister?" I asked.

"Yes. Siân. Keeping her eye on Rhys. She fusses, but once you've lost one child…"

"Oh!" I saw Willow freeze and knew I was doing the same.

Harry's brows knit anxiously. "Sorry?"

"No. It's just… We know what it's like, losing… My husband died a few months ago."

"Three months!" said Willow, fighting the words. "One week and three days!"

"Oh, good God," said Harry. "I'm sorry for that. Mrs McDonald said you'd had problems, needed to get away, but I didn't know."

"It's all right. But it's all still so raw. I can understand just how your sister must be feeling if her child died."

"Ah. No. I'm sorry, I put it badly. Gaynor just took off. Gone to London, we're told. Back in February. Bit of a shock for Siân, for all of us. Weren't expecting it. Now she's worried about Rhys going the same way. Different with boys though. They don't get in the same sort of trouble."

"Ah." That sort of trouble, did he mean? Was it still a problem in this day and age? I thought of Willow, of her 'in trouble.' That would be something to face, but not a disaster. If she disappeared from my life, that would be the real tragedy. I turned to look at Harry's sister again, but she was trudging away, Rhys in reluctant tow.

5

I stood on the quay and watched my daughter and Harry welcome the latest batch of tourists to the Lotte Lenya. Willow might have been doing it for years instead of one week. Once the last passenger was settled, she turned to give me a languid wave. Perched at the prow, she seemed suddenly so alone, despite the passengers babbling in front of her. Even from this distance, I could recognise the cloud of introspection enclosing her, though probably no one else would notice it.

She'll be okay, said Adam.

"Says who?" I muttered under my breath.

Says me. She's searching for a way through. She'll find it.

"Will I, though?"

Yes. You will. That's an order.

"Oh well, thanks for telling me."

I watched the boat chug out of the harbour, Willow already addressing her audience, arm raised to point out something about the sea wall. Harry Roberts would look after her. He probably knew more about our situation now than anyone except Carla. I couldn't decide if it felt intrusive or reassuring. Best to settle for reassuring. If my stalker tracked us down here, Harry was just the person to have around. But I'd almost stopped dwelling on my phantom tormentor. She hadn't found us. We were free.

The Lotte Lenya was out of sight now. Still I stood.

That gallery isn't going to go away if you stay here long enough, said Adam. *Get to it, woman.*

"Bully," I said, reluctantly turning towards the gallery. In her last skype call from New York, Carla had made me promise to introduce myself. I took a deep breath, chin up, and went in.

"The owner's called Yvonne Wright," Carla had said, and there was Yvonne, in floating silks and clusters of rings, a Bohemian uniform, advancing on me with a smile the moment I entered.

"Hello. I'm Nicki Bryce. Friend of Carla McDonald? You have one of my pictures on display." I nodded at the canvas.

Yvonne's eyes widened in enthusiasm. "Nicki Bryce!" She grabbed my hand and shook it. "Fabulous. I'm an enormous admirer, you know, and so are some others in the area." She raised a pencilled eyebrow archly. "We have another round the corner, although it's already sold. Carla often brings me two or three of your works and they always create excitement."

I smiled. Bemusement was a more normal reaction.

"I'm so glad I got to meet you personally," said Yvonne. "Are you staying at the cottage?"

"Yes. Carla's given me free rein while she's away."

"Wonderful! Well, anything you produce, you know, if you want a ready market. Usual terms of course."

"Thank you," I had no idea what the usual terms were, since Carla always handled such matters for me. I really should ask her about them when we next spoke. "When I have something finished, I'll bring it along."

"Wonderful!"

"They do sell, then?"

"Oh yes! Not to your average holidaymaker maybe. But we have some serious collectors, even out here in the sticks. Oliver Wyatt." She almost whispered the name, as if it wouldn't do to take it in vain. "Definitely your market. Big money." She rubbed finger and thumb together. "I mean seriously mega money. Millionaire doesn't begin to cover it. Keeps me afloat, to be honest."

From a financial point of view, it was encouraging that a hard-headed businesswoman lurked behind Yvonne Wright's arty front, one who knew how to sell my work. If I could just get round to producing any. So far, I had only managed to dump my gear and set up an easel in the tiny barn that Carla had designated my studio. I was still waiting for inspiration.

Promising that I would bring her something, I went off to grab a bite to eat at the Bell, sitting at one of the tables outside, as I watched the Lotte Lenya finally hove back into view. She moored and Willow leaped up onto the quay, stooping to help the passengers climb out in her wake. I smiled, watching her pocket several tips. Another hard-headed businesswoman. She looked good. Liberated. Fair hair tied back off her face, which was still too pale for my liking, but there was a hint of colour in it now. My mermaid.

A car screeched.

A car screeched, a crash and Adam was flying through the air. Screams. Blood.

I couldn't breathe. I had to breathe. I gripped the planks of the table till the pain in my fingers forced air back into my lungs. How long was this going to go on? How long was every screech of brakes going to have me reliving Adam's death? I felt the bile rise, clutched the table again and steadied myself.

The culprit down in the carpark was a shimmering ice-blue sports car, with open top and leather seats, demanding to be envied. People obligingly turned to look. A young man sprang out. Dressed in jeans and t-shirt, but probably both were designer brands. He walked as if they were. Halfway to the Bell, he glanced around and changed his mind, heading instead towards Willow. The tiger in me began to growl. He had already become a demonic threat in my mind, and now he was homing in on my daughter. He was tall, slim, confident and wickedly good-looking, guaranteed to raise the hackles of any protective mother and the interest of any innocent daughter.

I had always given Willow free rein to organise her ever-changing cast of boyfriends. None of them had had proved to have staying power when Adam died and Willow started locking herself in her room. Just too diffident, probably, but there was nothing diffident about this one as he strutted towards Willow. At eighteen, my daughter might be considered an adult, but she was still hurting and vulnerable and I had no idea how she would react to a full-frontal attack, so I rose and went over to meet her and the young man who was very obviously chatting her up.

Willow saw me coming and shrugged, meaning… I wasn't sure, but she didn't look desperate to be rescued.

Some boys reacted with tongue-tied embarrassment or defensive hostility to the parents of girls they fancied. Not this one. He was leaning on the bollard next to her, and glanced round casually in my direction, self-assurance oozing from every pore.

"Hi, Mum," said Willow, airily.

"Mrs Winters?" said the young man.

"She's Nicki Bryce," said Willow.

"My mistake. Sorry. Mrs Bryce. How do you do?" He offered his hand. "Alex Wyatt. I hear you're staying in the area for the summer."

"For a while, yes. I've just heard the name Wyatt. Is Oliver Wyatt your father?"

"You know the Boss, do you?" He used the term with good-natured irony.

"Know of him – and only that he's bought some of my paintings."

"Sure, he's quite a collector. Of course! I remember the name now. You're the artist. Great. Very nice to meet you, Mrs Bryce." Alex Wyatt was a young man who knew how to hold his own in any company, a skill probably honed at great cost by a school for the entitled. "You don't mind if I invite your daughter for a drink, I hope?"

"If she doesn't mind."

"I don't," said Willow, with a slightly challenging glance at me before sweeping young Mr Wyatt off towards the pub.

"Are you driving?" I called after them.

He smiled back at me. "Just a non-alcoholic lager."

Liar, I thought. He had charm. I resented him directing it at my daughter, but did over-privilege and squealing brakes really make him a villain? If I interfered at this stage, Willow would never forgive me.

"She's off with young Wyatt then," said Harry, who had finished tidying up the boat. He gazed after them inscrutably.

"I hope she shares the tips with you," I said.

He grinned. "She earns them."

Behind him, I could see Harry's sister Siân approaching, arms folded. She was a big-boned woman, strong but with an air of weariness, nodding to me with an expression of muted sympathy.

"Mrs Winters, you'll be."

"Yes."

"Siân Hughes. Harry told me about your loss. Sorry to hear it. I lost my Gwyn seven years back. A terrible thing, losing your husband."

"Yes." My throat tightened as I fought to still the instant trembling. A terrible thing, especially when it wouldn't stop replaying, again and again in my head.

She unfolded her arms to grip one of mine. "Any time you need to talk, get it off your chest, you come and find me. Harry will tell you where. Up at Maes Waun. Any time, you hear?"

"Thank you," I said, because it was all I could say. She had opened all the rawness of the wounds again.

6

I'd walked to the village again, supposedly because we needed a bit of shopping, but really in order to put off painting. I had daubed some paint on a canvas, but my mind was still refusing to open itself to ideas. I couldn't spend all day cleaning brushes as an excuse for getting nowhere.

The Lotte Lenya was just disappearing around the harbour wall as I arrived, and I had a moment of panic, picturing Willow sailing away from me. What if she sailed away forever? Adam was sailing from me...

Blinking back tears, I refocused. There was Harry's sister walking, heavy-footed, up what passed for Tregelli's high street. Any time you need to talk, she'd said and though I instinctively recoiled from the thought, I found myself longing for it too. Maybe she was right. Maybe I did need to let it all pour out. Everyone had recommended counselling, but I'd had no wish, to talk about Adam and the accident with some professional stranger. Mrs Hughes, though, was a woman who had been through it herself. She would understand.

On impulse, I hurried after her. "Mrs Hughes? Hello."

She turned, dull eyes brightening as she saw me. "Mrs Winters. Hello love. How are you keeping?"

"Okay. It's Nicki, by the way. I was just wondering if you had time for that talk you offered." I hesitated. She looked exhausted. "But maybe not now. You're tired. You must want to get home."

"Oh, I'll be all right, nothing that a cup of tea won't fix. And call me Siân. Come on, walk with me."

"Let me carry one of those, then." I took one of the bulky bags that were weighing her down.

"That's kind. Heavy, mind."

"What's in it?"

"Just cleaning stuff. Sometimes they've run out of what I need, so I bring my own."

"Is there much cleaning work around here?" I'd thought of it in terms of cities with office blocks.

Siân snorted. "Enough, with a couple of days at the supermarket. I do the school, of course, and the rest is houses. Most of them's holiday cottages now. I've got my work cut out this week, getting them ready for the hols."

"Of course. You don't clean for the McDonalds, do you?" I wondered if I had done her out of some employment at our cottage.

"Carregwen, is it, where you're staying? No, Mrs McDonald's never had me in."

"Well, it's only the size of a postage stamp."

"Nice woman though, for a…" She paused.

"English?" I suggested.

She gave a deep-throated chuckle. "They're not all bad."

"I hope I'm not."

"Good God no." We had turned up a side lane between garages and workshops on the drabber landward side of the village. "Here we are." Siân nudged me into a cul-de-sac of former council houses. "Number Two." At the front door she dropped her bag on the step while she fumbled for a key. "Just get the kettle on and I can put my feet up for an hour."

Five minutes later, she had me settled in a great corduroy armchair, clasping a garibaldi and a heavy mug of mahogany tea.

"Well." Siân planted herself firmly on the sofa opposite, legs apart, leaning forward. "So tell me about it. You lost your husband." She shook her head as she took a gulp of tea.

My mouth dried. From being impatient to talk, suddenly I couldn't. I sipped. "Tell me about yours."

"Gwyn? Oh, accident at work. He was a builder, see. Scaffolding came down. Died three days later. Terrible days. I still feel empty inside, thinking about it. And it shook the children so bad. Only seven, Rhys was. And Gareth supposed to be preparing for his GCSEs. Mind, he was a wonder. Don't know what I'd have done without him, to be honest."

It was terrible but, because it was her tragedy and not mine, I could allow myself to respond instead of freezing up inside. "An accident at work? That's awful. Was anyone held responsible?"

"Well." She shrugged; a battle lost. "There was talk, but nothing happened. Boss went bankrupt."

"Oh God, and you were left with the children and no money, I suppose."

"Pff." Her response said it all. Adam's death hadn't left me destitute. Money wasn't a major issue, but for Siân Hughes, it had been a big fat spider sitting on her grief from the start. "Couldn't pay the mortgage. Repossessed. At least we weren't thrown out. Mr Wyatt bought it, kept us on as tenants."

Wyatt again. "That was good of him," I said cautiously.

"Hmm. Yes. He owns two others here in Maes Waun. Him or his company. I think he'll have the lot, if they can be persuaded to sell, and then God knows what. Redevelopment probably. Anyway, it's kept a roof over our heads so far. Well." She looked at me hard. "What happened with your man?"

"I…" Where to begin? With me being irritable because we were out of milk and I was in the middle of cooking, and it was his fault for using so much on his cereal? "He went to buy some milk from the Spar round the corner. He was coming back, almost opposite the house. A man called Denis Anderson came speeding down our road, blind drunk. He clipped a cyclist, swerved, mounted the pavement, and struck Adam. Adam was thrown across the road, hit his head on our gatepost, died before the ambulance got there."

I spelled out the bald facts as the only way to put it into words. Like a newspaper report, it set it at one remove. Almost. Even telling it like that, I couldn't stop the tears streaming down my cheeks. But Siân wouldn't mind. She wouldn't grow anxious and embarrassed in the face of raw emotion, just as I wouldn't if she burst into tears.

She nodded. "And the man, Anderson?"

"He tried to drive away but people in the street hung onto him until the police arrived. He claims that someone else was driving. Some invisible man who ran off without anyone else seeing him. Such a farcical story. Why couldn't he just admit it? But no, he's sticking to it, making us wait for the case to come to trial."

Siân gazed at me for a minute, reaching out to take my hands, stroking them. "So, it's not over yet then."

"No. Not over. Will it ever be?"

"In some ways. In some ways not. You can't go back, undo it. It never leaves you. But you have to go on, start again. Just different."

"Yes. Utterly different. Whenever I try to look into the future, all I see is blank. I don't know what I feel, half the time. Anguish, rage, or just numb."

"I know. I know. You just stagger on, getting through the moment, the day, the week, wondering how you'll cope with the next. But you do. In the end, it hasn't gone, but there's something else waiting for you."

"In the end. How long before the end?"

"It comes when it comes. And meanwhile, you have to go on for the children. Your daughter."

"Yes. For her if nothing else." I glanced round the room, wiping my cheeks dry. Photos on the mantelpiece. Wedding, bridal veil, self-conscious groom. Three children, Rhys, the stalwart Gareth presumably, and a girl. Long dark hair, strong features, Celtic beauty. Gaynor, who had run away.

My throat caught again, remembering Rhys's sullen resentment on our boat trip. How much of that was down to the death of his father? Had Gareth failed his GCSEs as a result? Was that fatal accident responsible for Gaynor going off the rails? How would my child be damaged, her life wrecked even, by Adam's senseless death?

"Have you heard from your daughter?" I forced myself to ask, wondering how I'd begin to cope if Willow just walked out on me.

Siân pushed herself to her feet and rearranged things pointlessly on the mantelpiece. "Had another postcard."

I could see two, partially tucked behind a mirror, a beefeater in full regalia, and a night-time scene of the City from Tower Bridge, the illuminated Tower defiantly medieval in juxtaposition to the clutter of commerce. Would a teenage girl from Tregelli find London thrilling or bewildering?

Siân pulled the postcards out, turned them over, staring at them for a moment before coughing to clear her throat. "Seems it's what she wants. Got a job. Something to do with the theatre. Gareth says she's on that internet thing."

"Is she an actress then?"

Siân shrugged. "I don't know. Wants to be, it seems. Well, I'd best clear these mugs away."

While she did so, I picked up the postcards and read them.

Dear Mum. Don't worry, everything's fine. I'm being looked after. It's all been sorted. Love, Gaynor.

The handwriting was a nervous scrawl. It must have required an effort to write something like that to her mother. On the second card, the writing was stronger.

Dear Mum. I'm doing well. I've got a great job at a theatre, would you believe, not to mention a great bunch of friends. I'm really starting over, so don't worry about me. I've got a new life here. I WON'T BE COMING BACK MAM. Gaynor.

God. How on earth would I feel if Willow did that to me? How did Siân cope with this as well as her old grief for her husband?

I tucked the postcards back behind the mirror and followed her to the kitchen. She was rinsing the mugs, tears on her cheeks. I squeezed her arm. "I'm so sorry. Life is shit, isn't it?" I turned the squeeze into a full-blown hug. "If there's anything I can do…"

"No, no, love, you go. You'll have things to do. I can manage fine."

I sensed that to stay would be to intrude. "Thanks for listening to me."

"No, thank you. Just remember, you need a shoulder to cry on, you come to me. We know what it's all about, don't we?"

"Yes. We do."

7

I saw Siân, on the Friday, waiting for a bus so I offered her a lift and we went together to the supermarket where she worked. Scanning other people's purchases and cleaning other people's houses was her life now. It paid the rent. She'd once had other ambitions, I learned.

"Tell you what I really wanted to be," she confided, as we sat over a coffee in the supermarket café. "Veterinary nurse. I'd started a course and everything, and then I got pregnant with Gareth. Eighteen, I ask you. Well, that was that."

"You couldn't stay on at your studies?"

"I thought about it, talked it over, but there was no way Mam could cope with a baby while I finished college, not with my dad to look after, with the cancer. So, I had to give it up. Gwyn and I got married. He did his best, I'll say that. We always got by, until the accident. But I really thought, with Gaynor it would be different." She pulled a face as she stirred her coffee. "I said I'd help."

"She was pregnant?"

"She said it was her problem. Had to do it her way. Went off and all I've had since are the postcards."

I remembered the first brief message. *I am being looked after. It's all been sorted.* "Do you think she's had an abortion?"

Siân stared into her cup. "I don't know what to think. I'd have looked after the baby for her. She could still have gone to Bangor. I thought that was what she wanted, university, but there you are. People change. Some things you can't fight. You just keep an eye on that girl of yours."

"Oh, I will. I'm sure I can trust her…" Could I, though, after our emotional earthquake?

Siân nodded kindly, pitying my gullibility. "What about you? You went to college, I bet."

"Yes. Camberwell. That's where I met Adam. He was at King's. London."

"Ah. So, you know it well then."

"What, London? Yes, I did." I knew what she was angling for. "There are a hell of a lot of theatres in London. Do you know which one Gaynor works at?"

She shook her head. "Gareth's asked, on the internet, but she hasn't answered. I was wondering whether to go there and ask around."

Ask where though? How likely was it that Gaynor would be working at one of the big West End theatres? There were more tiny ones scattered around than stars in the sky. Not to mention less savoury locations that wishful thinkers might refer to as theatrical. If Gaynor had finished up in a strip club or some such place, it was hardly surprising she was being cagey about precisely where she worked. "I don't think you'd get anywhere," I said. "Probably better to wait for her to contact you. I'm sure she will in the end."

* * *

Things seemed to change overnight in Tregelli. The school holidays started and the village became a bustling mêlée of hikers, boaters, swimmers, sunbathers, screaming children and men in shorts who should know better. The Bell was a battle zone, the bar impossible to reach. I didn't want to drink there, but I was missing the food.

Chloe, the landlady, caught me hovering outside, as she delivered an armful of lunches to one of the outside tables. She nudged me towards a bench at the end, overlooking the harbour, that was still free. "What can I get you? I'll bring it out."

"Thanks!" I ordered a mineral water and a crab sandwich and settled myself on the bench. Alone… and uncomfortable. When Adam had been alive, I'd settled myself countless times in a pub with no husband in sight, and never given it a moment's thought. Now I felt vulnerable, and humiliated that I did. I had never felt dependent when married. Why couldn't I cope with independence now?

I spied Siân plodding across the carpark, laden as usual with her cleaning gear. "Siân!" I shouted louder. "Siân!" She looked up and I beckoned. "Come and join me." I shifted along to make room on my bench. "Bet you'd be glad to take the weight off your feet."

"I would too. You okay, love?"

"I am now. Can you stop for a bit? I've ordered some sandwiches. Share them with me."

She considered the offer for a moment, then settled herself heavily beside me on the bench, as if the need to take the weight off her feet really was her primary consideration. "Getting hot."

"Have you got many more houses to do, today?"

"A couple more. So, how are you keeping? Your girl okay?"

"So far, I think. She's enjoying her role as first mate on the Lotte Lenya."

"So Harry reckons," said Siân. "He's got a lot of nice things to say about her."

I smiled. "And she seems to seeing a lot of a local boy. Alex Wyatt. She's been out ..." I stopped as Siân gave an involuntary flinch. "Problem?"

She recovered herself, gazing out hard across the harbour. "No. I suppose not."

"You don't like him?"

"Never spoken to him." She licked her lower lip, debating, before adding, "Gaynor knows him."

"Oh? Good or bad?"

"She thought good. They were, how do they say it these days, quite an item for a while. Or that's what I thought. What she implied. He never came to our house, of course." She was wrapping herself up in cautious wording.

"You think he was the father of her child?"

"She wouldn't say. But I think he was."

"I see. Yes."

"You tell your girl to watch herself."

"I will."

Chloe appeared with a tray, squeezing round a fat gent to get to me. "Here we are."

"Thanks. Any chance of a drink for Siân too?"

"Oh no." Siân was on her feet. "Don't worry about me. I can't really stop. Need to get on. But you keep an eye on Willow, okay?"

I couldn't dissuade her. A moment before, she had been at ease, but with a couple of idle words she had closed up, glaring at an alien world in which she didn't belong. She clearly wanted to be out of it. With a sigh I watched her go and made a start on my crab sandwiches.

8

Yvonne appeared out of a back office as I entered the gallery. "Nicki Bryce. Wonderful. Have you brought me another painting?"

"I'm afraid not. Still working on it." I was working on three, theoretically, and had set all of them aside, to think about them.

"Just kidding. But don't forget, if you do have something…" She paused, looking round as the doorbell jingled, then she straightened. Stiffened almost. I could see her slipping into her business pose, all charm and authoritative confidence.

An elderly woman had come in, though for a moment I mistook her for a child. She was small and delicate, and I immediately thought of a doll dressed up as a princess, despite her tweed skirt and quilted jacket.

"Mrs Wyatt, lovely to see you out and about. How can I help you today?" Yvonne stood before her, almost rubbing her hands together. "We have some new work by Howard Galloway and I know you were interested in one."

"Yes, yes. Oliver. Where are you, Oliver? There was a bronze, a Paston bronze…" Her words were clipped but uncertain, as if she wasn't quite sure exactly where she was. She gazed around, passing over me as of no interest. Mrs Wyatt? Too old to be Alex's mother. Grandmother maybe.

She was searching for something in the depths of the shop and... I could swear that she pocketed something from a collection of pewter figures. They were only a couple of pounds, but even so. I tried to catch Yvonne's eye, but she was determined not to look my way.

The old lady clasped her hands. "It's still here. Oliver! Come and look. Tell me what you think."

A man had followed her into the shop. Tall, broad-shouldered, with the same good looks as Alex but strengthened by maturity – in his fifties, maybe. He nodded pleasantly at me in passing, and there was shrewd observation in his gaze. I had a discomforting sense of being catalogued.

"Ah. Yes. The bronze. You like it, do you, Mother?" He sauntered over to examine an abstract figure, his head on one side, lips pursed. Calculating.

"Yes, I think I'll have it," said his mother decisively. "Can you deal with it? Now..." She moved on to study other pieces, leaning close to do so. I watched, amazed, as she pocketed something else.

"Shall we..." Oliver Wyatt ushered Yvonne back towards the desk.

Her eyebrows shot up expressively in triumph as she passed me, then she stopped. "I should have said. Oliver, this is Nicki Bryce, the artist. You have a couple of her paintings."

"Nicki Bryce! Indeed I do." He offered a hand. "Oliver Wyatt. Delighted to meet you." His hand was firm and dry, nails far better manicured than mine. His accent was less strained than his mother's. Easy. Confident like his son. "You're quite a find. I bought the first one on a whim, and my adviser assured me you were a very sound investment."

It was, I presumed, a businessman's idea of a compliment. "That's nice to know."

He gave a twitch of a smile. "And since I actually admired the work…"

"That's even nicer to know."

Little Mrs Wyatt was upon us, pushing her way in between us. "Oliver? Are you being distracted? The bronze." She was trying to turn him away.

He merely chuckled, refusing to be turned. "Mother, this is Nicola Bryce. She's painted that picture in the drawing room. The one with the horses?"

I remembered the picture. I gave him full marks for knowing they were horses. My abstraction of the essence of horse, a flurry of galloping.

"Ms Bryce, this is my mother, Fabia Wyatt."

"Charmed," said Mrs Wyatt, offering the tips of her fingers as she eyed me warily. "Delighted to meet you. You are just visiting the area?"

"I understood you lived in London," interjected her son.

"Close. St Albans."

"You're not staying?" demanded Fabia.

"Just for a while. At Carregwen. You know it?"

"Of course we do!" said Oliver. "We're neighbours of a sort." He handed a credit card to Yvonne, then paused. "I believe I've encountered your daughter. Yes, of course. She mentioned her mother was an artist."

"Willow's been seeing something of your son, Alex."

"That's right. He introduced us. Willow…"

"Willow Winters. She's never quite forgiven me for that."

A cloud of anxiety had settled on his mother's face, her fingers twitching nervously. He was clearly aware of it, his tone a little brisker as he steered her towards the door. "Children always need something to rail against, don't you find? Yvonne, you must let me know when any new Nicki Bryce appears in your gallery."

"Oh absolutely!"

"Yvonne!" I whispered urgently as she opened the door for them.

She turned briefly back to me with a very soft "sh sh sh." Once they were safely ushered out, she gave me her full attention again.

"Do you realise she was putting things in her pocket?" I asked.

Yvonne smiled, unconcerned. "Any idea what? I'll make a note in case he doesn't find them."

"A little dragon for one thing. You knew she was doing it?"

"She does it all the time. Don't worry. Oliver always pays for them later – or sends them back if he really doesn't want to give them house room. It's her little foible. All the shops know about it. We have an unspoken agreement."

"And you don't mind?"

"Me? No. The more she nicks, the more Oliver pays out. Who's complaining? Fabia is our resident eccentric. Insanely jealous of any woman looking too fondly on her boys. It's a joke but she is quite harmless, honestly."

I felt faintly disgusted. Jealous mother and kleptomaniac? I sympathised totally with compulsive disorders but I couldn't help feeling that if Siân or one of the other locals had a similar "foible," they wouldn't be so readily tolerated. The Wyatt name, or rather the Wyatt purse, obviously held sway round here. Not just Siân's landlord, but lord of the manor. "Well, I hope you get paid for your pewter dragon. I'd best go. I think Willow's back."

Sure enough, Harry's daily jaunt in the Lotte Lenya had ended and Willow was on the quay, talking to a customer.

I waited for her chat to finish. "Good trip?"

"Not bad. Two of the children threw up."

"Poor things." I hesitated. I didn't want to risk prying insensitively, but I needed to know how things stood. "Any plans for the rest of the day? Are you expecting to see Alex Wyatt again?"

"Maybe." Instantly defensive. "Probably. Why?"

"I've just met his father, who buys my paintings as an investment, apparently."

"Oh yeah." She laughed. "Alex says he's rolling in it. They've got, like, an apartment in New York and a villa or something in the south of France and everything."

"Ah, now I understand Alex's appeal."

"That's not it! That's rubbish. You just don't like him. What's wrong with me seeing him?"

"Nothing. I just want you to be cautious. I don't think he treated Siân's daughter very well. People with money to fling around tend to assume they're entitled to whatever they want, without having to consider the feelings of others."

"Yeah, yeah." She flicked away my warning. "Alex is okay. Anyway, he has to think about others, 'cos he's going to go into politics. He's doing PPE at Oxford."

"What else! I suppose you have to put on a good act of concern and interest if you want people to vote for you."

"You're just cynical."

"This is true."

"Alex is okay, really."

"He'll be standing as a socialist, will he?"

She glanced at me sideways, then laughed. "Not even LibDem. But does it matter? It's nothing serious, you know, him and me. It's just…" She sighed. "Fun. That's all."

"Good. I'm glad. You deserve some fun." I couldn't simply leave it though. "But please take care it stays fun. I don't know, but Siân thinks he got Gaynor pregnant and then he whisked her off to London for an abortion and a new life doing something iffy on the stage."

"Oh, come on. You make it sound like Victorian or something. Fallen women driven into brothels. She wouldn't be doing anything she didn't want, would she?"

"I don't know. Maybe she's just after stardom. Isn't that what everyone's supposed to want these days? Or maybe she felt trapped with no other choice. I don't know how or why or whatever, but I do know Siân is devastated. If you see Alex again, can you ask him to persuade Gaynor to contact her mother again? Just a word would do. A proper word, not just a few postcards and Facebook messages."

She shrugged. "Okay, maybe I'll ask him. Maybe."

"And take care."

"I won't get pregnant, Mum. I'm not that stupid. Come on, are we going home? I'm starving."

She'd changed the subject and it was just as well. A moment more and I'd have pushed too far.

9

Four o'clock in the morning and I was wide awake. Not uncommon. I hadn't disturbed Willow with my nightmare shouting for a week or more, but I would still wake in the small hours, wrapped in a ball of misery that had me hugging myself to ease the pain.

But this waking was different. For the first time in months, I woke not with a sense of dread and loss but alert and fired up, buzzing with creativity, wanting to be out and doing. I listened. Nothing from Willow above. She was fast asleep. I sat up and, without thinking, I turned to Adam to apologise for disturbing him.

About time, he said. *You just going to lie there? Get up. Get at it.*

I got up and dressed quietly. Willow could easily sleep on for another five hours. I stepped out into the dim chill before dawn and crossed to my studio, a stone barn converted to a summerhouse, with a glass wall looking out to sea, perfect for sitting with a G&T, and not bad as a painting den. It lacked running water, but it had electricity and my hand hovered on the light switch.

I stopped. The darkness was mystical, heightening my other senses even as it dulled my vision. The feel of the breeze on my cheek, the wood grain of the door, the dew on the grass brushing my ankles. The sound of birds beginning their chorus, twitters from the garden and raucous shrieks from the cliffs, and the soothing, rhythmic whish of waves on rocks. The smell of damp fresh earth and ozone.

You want me? This is all me now. Come and join me.

"All right." All my senses were tingling, yearning to be fed, as if I had just hatched out of some imprisoning egg. Even sight seemed renewed, as my eyes accustomed themselves to the dark, and pallor began to soak into the sky behind the eastern hills. I didn't want to hide in the artificial glare of the studio. I wanted to go out and immerse myself in touching, hearing, tasting, seeing.

I would walk along the coast path. I pulled on walking shoes, but I would take nothing to encumber me, not even a camera; I didn't want to record anything, but become it. Be one with Adam.

Clambering over the stile onto the cliff-top path, it was as if the whole world had become my body. The wash of the waves below seemed to pulse in rhythm with the blood in my veins. The same light welling up behind the horizon, was welling up within me, spilling across the placid sea, cool and unearthly, mist drifting among the rocks. In a few hours the sun would have burned away the cellophane wrapping of the new day, blinding light strobing from the shook foil of the sea, and the hot and bothered dust would settle, but for the moment everything was washed fresh. A deep-down silence defied the gulls' clamour. I was one with primeval rock and ocean, a world that no one else shared, except Adam. In that fleeting amnesty between day and night, we were one again.

I didn't want people. I turned away from Tregelli harbour, drinking in a new world; the folds and crumbling cracks of the rocks beneath my feet, lichen on a stone gate post, cresses in the peat brown water of a rivulet that oozed through a reedy hollow before jetting crystal-pure down the rocks to unseen shingle. A kestrel hovered over the cliff face, a spider's web shimmered with silver on the gorse, a swathe of daisies on the stony bank, petals clasped, waited to open out to greet the sun.

I embraced it all, an elemental world that had no mark of humankind on it, except the bare earth and rock worn clean by a thousand feet. Walking in the footsteps of others, back through millennia.

Then, at a stile, a sign stated 'Cliffs kill.' The path beyond made a sudden turn around the brink of a deep inlet, a crocodile bite sheering through cliffs. Cliffs with caves. I could hear the subterranean boom as waves rushed in, deep beneath my feet. The rock under me vibrated. Far below, the sea in its narrow confine was concealed in indigo shadow, heaving to escape. I wanted to wave a wand and release it from its prison.

Or perhaps it wasn't a captive after all, but an assailant, hammering its angry way through the locked portals of the land, demanding redress against presumptuous invaders. Perched on the stile, I could see a quay of sorts, concrete meshing the jutting rocks at the base on the daunting cliffs. I'd seen that quay from Harry's boat. "Just a private landing site," he'd said, and it was very private. Absurdly private. There was no obvious access to it except by boat – like the sleek motor launch that was tied up there now, deep in shadows as it rose and fell on the waves. There was no one on board, so who had moored it there and where had they gone? They couldn't have ascended those cliffs, which were not merely sheer, but overhanging. Perhaps the sailor had swum across the inlet to the headland on which I was standing? No sheer cliffs and overhangs on this side. Instead, it tumbled down to the waves in giant steps of shattered rock and heathery turf. Even I could climb it.

I had to do it, to defy the presumption of that inaccessible quay, claiming privacy where it had no right. I had to get down there, squat on the lowest rocks and dabble my fingers in the salt water, to claim the waves as my own.

Show the buggers, said Adam. *You can do it.*

I started scrambling. Halfway down, Adam turned, hands on hips, to shake his head at me. *You're on your own now, Nick.* Relenting, he reached out, and then his outstretched hand vanished.

I stopped, teetering precariously on a rock. I must be mad. What tricks was my mind playing, to bring me out here, at some ridiculously early hour, scrambling down rocks in order to claim the ocean? Was I experiencing some sort of religious epiphany, opening myself to a deep spiritual union with the world, or had I unlocked some sort of natural LSD, a mixture of heightened sensation and hallucination? Whatever it was, I was there, all alone, with no one to call on to help me if I fell. Adam's hand had vanished. I was bereft. For a moment a thought overwhelmed me that if I slipped, went tumbling down and let the waves consume me, I would be with him properly, one with Adam and all the rest of it, forever. Not suicide, no, just out of everything.

I shook away the thought. My daughter was waiting for me at home. I had to be there for her, in charge, strong. Or pretending to be strong. I would have deal with this, like everything else. Either get myself back up to the coast path and home, before she woke, or keep going down to finish what I had started.

I had to finish. I went on, ending up at last on a perch of wiry grass and dried thrift, just a couple of feet above the surf. I reminded myself I was an artist. I absorbed the perpetually shifting patterns of the breaking waves and scintillating spray, among the blues and greens and purples of the water and the ink-black of the rocks that lurked in shadow, the aquamarine and ash grey where the golden light of the new sun was edging down into the cave-riddled cove with cliffs that kill.

I was sitting out in the light, cupped by land, sea and sky. The head of the inlet, the mysterious quay and the launch were still enfolded in twilight, but the mystery was explained. The inlet ended in a gaping cave and the quay ran into it but only for a couple of yards before ending at a bastion of black dripping rock. A tunnel had been cut into the rock barred by an iron grill. Squinting into the gloom, I could see a padlock and a metal sign with a single word. "Private." I guessed it said private, keep out, mine, not yours. I could just make out, through the grill, metal steps, rising into darkness.

"What is that about?" I asked.

There was no one to answer. A distant tanker was edging its way like a giant slug along the white horizon.

"Where does it lead?"

Into darkness, said Adam, somewhere behind me. If I turned, he would vanish, so I sat staring at the water, and he appeared. How was that? Two eyes were staring at me. Two huge dark eyes fixed on my face. I blinked. A seal's gleaming round head had broken out of the waves a few yards out by the rocks that formed a sort of breakwater at the mouth of the inlet. He bobbed there, surveying me solemnly.

"The great Silkie," I said. "Hello, Adam."

He stared back at me, until, satisfied that we had communicated, he flipped and disappeared back into the deeps, a black glimmering illusion gliding into the cove, beside the quay, towards the gaping cave.

"Don't go!" I called, a wave of desolation seizing me. "Where are you going?"

Into my grave, said Adam the seal, and the secret door onto darkness suddenly swallowed everything. A tomb.

The sun, topping the brink of the cliffs, flashed on the burnished flanks and glass of the motor launch. It jarred. It did the trick. The spell was broken, like crystal smashing as the bald bright day claimed its cruel grip on reality. The coast path would be busy soon with sturdy hikers, earnest joggers and idle strollers. People everywhere – except the one I wanted on those dark steps behind that locked gate from which there was no return.

My head was spinning, the anguish overwhelming me again, and it had to stop. I curled my fingers into my palms until the pain shook me back into cold sense. I needed to get back, to snap out of this, whatever it was, fantasy, delusion, mockery.

I clambered back up the headland, my feet slipping on crumbling rock, tears of frustration mixing with those of grief. I nearly lost my balance a couple of times, but I made it safely back to the coast path, rimmed with seeded foxgloves and white daisies, the warming air already rich with the coconut scent of gorse. Leaning on the stile, I breathed deep, waiting to regain my equilibrium. Be calm. Be rational. Think about something other than graves. Who owned that bloody quay anyway? Who dared to claim the sea and rocks as private?

Nursing that small germ of anger, I climbed onto the stile, standing on tiptoe to gaze inland, over the bank of tangled hedge and wire. Small strips of pasture ran either side of an overgrown ravine in which I could just see the tops of a couple of buildings, or what were left of them. Brick-built sheds, one totally derelict, one with its corrugated iron roof still clinging on. Did they line up with the steps in the rock down below? They must do. There was nowhere else that the steps could lead. Further inland, a line of pines, bent by the wind, protected a clump of parkland trees, gables and chimneys protruding among them. A big house fit for a man who kept a motor launch at his own private quay. Probably fit for a man who had a pad in New York and a little place in the south of France. Oliver Wyatt. It had to be him. Who else would have the presumption to claim a chunk of the coast?

"Bastard!" I shouted.

Fuck Oliver Wyatt, said Adam.

"Yeah, fuck him!" I felt my pulse slow. "I thought you'd gone."

Me? No. Never. You're going to go, though. You've drunk it all in. Now go and paint it.

10

That afternoon, Willow, back from her boat trip, came out to find me in the studio. She offered me a mug of tea as she stared at my canvas. "Is that…?"

"What?" I looked at what I'd done. Just colours, inspired by my early walk, misty light on rock and sea, shadows and depths, a million dancing shards of colour.

"Dad," she said. "Is it Dad?"

I stared at it. It was everything I had seen that morning, the darkness of the grave but all the brilliance of life too.

"Yes, it's Dad," I said. Why hadn't I realised? My grief was as much a part of my creativity as everything else. "It's enough for today. Come on, let's go in."

Time for a little domestication. Willow loaded the washing machine. I made a half-hearted attempt at tidying up the living room. Books, magazines, leaflets; amazing how they had managed to scatter themselves everywhere. I leaned down to pick up a folded sheet of paper, one corner jammed under the front door.

My neck was prickling the moment I touched it before I even consciously thought about it. Folded paper, thrust under the door, pushed and snagged as Willow had come in. The nausea was rising as I opened it and read.

I know what you are, you slut. You're not wanted here. Go back to where you belong or you'll be sorry.

I couldn't move. Our stalker had found us then. All the enlightenment of the morning disintegrated in a tornedo of utterly incomprehensible confusion in which nothing made any sense. Nothing. There was no sense in anything. My monster had come to reclaim me and squeeze all the sanity out of me. Why? Why? Why?

The paper was pulled from my fingers. I turned, fighting to hold myself upright, expecting to find Willow in tears of terror, but no, her face was rigid with fury as she read the words.

"Right!" she said. "Very funny I don't think!" Before I could respond, she'd flung the door open and was storming off towards the village.

"Willow!" I thought I was shouting, but no sound came. I was voiceless, frozen. And then I was shaking. I poured myself a gin. It couldn't be happening, not again, and yet it was. I sat at the window, nursing the bottle, staring out blindly, waiting for a hooded figure to appear. Waiting, waiting. Waiting.

A hooded figure appeared. By then, I was so drunk, it took me a moment to realise it was Willow returning. She came bouncing in, merrily. "Well, that's fixed that."

"What have you done?" Murder in the undergrowth? A knife in the dark? My tormentor hurtling from the cliffs?

"Had a few meaningful words, you know." Willow stopped laughing. "Oh Mum! How many have you had? Is this because of that sick letter? Don't let her upset you, stupid woman. We've got her sorted. Come on, I'll make you some coffee."

She didn't make sense, but then why would she? There was no sense in the whole universe anymore.

* * *

One result of getting blind drunk was that I didn't lie awake worrying about it. Willow must have put me to bed, and I woke, eventually, convinced that someone had buried an axe in my brain. My stalker of course. I staggered up and checked by the front door for more notes. Nothing. I stepped outside to peer at the cottage. No graffiti. I made my way to my studio, expecting to find my latest picture slashed, but it was exactly as I had left it.

I stumbled back to the cottage. Coffee. I needed coffee. I must have made a noise clattering kettles and cups because Willow woke.

"Mum?" She was peering down from her high perch. "Are you okay?"

"I will be. Once I've had a couple of paracetamols."

"You really hit the bottle yesterday." She was slithering down the ladder. "What brought that on?"

"What brought it on?" I almost laughed. Then stopped. The day before had been weird from the start. Was any of it true, or was it all a figment of my delusional imagination? The letter from my stalker? The early morning walk with Adam? The cave and the quay and the steps leading up into darkness? "She's found us, hasn't she?" The memory came back to me of Willow telling me she'd fixed it. "What did you do to her? Did you catch her?"

Willow's nose crinkled in puzzlement, then enlightenment dawned. "Oh my God. That letter. You thought it was from that nutter back home, didn't you?"

"Wasn't it?"

"No! It was completely different writing. You must have seen that. The nutter uses felt tip. This was all la-di-da fountain pen stuff. Yeah?"

"Yes." I sat down. "The nutter back home…"

"She'll never find us here, whatever her loony game is. Her and her notes and the graffiti and the dog shit. She's there and we're here."

"Yes. I know." Of course, I knew. My stalker was still in Hertfordshire because the neighbour with whom I'd left an emergency key had phoned to tell me more graffiti had been sprayed on my front door. I was not to fret about it, her husband had scrubbed it off. Did I want her to tell the police? No, I didn't. Something about not wanting to bother anyone. I couldn't explain why I was so resistant to reporting it, except that Adam's death was enough misery. I couldn't cope with anything else. "Who was it, then?"

"It was for me, Mum, from Alex's barmy gran. He warned me she'd probably play up if she saw us together. Apparently, she does it with all the girls he brings home. I was furious, but Alex said all we had to do was tell her I was a princess, from darkest Peru, or something like that. She's such a snob it would make her behave herself. So anyway…" She grinned at me, mischievously. "I told him, didn't I? About Grandad being a real lord. And Fibs lapped it up. Even apologised for the letter. Alex was wetting himself it was so funny."

"Funny!"

"Okay, well I suppose it wasn't funny really. Just her reaction. You're not cross about me mentioning Grandad?"

"I'd rather you hadn't. Oh well. I'll just have to live with it."

"Anyway, no more silly letters from Fantasy Fibs, so you needn't worry."

"No. Of course I won't."

"Right. I'm going to have a shower, then." She sloped off, trailing a towel, leaving me trying to get to grips with new sensations.

First of all, anger, that Wyatt woman had written vile letters to my darling Willow, calling her a slut. How dare she?

Then impressed astonishment. Willow had understood who the note was from, and she hadn't sat cowering. She had stormed out to deal with it. My daughter. Where had she got that strength from?

Obviously not from you, said Adam.

"No, because I just cower."

Get a grip, woman. If our daughter can, so can you.

"Oh, shut up." He was right, of course. I needed to be the adult Willow obviously was, someone capable of dealing with things, including Fabia Wyatt. Willow's solution, at Alex's suggestion, didn't seem to me to be entirely satisfactory. I might have to go and see the woman myself.

I dug out an ordnance survey map of the area from clutter on the dresser and spread it out. Tregelli. I traced the narrow winding lane to it from the main road inland.

The harbour wall. The Bell, of course. Our own cottage was a tiny insignificant square on the cliff top. Westwards, the coast ebbed and flowed in a series of jagged headlands and hidden coves. Pendiawel. There was the inlet with the private quay, and the house amongst its cedars and purple beeches, was marked clearly enough. Cwrt y Frân. I'd seen it with my own eyes, but having followed the contorted route of the coast, I hadn't realised how close it lay to our cottage. A dozen times I must have passed Bethel Lane, which turned off the narrow road along the creek just two hundred yards before our own zigzag track, but I'd never thought about where it went. It led ultimately to a farm and a chapel, but halfway along stood Cwrt y Frân. The house itself, hidden by a rise in the land, was just three small paddocks away from us.

Oliver Wyatt had mentioned that we were neighbours of sorts. I felt affronted that his property was almost touching us. In fact, the fields between us were undoubtedly part of the Cwrt y Frân estate, just over the tumbled wall and shaggy hedge that rose next to our cottage. The Wyatts could all be lined up there, watching us.

"Yeah, that's Alex's place." Willow was beside me, rubbing her wet hair with a towel.

"Convenient if you're spending a lot of time there."

"There? Hardly. At least not in the house, not with his mad gran getting so shirty with visitors, but they've got a swimming pool."

"There's a surprise."

"Indoors. Heated. Very posh. Bit daft though, isn't it, having a pool in an old barn when you've got all the sea out there."

"Yes, a bit daft. You've been swimming there?"

"Yeah." She looked at me sidelong. "You're worried that counts as an engagement?"

"No." My laugh died. "You're not…"

"No, Mum. We're just messing around, you know. It's summer. He's got a pool. We swam in it. End of."

"I know, I know. As long as he's not leading you…"

"Mum! No one's leading me or seeing me off. I can look after myself, okay? I'm just chilling."

"Before you go to university."

"Don't hassle me, please!"

"Sorry, sorry." I crept back to the kitchen.

11

The next day, when I sat beside Siân on a bench overlooking a scrubby patch of playing field beyond the pub, watching Rhys kicking a football around with some other boys, I was still thinking about Willow.

"I'd hate her to miss out because Adam's death has turned her world upside down," I said. "She's had good offers from Exeter and Newcastle, and I know her grades might not be quite as good as they would have been if it hadn't happened…"

Siân was nodding, saying nothing. I kicked myself, remembering belatedly that she had been expecting her daughter to go to university too, until Gaynor had opted for the bright lights of the theatre instead.

"Sorry," I said. "I'm wittering on about Willow and you've already been through the wringer."

Siân shrugged. "Well. What would she be studying then? Your girl."

"Foreign languages. She's always had a good ear. She fancies trying Chinese… or did."

"Nice. Useful, I expect."

"Mm. What was Gaynor planning to do?"

"Oh, environmental science. Saving the planet."

"Really?" The switch to acting was quite a leap. But trauma does that. It was trying to make Willow leap and I was determined to stop her. "I suppose Gaynor was badly affected by her father's death."

"They all were. I thought she'd come through it, though. Until Alex Wyatt got his claws into her." Her voice shook with bitterness. No hesitation now about laying the blame squarely on Alex. We both glanced back towards the quay, where he was perched on the bonnet of his sports car, overlooking the harbour, idly tapping his phone. He was waiting, I guessed, for the return of the Lotte Lenya, which was just rounding the harbour wall.

"She went there, you know." Siân was staring at him as if she would happily bore a hole through his heart. "Before she disappeared. Off to London."

"To Cwrt y Frân? To see Alex?"

"Not him. He was away at Oxford."

"Oliver then. What happened?"

"Ha! Wouldn't I like to know!"

"Haven't you asked him?"

She gave me an old-fashioned look. "You think Oliver Wyatt would answer my questions? Anyway, he's never here. Always gadding off on business somewhere or other. Don't see him around for months, sometimes. He doesn't give me notice when he's in residence."

"He's here now. I met him in the gallery the other day."

"Well." She sniffed. "He won't let that boy of his take any blame, you can be sure of that."

Alex Wyatt, stretching extravagantly in the sun, didn't look as if he'd ever had to take the blame for anything. But he needn't think he could play around with my Willow in her vulnerable state and then shunt her off to an abortion clinic in London while he moved on to the next conquest. I rose. Siân rose with me, and we started along the road towards the quay as the boat gently eased its way through the moored vessels and chugged towards its mooring. A full complement, I could see. One passenger, a dark curly-haired young man was standing in the prow with Willow, chatting to her. As she readied herself to hook a rope over the bollard, he took it from her and completed the manoeuvre with a practiced hand. She was smiling, making a joke because he laughed. The next moment he had bounded ashore and was handing her up. They stood to either side to assist the remaining passengers.

We were still some yards from them when the last family skipped away, beaming, and Alex Wyatt sauntered over to Willow's side. They spoke, she turned back to the young man from the boat with a shrug of apology, waved to Harry and let Alex escort her to his car.

Harry and the young man watched them drive past Siân and me and away, the same guarded expression on both faces. Then the young man turned to us as we reached them and bent down to drop a kiss on Siân's cheek.

"Hello Mam."

She patted his hand and said something in Welsh before turning towards me.

"My Gareth. This is Nicki Winters. She's staying up at Carregwen for the summer."

"Pleased to meet you," said Gareth, pumping my hand. He was in his early twenties, well built, nice looking. A young Tom Jones. He was dressed in a rather grubby t-shirt and tattered jeans, but he looked as if he, at least, had recovered from the trauma of his father's death. He nodded vaguely inland, Alex's sports car no longer in sight. "Your daughter. Stole my job here."

"Now, Gareth." Siân nudged him. "Don't go giving Nicki the wrong idea." She turned to me in explanation. "Gareth's worked with Harry in the summer months for I can't remember how long. But he's got himself a job over at Rhyd-ddu Mawr this year, leaving his uncle in the lurch, so there's been no stealing, thank you."

"Only kidding, Mam."

"No loss to me," said Harry, scrambling up to join us. "That Willow's better looking by a long mile."

"Mm," said Gareth. "Not the only one who thinks so, are you?" A wary look passed between the three of them.

"I don't think she's serious about Alex Wyatt," I said, although I didn't really know how Willow felt. Knowing the story of Gaynor, I would rather she wasn't with Alex Wyatt. But if it was just fun, if he was taking her out of herself a little, I didn't want to drag her back down.

"You can be sure Alex Wyatt isn't serious about her," said Gareth and there was no disguising the anger in his tone.

"Now, now, boy," said Harry, with a cautionary hand on his shoulder.

There was an awkward pause. I was suddenly an intruder in their family affairs, someone around whom they had to be cautious. "I'd best get this shopping home," I said, waving my carrier bag. "I'll see you soon, Siân. Nice to meet you, Gareth."

Back at the cottage, I found myself mulling over the problem of Gaynor. I didn't want to stay on the side-lines and have Siân seeing me as a neutral spectator or worse, a double agent with a foot in both camps because my daughter had taken up with Alex Wyatt. Willow might get prickly if I started interfering, but I needed to tackle her more decisively about him. When she came in, I would sit her down and make her talk.

It didn't work out like that. Late afternoon, I caught the unnecessary revving of a powerful engine as a sportscar pounded its way up our track. I hoped he'd just hover long enough to watch Willow safely indoors, but no. The engine fell silent. They were out of the car, walking across to the cottage, Alex's arm around her.

I held the door open for them. "Both coming in?"

"Yeah, that's okay, isn't it?"

"Of course. I was just about to make tea. You'll have a cup?"

"Alex has a bottle."

Of course, he did. Champagne. None of your budget prosecco for Alex Wyatt.

"You'll have a glass, won't you, Nicki?"

I swallowed my annoyance at his presumption. "Why not."

He was already busy opening the bottle while Willow rummaged for glasses. Two wine glasses and a tumbler. There were no complete sets of anything in Carregwen. Alex didn't seem bothered. He poured as if he were the host, and we were welcome guests. I took a glass, thinking I really must find out if Carla owned the freehold to this place, or was Carregwen another Wyatt property.

"Cheers!" Alex and Willow clinked glasses and laughed.

"So, Alex." As he was here, he could answer my questions. "Since you're seeing so much of Willow, you won't mind me asking…"

"Mum!" said Willow, glaring at me.

Alex smiled; his charm switched to full, ready for the interrogation. "Sure, fire away."

"Mother's prerogative," I said. "You're at Oxford, that right?"

"For my sins." Why do people say that? It's such an irritating phrase. I'd always thought it and Willow knew I'd always thought it. She was glaring at me again.

"I know how difficult it is to get into Oxford or Cambridge," I said, certain that he'd been shoe-horned in with ease from an exclusive public school. "Your parents must be very proud."

"Oh. Sure." I detected a hint of pleasant irony.

"PPE, is that it? Keen to go into politics, yes?"

"Seems so." He didn't seem too adamant about it. Off-hand, rather, as if it had nothing to do with him. "I expect the Boss has some internship lined up with a bigwig in the Cabinet."

I felt a twinge of sympathy then, despite his apparent nonchalance, the boy had the golden path to success laid out before him, whether he wanted it or not. But then he probably did want it. He wasn't yearning for a career stacking shelves in Aldi. "Your father has a finger in a lot of pies, or so I've heard. Owns a lot of properties in the village."

He laughed, derisively. "Owns a lot of everything. Very smart guy, the Boss. Inherited a pretty sound company from Grandad and built it up into an empire. Likes to win, my dad."

"And your mother?"

The easy smile vanished, the jaw set, the face grew bleak. Just for a second, then he managed a shrug. "I wouldn't know. You'd have to ask her if you can find her. Fucked off years ago." The violence of the words belied the studied calmness of his voice.

"I am sorry. Really." I meant it. "Don't you keep in contact?"

"No." One word and clamped lips. Then he thought better of silence and managed a laugh. "Fibs says she ran off with some…" He paused, assessing me before choosing his words. ""Gentleman of colour". He's welcome to her. I don't want her."

It was so obviously untrue. I caught Willow biting her lip, tears in her eyes. I reached out to squeeze her hand.

Alex read the signals. "I am so sorry about your husband, Nicki. Will's father. It must be a terrible loss. But my mother isn't, believe me."

I needed to turn the conversation fast. Willow was refilling her glass with a dangerous urgency. I smiled. "That's your house just up the lane then"

"Yes. At least it's Fibs' place, in theory. My grandmother, Fabia. Have you met her in the flesh?" He was keen to get back to normal chat. "Well, you've already discovered what she's like. Eccentric, my father

79

says. Totally barking in her old age. I suppose being so long on her own in the house doesn't help. The Boss is Stateside or off round the world on business mostly, and with me at Oxford, she's only got the servants."

Willow snorted into her champagne.

I laughed. "Must be hard only having *servants* to talk to."

He shrugged apologetically. "I know. Thing is, my grandmother's turned into this crazy snob. Goes off on a fantasy, convinced she's blue-blooded aristocracy, grew up in a castle and all that tosh."

"It's harmless enough, as eccentricities go," I said, thinking that compulsive shoplifting was probably less so.

"Yes, she's always good for a laugh if you like the ridiculous. So, Willow, you game for this boat trip?"

"Sure." My daughter knocked back her champagne and slammed the glass down a little too emphatically.

I rubbed my eyes. "I'm not made of cast-iron like you two. It's way too early for me to be tippling. I need a coffee. Can you make a pot, Willow? I'm sure Alex wouldn't say no."

"Never do," he said, breezily.

"Okay." Willow trailed off into the kitchen, unaware of any ulterior motive on my part. Alex, on the other hand, was less gullible. He turned to me with ready reassurances.

"I'm not too drunk to be in charge of the launch if that's…"

"I might need a bit more convincing of that," I said, my voice low. "My daughter has been through quite enough and I don't want any more harm coming to her."

"Sure. Don't worry. I won't let anything happen to her."

"No? Tell me about Gaynor Hughes."

His easy smile vanished again.

"Don't tell me you don't know her," I said.

"Yeah, sure I know her." He'd recovered whatever composure he'd lost. "Used to hang around with her for a bit, actually."

"Hang around?"

"I saw her for a while, that's all. She doesn't mean anything to me now if that's what you're worried about. She's no one special."

"No one special," I repeated, anger igniting inside me.

It ignited in him as well. "Look, she's nothing. A little gold-digger, okay?"

"You mean she was only after your money?"

"And she got it, too. Or Dad's, as any rate. He paid her off, gave her what she wanted, which was a way out of here. End of story. She's nothing to me."

"Was it your child she was having?"

He had to pause for a moment to keep his temper contained. "If it was, she didn't want it, okay, got rid of it, cut me off, so what does it matter?" He was boiling internally, his eyes gleaming. Siân saw him as the hard-hearted villain, but he saw her daughter that way and, whatever the truth, there was a lot of hurt being nursed on both sides.

"I don't want to talk about her," declared Alex.

"You don't have to!" Willow was at the kitchen door, having heard enough to be convinced I was the wicked witch of the west. "How could you, Mum? Come on, Alex." She grabbed his arm and led him out through the kitchen into the paddock leading down to the cliffs. He half-raised a hand in farewell, or dismissal.

I wasn't feeling particularly proud of myself, or satisfied with what I'd discovered, but there it was.

Could have been worse, said Adam.

"Could it? I thought I failed dismally."

You had to ask.

12

I was rediscovering the therapy of work, and I had a couple of spare pieces finished now, still too wet for the gallery, but I thought I'd let Yvonne know she could have something soon. When I reached Tregelli, I found a gleaming Jaguar parked up outside the gallery door. The double yellow lines on the road had been blurred and scored by sand and salt, so maybe that was the driver's excuse. Or maybe he was someone who thought parking restrictions only applied to little people.

I hesitated and was about to turn away when Oliver Wyatt appeared in the doorway.

"Ah, just the person I was looking for." He hailed me with a raised hand before reaching into the jacket of his very smart suit and producing an envelope. "I return from London and find my mother demanding that I fulfil her commission."

I took the envelope and drew out a thick cream card, with gilt edging.

Mr Oliver Wyatt and Mrs Fabia Wyatt request the company of…

"Lady Nicola Bryce?" I couldn't help saying it aloud, with intense irritation.

He smiled politely. "You don't care for the title? I don't have time for them myself, but it's my mother's little foible. She's a stickler for what she sees as the social niceties."

I opened my mouth, then shut it again. Why bother? What did I care what Fabia Wyatt imagined about me? Besides, her son wasn't waiting for an answer.

"You will come, I hope. She's very insistent. A small dinner party this Friday, that's all. Nothing too formal."

Just slightly formal. A small dinner party in two days' time at the gracious mansion of Cwrt y Frân, with, no doubt, the self-classified elite of Pembrokeshire society. I couldn't think of anything I wanted less. But I had to speak to Fabia Wyatt about that vicious letter she had inflicted on Willow. Besides, I could see Siân's face as she said "Wouldn't I like to know?" She felt she couldn't interrogate Oliver Wyatt, but there was nothing to stop me.

"Thanks," I said, decisively. "I'll be happy to come."

* * *

"I love it," said Willow, when I showed her the card. "Lady Nicola!"

"That's thanks to you. You told Alex the truth about Grandad?"

"Oh yeah," said Willow, breezily. "It doesn't matter, does it? It's not as if you're really going to dine with fantasy Fibs."

"Actually, I said I would."

"No way!" Willow exploded in mirth, and then sobered rapidly. "Why? You're not going to go on about that letter, are you?"

"Any reason why I shouldn't?"

"Yeah! Every reason. We've sorted it, haven't we?"

"By letting her think I'm Lady Nicola? Anyway, it's not just that I want to talk about."

"Oh no, please, not that girl?"

"Gaynor Hughes. Yes, that's precisely what I want to ask about. For Siân's sake. How do you think I'd feel if you left home without a word? Especially if you were pregnant."

"I'm not."

"Good, but supposing you were."

"Look, it wouldn't happen, okay. You've just got it in for Alex, haven't you?"

"No. Not at all. Unless he did behave badly to—"

"Well, he didn't, so leave him alone. And don't go to this stupid dinner. You'll hate it. Alex says she's really gaga, so you'd only set her off again."

"Maybe, but I did say I'd go. Unless you want me to tell them I can't leave you on your own?"

"You're kidding." She dissolved into laughter. "What would you do? Ask Harry to babysit? Tell him I want boiled egg and soldiers for my tea? If you really must go, I'll be fine."

"There goes that excuse then."

* * *

Having decided to do this thing, I wanted to talk to Siân again first, so I walked up to Maes Waun and tried her door. I could hear her coming. The door swung open.

"Hello Siân," I said.

She stood there, blocking my way, her eyes accusing, hostile even. "What can I do for you?"

"Can I come in?"

Reluctantly, she stood aside and ushered me through to the living room. Gareth was standing in the kitchen door, his glance no friendlier than his mother's. He was wearing overalls, stained with mud or possibly manure, the sleeves rolled up as he wiped his hands with a towel.

"Put the kettle on," she said, and he retreated obediently.

"Well." She waited for me to sit, but remained standing, her arms folded.

I met her gaze, wondering what had caused the obvious antagonism. The memory of my stalker came back to me, vicious anger in her eyes. This wasn't the same. There's was nothing vicious in Siân's eyes, just hurt and resentment. I had made a bad mistake coming, though I didn't know why. I just had to go on.

"I've been invited to dinner at Cwrt y Frân tomorrow."

"I know," she said, her arms tightening around her.

"Oh?"

"Talk of the town, isn't it, Mam." Gareth was in the doorway of the living room now. "Lady Nicola Bryce to dine with the Wyatts."

"Oh God, who put that about?"

"Everyone," he said, his eyes challenging me. "Us plebs, we love a good gossip about our betters."

His mother chided him with a look, gesturing to him to go back. "Her ladyship will be wanting her tea. Better find the best china."

"Siân!" I stood up. "Look. I am not bloody Lady Nicola. That's complete bullshit, okay?"

She eyed me incredulously.

"Seriously. I'm not some inbred descendent of Norman thugs. I'm gutter material with the very best. Yes, my father was technically a lord, very briefly. Baron Bryce of Houghthorpe. But before he was given a life peerage, he was Ron Bryce of the T&G and until he went into the hospice at the end, he lived in the same council house where I grew up. And he only accepted the peerage because he thought he'd be playing a part in abolishing the House of Lords. We never let him hear the end of it though. Laughed him out of court every time it was mentioned."

Siân was looking at me, eyes narrowed, lips pursed. Gareth must have heard it all too. He was hovering with the tea tray, pulling a face as he considered one of the mugs with an obvious crack.

"I'll get another," he said.

Siân very nearly smiled. "And biscuits. If her ladyship would settle for a custard cream."

"Her ladyship would find a custard cream most acceptable," I said, hoping the worst of the misunderstanding was out of the way. What had she thought? That I had been slumming it when I'd visited her? That I'd been patronising her like some Lady Bountiful being nice to the peasants?

"Look, Fabia Wyatt has some form of dementia, and snobbish fantasies are, apparently, a part of it, so she's welcome to imagine I'm a duchess if she likes," I said. "I'm only going to this dinner so that I can quiz Oliver Wyatt about Gaynor."

"I never asked you to go prying." Siân was still touchy.

"No. But you did say you'd like to know what happened when Gaynor went there? So, I can at least ask. Sorry if you think I have no business poking my nose in, but Alex Wyatt is seeing Willow and I want to know… I want Willow to know how she's likely to be treated if things get out of hand."

Reluctantly, she nodded.

"I challenged Alex about Gaynor."

"You did?"

"Yes, and he seemed genuinely upset about the abortion and Gaynor leaving."

"So he says."

"He claims that his father gave her money to go." I thought it best not to suggest that Gaynor might have asked for the money. "I don't know if that's true, or why or what really happened, so I want to ask Oliver himself. Confront him in front of his posh guests, maybe. And find out if he knows where she is now."

Gareth was back with a replacement mug and a packet of biscuits, exchanging looks with his mother.

"Have you heard any more from her?" I asked.

A moment's hesitation. "Gareth's had one of them texts on his phone. I haven't got a mobile."

"Her phone's always switched off when I call, but I've been texting her." He pulled his phone from his pocket and clicked, studying the text that appeared there. His nose twitched as he did so.

I was still standing. I glanced at the screen.

Dywedwch wrth Mam i beidio a phoeni, rwyn iawn.

"What's it mean?"

Gareth exchanged looks with his mother again. "Well." He sniffed a laugh. *"Tell Mam not to worry, I'm all right."*

I'm all right. It wasn't much to appease all Siân's worries. It certainly wouldn't have mine. Either Gaynor was trying to hide the truth of her situation with bland reassurances or she really had moved on, determined to leave her old life behind. Both options must be equally painful for Siân.

"I can at least ask Wyatt if he has any idea where she is," I said. "Unless you'd rather I didn't."

"You can if you like."

"If it will help, that's all."

She shrugged.

"How's Willow," asked Gareth, handing me a tea.

"Okay, as far as I can tell. I think more up days than down, now."

"Thought I might go out on the boat with them again."

"Please do." An alternative distraction certainly wouldn't hurt.

13

I walked to my dinner engagement. Willow pointed out a short cut onto Bethel Lane from the end of our paddock, through a bit of tangled wood and down some steps. She hadn't warned me how muddy the steps were, and I was still trying to wipe my shoes clean when I reached the broad lay-by and the gates to Cwrt y Frân. Tall gates of ornate wrought iron, antique in appearance but electronically controlled.

A speaker crackled at me, demanding my name. I gave it, but when the gates silently swung open, I was half tempted to turn and go home. I didn't want to be approved by this world. But I had a mission, so I walked through.

Cwrt y Frân was modest as country houses go, more like a self-important rectory. It stood four-square, in uncompromising grey stone, at the end of a long gravel drive. Symmetrical rows of gleaming windows gave it an industrial air, eased a little by a porticoed entrance and an intricate fanlight over the door. A backdrop of purple beeches and cedars shielding it from the gales off the sea softened it slightly.

To the left of the house, tastefully masked by the rhododendrons that banked up on either side of the long drive, a large cobbled yard was surrounded by barns, stables and storage sheds, where, once upon a time, labourers could gather to pick up their scythes or jugs of cider. The buildings had all been converted to swish modern offices and garages, except for the one that now housed a swimming pool, faintly illuminated by concealed blue lighting, behind gleaming patio doors. Cwrt y Frân was a business centre and present-day employees would be working on laptops and drinking skinny lattés.

The yard was currently occupied by a row of neatly parked cars and a minibus. I was probably the last guest to arrive. Maybe they'd started without me, and I could just creep away? No such luck. I didn't even have to raise the big brass knocker. The door was opened, as I approached, by a woman I had seen once or twice in the village. Tall and heftily built but elegant and assured with it. She could have been Oliver's wife, except that I'd heard no mention of a stepmother for Alex.

"Good evening, Lady Nicola. Please come in." A slight Ulster accent. "Let me take your coat."

The housekeeper perhaps. I shrugged off my jacket. "Actually, I…"

Oliver Wyatt appeared out of nowhere, his hand outstretched. "Thank you, Veronica. I'll look after *Lady Nicola*." His smile was ironic.

"You do know I am no such thing?"

"I did enquire. Daughter of Ron Bryce. A chip off the paternal Marxist block, I assume?"

"Absolutely. I'll sing you all three verses of the Internationale if you like."

"I'll look forward to it." He laughed. "But can I crave your indulgence for a few hours? My mother…" He glanced up at the ceiling with a shake of the head. "Would you mind being a feather in her cap this evening? She has woven herself an alternative reality in her rather wandering old age. A little bird has told her you are the daughter of a lord and she's decided that he was an earl. I haven't had the heart to disabuse her. It's quite harmless, I assure you. Would you object to playing along for one evening?"

I groped for an answer. He was being a caring son, so I should be tolerant, but at the same time I resented it. Deeply. Of course I objected. "I quite like being who I am. Nicki Bryce, artist. Mrs Winters, wife… widow."

"Yes." He was serious, his hand squeezing mine. "I understand that. Of course. It's a lot to ask. But my mother has reached an age when there are few pleasures left and I can't bear to deny her. I shouldn't have asked it of you. Would you prefer it if I explained to her?"

I was being cornered. "Oh, God, never mind. All right, if you think it matters so much to her, I'll be Lady Nicola for an evening. I'm not exactly dressed the part."

He looked me over, amused. "She would have preferred it if you were wearing a tiara, but we'll have to make do."

"Come on then. Let's get it over with."

He offered me his arm, which I took after a moment's hesitation. If I had to play the part, I might as well do it properly. I allowed myself to be guided through into a large drawing room, in which a dozen or so guests were already gathered. They were all elderly. One had a walking frame, others wore the blank smiles or concentrated frowns of the deaf who couldn't quite understand what everyone was saying. But despite age and decrepitude, they were all dressed to the nines. The men, like Oliver, were in dinner jackets, the women in pearls and satin and the odd bit of dead animal. None of them looked comfortable in their get-up, but an effort had been made. I was wearing a dress for the first time since Adam died. It felt obligatory, somehow, for a dinner party, but I had only packed one. Sleeveless dark blue jersey. And my flat shoes were still not entirely spotless. Even the waitresses, in natty black outfits, armed with trays of sherry, looked smarter than me. Rather than feeling cowed, a sense of bolshy defiance buoyed me up.

Go on, Lady Nicola, whispered Adam, behind me. *Strut your stuff and show 'em.*

"Mother." Wyatt tapped his mother's shoulder as she was twittering with another guest. "Lady Nicola is here."

Fabia Wyatt turned. Oh my God, she was wearing a tiara. Her aging face was aglow with delight, undampened by my appearance. Maybe, in her mind, I was wearing ermine. "Ah. Lady Nicola. So glad, so glad. How delightful. You are so kind. Monica, let me introduce Lady Nicola Bryce. Lady Nicola, Monica Powell. Her husband Johnny is a Lieutenant Colonel."

"Retired," added Monica. I think she added, under her breath, "captain." She smiled bravely and shook my hand. "Bryce." She searched for some reference and couldn't find one. "Are you new to the area?"

"Yes, I am."

"She's taken a place in Tregeely for the season," said Fabia, with an aristocratic disregard for Welsh pronunciation. "Lady Nicola is quite a renowned artist."

"Ah."

"Her father was Lord Bryce, you know. The earl and my husband Sir William used to hunt together."

I flinched at the suggestion, then decided to block my ears. Challenging her about the malicious note to Willow would obviously be a waste of time. She had probably already eradicated it from her memory. I looked around as she talked, yearning for escape, if not from the house, then at least from her.

The drawing room was furnished in unforgiving Georgian style, but the walls were hung with paintings that demanded my attention. I caught a glimpse of one of mine and what looked like a Paul Nash and possibly a Gwen John. Side tables supported a gleaming steel sculpture as well as the bronze that Oliver had recently bought for Fabia. I wanted to look at them, but with Fabia's hand on my elbow I was being introduced to a string of sirs and lord admirals and double barrels. God knows where she had collected them or whether any of them really were who she claimed. They all seemed slightly bemused by her introductions, not entirely sure what was expected of them. One or two looked desperate for a nice cocoa and a comfy bed.

Why had I let myself be talked into this? A knotted ball of resistance was swelling inside me as Fabia plied me with questions, my answers tautly monosyllabic. Had I attended Glyndebourne yet this year? No. Did I ride much? No. What was my husband doing at the moment? Nothing! The question stung. She could hallucinate all she liked about me, but how dare she fantasise about Adam? I was grabbing every available glass of sweet sherry that passed within reach.

I found Oliver watching us with a smile. Was it a smile of gratitude or of amusement? I didn't care. I wasn't amused any more.

The smart woman, Veronica, who had opened the door to me, appeared at last and lightly tapped a gong.

"Dinner is served, ma'am."

"Oh. Oh yes, delightful. Now please, everyone… Ah, Oliver, come, come. You will lead the way, escort Lady Nicola in?

Oliver, biting back a smile, gravely bowed and offered me his arm.

I'd had enough of the pretence. I wasn't going to be paraded on his arm this time, but with a sigh of frustration I fell in step beside him. "You can tell me which knife and fork to use."

He smiled. "Spoons, mostly, for this lot. I'm not sure their teeth would manage anything that needs cutting."

I glanced sidelong at him as he directed me through double doors to a stately dining room. This was his mother's show, and it was just a game to him. "I expect you're more accustomed to working lunches in Davos," I suggested.

He laughed softly. "Working lunches, certainly. With fellow greedy grasping capitalists."

"Grinding down the workers."

"When we're not actually eating them." His humour was just enough to release the pressure valve and stop me running for home.

The dining room was occupied by a vast oval table, glittering with silver cutlery and candelabra. Oliver insisted on holding a chair ready for me, before seating himself to my left, at the head.

God, how long was this going to go on?

"I don't think you really need advice with the cutlery." Oliver was smiling mischievously, and I realised I was rearranging my silverware, positioning a spoon where it should be.

"No, well, I spent one summer working in a restaurant that was too up itself for its own good."

"Then you'll probably know what to expect at my mother's dinner parties. Nothing remotely exciting, but Veronica has hired decent caterers, so you won't be poisoned."

"That's reassuring."

Fabia, at the far end, was beaming at me, and pointing me out to another guest. "Her father, you know…"

Across the table, Adam looked at me, shaking his head in amused disbelief. "Get me out of this," I mouthed at him, but he had turned into a bald man nervously straightening his bow tie.

"Ah, now you are the artist, are you not?" The elderly gent on my right had decided to engage me in conversation. I had been introduced, but I couldn't remember his name. It didn't matter. He waffled on, asking the same questions over and over and obviously not taking in my answers. That was good. It meant I didn't have to answer. I didn't want to answer anyone, not even Oliver when he leaned towards me and murmured something. Out of nowhere, panic was wrapping round me, squeezing the air from my lungs.

Had I disappeared down Alice's rabbit hole? Conversation became a meaningless buzz, coming and going in waves like a swarm of bees. Faces blurred. I managed the consommé, then sat like a zombie through the next two courses. Sole and Beef Wellington. And wine. Different wines for different courses. Hands filling and refilling the glasses before me and my neighbour waffling on interminably, as soup and gravy dribbled down his front. Dishes of pineapple pavlova were being placed before us and he was still at it. As he leaned towards me to murmur in my ear, I zoned back in at last.

"Of course, he had a good innings and when it's your time it's your time, I say, but what a way to go. Utter shambles they say, blood everywhere."

Adam was sitting across from me again and as I watched, his eyes glazed, blood was pouring from his nose, his mouth, his ears. I couldn't breathe. I could only shake. I was going to faint.

A hand settled on mine, pressing it gently. "George. Could you see to Mrs Groves? I think she's been missed twice by the wine waiter."

"What? Ah, yes, yes, right away." My waffling neighbour turned away.

"Are you all right?" asked Oliver. "What am I saying? Of course you're not. I am sorry, I didn't realise. Your husband? Alex said he'd died, but I didn't realise… Oh, I am so sorry, Mrs Winters, Nicki. I had no idea I'd be placing you in such an appalling situation when I pressed you to come. I can't imagine you're in the mood for any company, let alone this geriatric pantomime. All right?" He was speaking softly, rubbing my back gently as my shaking calmed and the desire to vomit faded. Capitalist pig he might be, but he had wits enough to grasp the cause of my reactions. "Let's see if we can hurry on to the coffee and then I'll get you out of here."

I wanted to tell him I was fine, I didn't need rescuing. But I couldn't speak. I felt as if a plug had been pulled and all the sand had run out of me.

Oliver kept talking, occupying me so my waffler couldn't claim me back. He surreptitiously beckoned and the housekeeper, who had been hovering in the background, was at his side. He murmured something to her and she nodded, before gliding off down the table to whisper in Fabia's ear. Fabia frowned at Oliver. I didn't see the look he gave in reply, but her frown turned to smiling acquiescence.

"Shall we take coffee in the drawing room?"

There was a general bustle of chairs scraping, people struggling to their feet, cutlery clattering. I don't even remember rising, only Oliver guiding me smartly out of the dining room and placing a cup of black coffee in my hands before leading me to wide French windows, which he swung open.

"Come on. Are you warm enough? Let's get some fresh air."

I let him lead me out and I breathed in great gulps, my body beginning to relax. How long had every muscle in me been clenched? And how much wine had I drunk? The ground was solid beneath my feet, but the rest of the world seemed to be swaying in a high wind. I sipped the coffee. It was good and strong, thank God. I set the saucer down on a stone plinth and wrapped my hands around the cup.

"I can only apologise," said Oliver, guiding me down steps to a terraced lawn. He strolled beside me across the grass, close but not too close. "I presume your bereavement was more recent than I'd supposed?"

"Recent enough. Four months it must be now. Still seems like yesterday. He was hit by a car. Fatal collision is the correct term, I am told. Sometimes it just collides with me again."

"And I was simply trying to indulge my mother in her dotty old age, without thinking."

"Understandable," I forced myself to say.

He nodded slowly, as we descended more steps to another terrace. "It's guilt on my part, I suppose. I neglect her too much, leaving her all alone in this place. Far too big for her."

"Alex said it's her family home."

Oliver laughed, a deep easy laugh. "Not quite. That was a semi in Nuneaton, brutally suburban. But she's remodelled her memories. Her family has gradually edged up the social scale. Sometimes they're even Romanovs in exile. It all started when my father fell ill. I should have noticed the signs, the little obsessions coming on. When he died, she went to pieces entirely but somehow, she got through it by reinventing herself. So, no, Cwrt y Frân isn't the ancestral pile. My father acquired it as an investment, but never had a chance to develop it, so when he died, I urged my mother to move here and give up the London house."

He glanced sidelong at me. "I expect you've heard my mother's confusion includes a tendency to pocket things. No rhyme or reason to them. It's quite unconscious, but it was getting to be a problem, an embarrassment, to be honest, in London. I felt she'd be better off in a small community where she could be looked after indulgently, allowed to have her little ways without added complications. Veronica Erving looks after her splendidly when I'm not around and I have an understanding with the local shops. If they let me know, or I find something she's clearly walked off with, I return it, or pay for it and there's no need to involve the police. I've just returned a set of cutlery to the Bell." He smiled painfully. "Families. You do what you can."

"Yes," I said. "You do. In my case, I take care of my daughter. I assume you're aware that your mother's eccentricities include sending unpleasant letters to anyone your son takes a fancy to?"

"Alex told me. Unforgiveable of course, although he seemed to think that your daughter was happy to see the amusing side of it. I've had a word with Veronica to make sure it doesn't happen again, but I don't think you have anything to worry about. A few whispers of aristocratic lineage in my mother's ear and she's quite convinced that Willow is untouchable."

"That isn't how I would have chosen to deal with it."

"No, perhaps not. But it's done, and it means that she'll leave them in peace. I hope that Alex is managing to take your daughter out of her grief in some small way. He can be a little brash, like all the young, but he has a good heart."

"I'm sure. And yet..." He had conveniently given me the opening I needed if this evening of torture were to serve any purpose at all, but I no longer had the heart for confrontation. He was so sympathetic, so understanding, that I couldn't rise to the challenge as belligerently as I had intended. He was not the indifferent, callous oligarch that my talks with Siân had led me to imagine. I took a deep breath. "My daughter has a good heart too and I don't want it broken."

"Of course not. You're afraid Alex might do that? I'm sure he doesn't intend to hurt her in any way."

"She's not the first girl in his life."

"No, of course not. He's a good-looking lad and much too much aware of it for his own good, but I don't think he's ever behaved badly."

"What about Gaynor Hughes? How did he behave with her?"

"Gaynor Hughes!" He was taken aback. "The girl from the village?"

"She was involved with Alex, wasn't she? I've heard she was pregnant and you paid her off. That's one version at least."

It was his turn to draw a deep breath, a flicker of annoyance showing. "Hm. Is that how it's told? I suppose you think Alex had his wicked way with her, left her in the lurch and his brutal father sold her off to traffickers. And you're afraid the same might happen to Willow."

"Something like that. I didn't mean to paint it in quite such lurid tones, but Gaynor was involved with Alex, wasn't she? She came here and the next thing, she's sending postcards from London and her mother's frantic with worry about her."

His eyes narrowed. "That would be Mrs Hughes, wouldn't it? She's employed to look after some of my properties."

"A cleaning lady, yes. She thinks Gaynor was pregnant and you or Alex persuaded her to have an abortion and disappear."

"Right." He pulled himself together. "I thought I'd cleared this up, but I can see how things are being twisted. Let's set the record straight. Yes, Gaynor Hughes did go out with my son a few times last summer. As did quite a few others. You know how it is, and yes, I am afraid Fabia reacted to her exactly as she did to your daughter. But this February, as I was about to leave for London, I found the girl on our doorstep. She claimed that Alex had got her pregnant and I should give her money or else. Well, it was patently absurd. Her pregnancy wasn't at all obvious so Alex couldn't have been responsible. He hadn't been here since the previous summer. He'd either been in Oxford or in Switzerland over Christmas with me. I suppose she just imagined, rich man, try her luck with a feeble bit of blackmail. I'm afraid I was pretty brusque. I told her I'd call the police if she said another word.

"I expect I can be rather intimidating. I'm more accustomed to dealing with hard-nosed businessmen than pathetic little girls. She broke down, burst into tears, and I finished up feeling sorry for her. I invited her in and asked her to tell me all about it. After all, solving problems is my metier. She confessed that yes, she was genuinely pregnant, but she had no idea who the father was. She was in trouble, she was frightened, there'd been some terrible row with her family at home and all she wanted was to get away. She had this dream of being an actress, film-star, you know what these girls are like. She was looking for escape, a solution to the unwanted pregnancy, a new life, and she was desperate. I'm actually quite soft-hearted. She was a sweet little thing in her way when she wasn't resorting to extortion. And, if I'm honest, I wanted to avoid her turning up at Alex's door in Oxford and making the same demands. So, I agreed to help her. She obviously didn't have anyone else who could. I offered her five thousand pounds and she jumped at it."

"You did pay her off."

"With peanuts. And I did more than that, I hope. I knew a clinic that could help her and contacts in the theatre world who could possibly offer her a job as a first step in the life she wanted. I didn't just brush her away. I was about to leave for London anyway, so I drove her there and left her in the hands of people who could take care of her."

"Where is she now?"

"Still in London, I assume. You mean, a precise address? I could enquire if you like, but... you must understand, she really didn't want people coming after her. I don't know what had happened at home, but she wasn't a happy girl. An argument about the baby perhaps? She genuinely wanted to escape." He gave a twisted smile. "I imagine Tregelli can be quite a suffocating place if you have nowhere else to go."

I said nothing. It was true I had only heard Siân's side of the story. She blamed Alex but how many other boys were there in Gaynor's life? A girl gone off the rails. Siân had hinted that she and Gaynor had had a difference of opinion about the baby. It was possible that Gaynor was determined to have an abortion and Siân disapproved. And I really didn't know what other strains there had been between mother and adolescent daughter. There had been plenty between Willow and me in her earlier teens.

One thing was certain: I didn't want anything dividing Willow and me now. I shivered.

Instantly, Oliver removed his jacket and placed it round my shoulders. "You're cold. Can you face going back to the house?"

"I'd rather not, to be honest."

"No. Really you want to go home to your daughter. Of course you do. Come on, I'll drive you."

"No need. It's only round the corner."

"I'll drive you," he said firmly. "You've already suffered enough for one day."

"You've been drinking."

"Very little. And as you say, it's only round the corner."

I was there. Again. There. Reliving that moment that lasted an eternity, endlessly repeated and yet had been over in a flash. Adam across the road, a milk carton raised triumphantly as he grinned at me and then, roar, skid, crash, and Adam crumpling into a car bonnet, catapulting across the road, smashing into the gate post. I could feel the bile rising, my whole body shaking.

"No!" It came out as a croak. "No one is drinking and driving me anywhere."

He squeezed his eyes tight shut, cursing himself. "Sorry. Of course. But I'll walk with you. No argument. Come on, no need to face the gathering again." We had returned along an acre of tiered lawns and shrubberies to the paved terrace by the house. The housekeeper was waiting by the open French windows.

"Veronica, will you bring Mrs Winter's coat? We don't want to go back in the house."

"Yes, sir." She brought my jacket, and he helped me on with it before reclaiming his own.

"You'll explain to my mother?"

"I've told her Lady Nicola has been summoned by a royal equerry." Veronica Erving gave me a twitch of a smile. "She seems to be happy with that."

"Good. Come." Oliver ushered me on. "Let's get you home."

I heaved a sigh of relief at being permitted to escape. He walked with me down the long gravel drive, the gates that opening silently at his approach. I let him escort me along Bethel Lane but at the muddy steps up to our acre I insisted that he turned back. "I'm fine now. You really don't want those shoes getting plastered in mud. Please." I insisted as he looked about to argue. "No. Go back to Cwrt y Frân. Tell your mother Lady Nicola apologises for her absence. And thank you for your understanding."

He pressed my hand. "Thank you for yours. I can only beg forgiveness again for having put you through this. I'm sure you want nothing more than a quiet time with your own thoughts. But Mrs Winters, Nicki, please be reassured. I know my son. He may seem an over-confident young buck, but he had vulnerabilities of his own. He'd do nothing to hurt Willow or any other girl."

I nodded and watched him walk away. My head ached. My heart ached. I'd had enough.

14

"Wait!" I was half running to catch up with Siân as she trudged between jobs.

She managed a smile. "You survived then. Dinner with his lordship and the Queen of Sheba?"

"I had to leave early. There was only so much I could take."

She nodded, breathing heavily, waiting for whatever I might have to tell her. I could see her knuckles tightening on her heavy bags.

"I did manage to speak with Oliver Wyatt though. About Gaynor."

"Yes?"

"He admits he gave her money and took her to London. And he fixed her up at a clinic and put her in touch with some theatre contacts."

Siân came to a halt, staring fiercely at nothing. "Where is she then?"

"He says he left her with people and she's gone her own way. He said he could find out where she's living now, but... Siân, did you have a bit of a row with Gaynor before she left?"

"No!" She said it angrily, too quickly. "Is that what he's saying then? That I drove her away?"

"He says he thought she was unhappy." I didn't want to suggest that she was desperate to get away, but I'd already said too much.

"That's that then," said Siân.

"Do you have time to stop for a cup of tea?"

"No. Not now. Too busy. Another day, all right?"

* * *

"This one… no, here. This one. Look. Me at the wheel." Willow tilted her phone so I could get a better view of the screen. Alex Wyatt's Instagram posts. He believed in keeping the world informed of his conquests. There was Willow, smiling, hair flying, as she poised at the wheel of the Wyatt launch.

"Let me see the rest," I asked.

"Why?"

"I like looking at pictures of my daughter. My clever daughter. Is that all right? Are there some I shouldn't see?"

Willow thought hard for a second, then shrugged. "No, they're fine. Here." She handed me the phone. "Help yourself." She rose from the sofa beside me. "I'll make some lunch, shall I?"

"Please." Left to myself I scrolled through a couple of dozen photos of Willow – being excited, being serious, being silly, Willow posing, Willow caught unawares. My daughter living a life independent of me. She had received her A level results that morning and now she was free to confirm her place at university, whichever she chose. If she chose. She was still being cagey with me about whether she'd go or not and I was praying that she'd do the right thing. But a deeply buried niggle inside me was starting to question what the right thing was.

If she doesn't want to go, she won't leave you, like I did.

"Is that really what I'm afraid of?" Maybe that was why I was so wary of her friendship with Alex Wyatt. Not fear of harm but fear that he would take her from me. I couldn't cope with that idea just now.

Selfish cow, aren't you?

"Yes. I am."

Angry with myself, I turned back to the phone, flicking through endless shots of Alex's busy life. More photos of Willow, and other young people outside a pub. Photos of friends at Oxford. No scenic shots of Magdalen bridge but plenty of fellow students grinning, leaping, playing the fool. Who'd take a picture of earnest work?

More photos of a ski resort, taken at Christmas, more friends, a couple with his father. One with Fabia looking vague, with Veronica Erving looming up behind her.

Pembrokeshire. Yet more friends, mostly male and rowdy. And one amongst them of a girl I recognised from the photo on Siân's mantlepiece. The same strong, striking features, the same long dark hair, Alex's arm around her shoulder. She looked happy, he looked slightly drunk.

I sat there staring at it, half my mind on the girl in the photo, smiling out of the past, and half on my problems of the present.

"What's up?" Willow, wiping her hands dry, slid back beside me. "What's that? Oh. Is that her then? Siân's daughter? Still obsessing about her?"

"I'm not obsessing. I'm just thinking how I've messed up things with Siân, without meaning to. I should never have gone to that dinner, should I?"

"No, you shouldn't. Sounded like a real heap of laughs."

"I didn't go to be entertained. I only meant to ask about Gaynor for Siân's sake, but all it's done is drive a wedge between us. I don't know what to believe. Siân says she didn't row with her daughter, but would I admit it if you and I had a flaming row and you stormed out?"

"Yeah. You would. You'd beat yourself up about it."

"Maybe. But would I want to tell the world that you'd gone because you couldn't stand home anymore? The fact is, I can't expect to blunder into other people's lives and understand the truth of it all after a couple of chats over tea. All I know is that I feel desperately sorry for Siân, whoever was at fault."

"Yeah," said Willow, looking at the picture again. "Nice bag."

"What?"

"Her bag. I like it."

Gaynor's hand was resting on a shoulder bag of patchwork leather, its fringe fluttering in the wind, glinting with something silver. I saw family rifts and my daughter saw a fashion accessory.

"I'll ask Gareth about it," she said, getting up again. "Salad okay?"

"Yes, fine. We'll have a proper celebration meal tonight."

"Celebration?"

"Your results. Your brilliant grades. Your chance to go…"

"Oh that. Yeah, sure."

"If you want to discuss it… University? I just…"

"Chill out, Mum, leave it to me."

"I know you're tight with Alex at the moment, but he'll be going back to Oxford. So…"

Willow laughed. A remarkable healthy, almost care-free laugh. "Yeah, back to the grind. Says the social life is wicked. Reckons the rest of it's a waste of time."

"But…"

"But then Gareth says grab it with both hands."

"Gareth? Siân's Gareth? I didn't know you saw that much of him."

"Yeah, now and again. You know. Like Alex." She grinned. "I'm just chilling. Not making life choices. Except for university. And yes, I am going. Exeter, okay?"

"Oh. Oh!" I jumped up and hugged her.

"And since it worries you so much, I'll get Gareth to tell me what was going on with his sister, if there was a big row or anything. Happy?"

"Blissful," I said.

15

Willow remained irritatingly blasé with me about the need to make arrangements for university, but she kept her word and asked Gareth about his sister. He claimed to know nothing about any violent argument between Gaynor and mother, everything had been fine, so what more could I do?

August was drawing to a close and the end of summer was to be celebrated with the Tregelli regatta, a two-day annual event. Bunting went up in preparation for parades of boats, races, and imbibing. I might have let it pass in a mystifying haze, but Willow was going to be involved, so I decided to join the crowds on the quay and watch. She would be on the Lotte Lenya with Harry and his nephew Gareth, for various technical reasons to do with umpiring and safety, too complicated to explain to me.

I saw Siân and waved, and she came over, almost smiling. "You a fan of water sports then?"

"I'm about to find out. Is Rhys taking part in any of the races?"

"God, no. Not a great fan of anything wet. Just his music."

I laughed, remembering our first boat trip with Harry. "Gareth's not so reluctant."

"No!" She was almost animated. "Always loved messing around on the water. Pity he's not got a boat or he might have a go tomorrow. The sailing, you know."

"That's tomorrow, is it? I don't know anything about regattas."

"It's all the fun stuff today. The kiddies and swimming and what not. Tomorrow they get serious." She was interrupted by a loudspeaker, announcing the first race, a swim across the harbour. "Well, I'd best get on. No rest for the wicked."

"Aren't you staying to watch?" I indicated my basket with its flask and sausage rolls. "I've got plenty."

She shook her head. "Signed on with the WI brigade, keeping our village tip-top." She held up a roll of black bags. "Place would be a pigsty if we don't keep on top of it."

"Of course. Do you want some help? I can't just stand here while you're working."

Her smile broadened as she patted my arm with her free hand. "We know what we're doing. You stay and watch the races now."

So I stayed and enjoyed the spectacle of fun and games in the water. Shrieks and laughter ringing across the creek. In the afternoon my phone purred in my pocket. A text from Willow, out on the Lotte Lenya.

Alex says I can go on their yacht tomorrow and his dad says would you like to come too?

I looked out across the harbour, currently hosting a shambolic fancy-dress race on inflated tyres, water splashing, glinting in the sun, thinking that it was rather tame to be sitting on a deckchair with a flask.

Go on, whispered Adam in my ear. *You'd love it. You loved that trip on the Lotte Lenya, didn't you? Even*

113

better under sail, skimming over the water like an albatross.

"Yes, but with Oliver Wyatt?" Apart from a friendly wave from his Jaguar as he passed me in Tregelli, I hadn't had any further contact with the lord of the manor since the ghastly dinner party.

Thinking about him too much, are you? So, he's gort a yort. That's enough. Go for it.

"Oh, what the hell." I tapped a reply to Willow. *Yes please, if I won't be in the way.*

* * *

The following morning, I waited with Willow on the quay, as ordered, to be collected by the Wyatt boat.

I looked around for signs of it, surely one of the smarter sailing boats in the harbour, limbering up for the day instead of snoozing gently in their moorings as usual. I shaded my eyes searching, but I couldn't see Alex or his father among any of the crews gathering on decks, busy with sails and tackle. I totally ignored the launch heading in to edge up to the quay, until Willow nudged me.

"Oh," I said. "I thought we were going to be in a yacht."

"We are," said Willow, as Alex reached up a hand to help me in.

He grinned. "Hi, Nicki. Don't worry, this is just the ferry."

"I see."

We were off. As we rounded the harbour wall, I glanced up at the crowds already ensconced with cameras, deckchairs, hampers, preparing to enjoy the day, despite ominous clouds in the west.

There was Siân, with a couple of other jolly ladies armed with plastic bags. I found myself squirming, hoping she wouldn't glance my way. I didn't want her seeing me sitting in pride of place on the Wyatt launch. Her eyes glanced with fleeting interest over the passing boats, and for a moment I thought I'd escaped. But then she saw me and did a double take. I tried to smile bravely and raised a hand. Expressionless, she raised hers slightly in return, then turned her back and continued talking with her companions.

"Damn." I said turning desperately to face the open sea.

"What's up," asked Willow. "You're not seasick, are you?"

"No. No, I'm fine. Where's this yacht then?" There were a dozen or more sailing dinghies skidding across the bay, but most could hold only a couple of people.

"There she is." Alex pointed and I looked further out, my heart swelling at the sight of tall white sails billowing taut as birdwings, as a much larger boat came racing towards us, sleek as a dolphin, tilting in the water, spray rising around it. It was a perfect image of freedom, between purple-blue sea and mostly blue sky, or would have been if a bloody great passenger ship behind it had not spoiled the view. Then it drew nearer, near enough for me to see that there were four youthful and energetic sailors on board and none of them were Oliver Wyatt.

And it dawned on me. The Wyatt yacht was the bloody great passenger ship. Perhaps not an actual cruise liner or the Irish ferry, but still a monster, with three or four tiers of decks, sun loungers, crew in crisp white uniforms handing round trays of champagne and a host of smartly dressed passengers casually raising binoculars or throwing back their heads in hearty laughter. It was the sort of ship in which Blofeld plotted world domination.

"I thought yachts had sails," I said lamely.

Alex laughed. "Only sailing yachts."

"My mistake."

"Here we are." With nonchalant skill, he turned the launch in a wide circle to approach the monstrous ship up its gleaming rear. At least I didn't face the indignity of being hauled up a ladder on the towering hull. We were simply handed onto a landing platform by a couple of uniformed flunkies and ushered up polished wooden stairs to the deck above, where Oliver Wyatt was waiting to greet us.

He smiled as he shook my hand. "Glad you were willing to indulge us again, after my previous faux pas."

I managed a smile in return, praying that Siân wasn't watching us from the harbour wall.

"Nicki was hoping for sails," said Alex, pulling Willow off into the interior with a departing wave at me.

Oliver laughed. "Ah. I'm afraid that for all her virtues, the Artemis is not quite that green."

"I wasn't expecting a Dreadnought."

"Now, now, she's nothing terrible. Quite modest for her class, barely sixty metres."

"Barely nothing. Come on! Swimming pool?"

"Yes, a small one. And Jacuzzi. Gym. Cinema."

"Precisely. She's serious bling. Admit it."

He laughed again, a deep hearty chuckle. "Maybe, by some standards. But she's not a personal indulgence, you understand. She's a corporate asset, our very willing working girl, earning her keep satisfying some very well-heeled clients." He was making light of it, but he could see I found the analogy distasteful, and immediately he was serious. "I'm sorry. A poor joke. But in the business world, it's a sad fact that excess spells success. Bling like this is what investors expect, if we're to part them from their money."

"You're not winning me over."

"No, I don't suppose I am. You are too feisty a revolutionary firebrand and I'd hate to see you tarnish your principles for a capitalist reprobate like me. But can I at least tempt you to a glass of champagne? Or a cocktail? Quickly, before my mother arrives to press her sherry on you. She'll be over the moon to find you here."

"Does she still think I'm Lady Nicola?" I accepted a glass.

"I haven't had the heart to disabuse her. But I will if you find it upsetting."

"No." I took a swig and shrugged. "Let her keep her delusions. Why not? Everything feels fake today."

"We are such stuff as dreams are made on."

"Quite." I was absurdly annoyed with him for getting the quotation right and snatched another glass as he guided me round the yacht. Boat. Ship. Liner. Whatever it was, there was too much of it. And whatever my dreams were, they didn't feature a thing like this.

He was astute enough to appreciate, once we'd reached a canopied dining area with a well-stocked bar, that I wasn't impressed.

"We have been known to take a couple of deckchairs and join the spectators on the harbour wall," he said. "The Artemis is only here this year because we're entertaining a contact from the States. Calvin Eastermann. Calvin! Come and meet Nicki Bryce. The artist I was telling you about?"

"Ah." Calvin Eastermann was a slim, taut-featured, east-coast American, with a ready smile and annoyingly perfect teeth. He shook my hand. "Hi there. So, Nicki Bryce. Oliver says you're a rising star, going places, and I always trust his word on art as with all investments. I'll be looking out for you in future."

"Calvin was intrigued when I mentioned a village regatta," explained Oliver.

"For my son," said Eastermann. "Cal… Where is he? Ah, there's the boy."

The boy, Calvin Eastermann Junior, was a strapping six foot three, his muscular arms around Alex and Willow, as he herded them towards the bar.

"Who's the gorgeous nymph your son's snapped up, Oliver?" asked Eastermann, assessing Willow like a slab of meat.

"My daughter," I said.

"Is she? Great looking girl. Alex had better watch out or Cal will be stealing her away."

"My daughter isn't property to be stolen," I said, stiffly. Oliver might be in the business of buttering up Mr Eastermann, but I wasn't.

Oliver stepped in before Eastermann's lip had time to curl. "I imagine Cal's going to have all his thoughts on the race today." He smiled at me. "Cal's something of a sailor, and he fancied trying his luck. There's a laser-class so we picked one up at the marina."

Cal Junior, lolling against the bar, turned to face us, eyebrows raised, sensing that we were talking about him.

"Not drinking before your race?" suggested his father.

"No sir!"

Alex discreetly shifted a glass along the bar. "How do you fancy your chances?"

"Oh, pretty good, pretty good."

"Eastermanns like to win," said his father, with a humourless smile.

"Yes sir!"

"Going to show the hicks how it's done?" suggested Alex. "Might have a run for your money, you know. It's only a village thing, but we get some serious competitors come to take part."

"Oh sure. Bring them on." Cal's breezy confidence was aimed, I suspected, at his father. What would happen to him if he didn't win? Sent to bed without supper maybe.

I caught Willow's rather glassy eyes, which flashed wider as they met mine. Her smile was forced. She turned and whispered in Alex's ear.

"Okay, Wills, you know where it is."

"Yes, I know." She sidled into the interior.

I was about to follow, but Eastermann was in my way. "There's talk of selecting him for the Olympics." Behind him, Oliver's eyes rolled.

"Is there? That's nice."

"You don't sail, yourself, Nicki?" He'd placed himself in front of me, invading my space, demanding my attention, as if I were a challenge he had determined to conquer.

"No. I'm a complete landlubber, I'm afraid."

"You should try it. Oliver…"

"Please, excuse me for a moment." I skirted round him and hurried off to find Willow about to enter a luxurious bathroom, her phone in her hand.

"Are you all right?"

She turned to me, pulling an expressive face. "God! Cal Eastermann is a total git. Tried to bloody grope me. I'm phoning Gareth. He said he wasn't sure whether he'd race. I'm going to tell him he's got to. Maybe he can borrow a boat."

"Cal's father is expecting him to compete in the Olympics."

"Yeah, well, he can carry on expecting. Gareth's pretty good too. Won plenty of races in Cardiff."

"What was he doing in Cardiff?"

"Electronic engineering." I could hear her phone dialling. "Not sure he'll be able to do much sailing in Manchester." She saw my raised eyebrows. "His PhD. Just heard he's got his funding. Starts there any moment. Ah. Gareth! Listen." She shooed me away, clamping her phone to her ear, and whispering to me. "I'm supposed to be having a pee." She shut the bathroom door.

I turned back, feeling lighter now that I was embroiled in a conspiracy with my daughter. Oliver was still chatting to Eastermann by the bar. He saw me coming and his lips twitched a warning smile. I realised why when Fabia Wyatt stepped forward to greet me, clasping my hand, Veronica Erving one step behind.

"Lady Nicola, how lovely that you could join us." Fabia was wearing a jaunty yachting cap and beautifully tailored blazer over a linen dress. Predicting that it could be breezy on a boat, even in fine weather, I was in jogging pants and an aging hooded fleece, but she didn't seem to notice. She beamed up at me. "I was so thrilled when Oliver told me you could join us today. We've been quite in raptures, haven't we, Erving?"

Veronica Erving's eyes crinkled in sardonic mirth. "Entirely, ma'am."

"You cannot imagine how much I appreciate your company. There are so few people in the area that one can mix with. Would you care for a sherry?"

"Thank you." I was fighting to contain my laughter. "I think I'll stick to orange juice for now."

The barman promptly produced an iced juice.

"So, tell me, Nicola… can I call you Nicola? What are you working on, these days?"

"Pieces for an exhibition in November. In London." Playing along with Fabia was presumably payment for being on this boat thing. Did it really hurt? "I'll make sure the gallery sends you a VIP invitation."

"Oh, that would be charming. And here's your daughter. I hear an engagement is about to be announced!" She didn't notice my astonishment, which quickly subsided as I caught Veronica's surreptitious shake of the head. "Such a lovely smile. Could it be the smile of a beautiful girl in love?"

"It's possible," I said. Or the smile of a girl who'd just succeeded in spiking some gilded guns.

Alex, with unexpected tact, jumped in to claim his grandmother as Willow hooked her arm through mine. "Shall we go out on the sun deck and watch the first race?" She added in a whisper, "Thought you needed rescuing from Fantasy Fibs."

"I was coping, thank you, but yes, let's go and watch some real boats, while you tell me all about your forthcoming engagement."

Willow's roar of laughter reassured me that it was just Fabia's imagination on overtime again.

I knew nothing about sailing, but today's races, out on the open sea, looked serious. One was already underway, a flotilla of sails herded by a launch and an inflatable as they surged towards an orange buoy so distant it was barely visible. I couldn't make head or tail of what was happening. Three or four other guests were already out there, watching intently

They glanced at us, not sure if we were guests or staff. Others were arriving on deck, Oliver's people, not Fabia's flotsam from the local nursing homes. Men and women at ease in this luxury setting. Power and indolence vied with each other, vibrating in the air. Champagne and conversation flowed. Some of the talk concerned sailing, but most revolved around high finance and mega deals, all equally meaningless jargon to me.

"Do you have the first idea what everyone's going on about?" I asked.

"Not a clue," said Willow, as we both reached for glasses, orange juice discarded.

Across the deck, Fabia was being settled into a chair by Veronica Erving. She was looking around anxiously, searching so, shamelessly, I ducked behind some others. Cal Junior, jawing with Alex, caught his father's eye as Eastermann emerged with Oliver. He yawned and stretched, flexing his muscles before coming our way, Alex beside him. "Best get going then. You guys cheer me on, okay? Remember, 3598." He smacked Willow's rump in passing, or would have done if she hadn't skilfully moved at the last moment.

Alex exchanged a meaningful look with her and urged him on to the rear – stern – end – thing. He was back with us in time to see Cal sail past, heading for the harbour on what looked like a skateboard with sail. He was leaning far out, throwing us a casual wave, and I could see that to attain the albatross illusion, a sailor needed the muscles, agility and stamina of a prize fighter. Nothing relaxing about it. Perhaps it was just as well the Wyatt yacht had no sails. Less of an albatross, more like a bull-elephant done up for a durbar, and I need do nothing but lounge and watch.

I tried to listen for the more knowledgeable comments on techniques and manoeuvres amongst the background rumbling about share issues and bull and bear markets, but I couldn't make head or tail of any of it. Alex had drawn Willow to one side, explaining tactics to her, just beyond earshot. She nodded occasionally and then surreptitiously glanced down at the phone when it vibrated in her pocket. She flashed a broad smile at me.

I smiled back innocently.

A waiter presented me with a platter of canapés and Oliver, coming towards me with Eastermann, plucked a champagne bottle from a passing tray and topped up my almost empty glass.

"Enjoying the show, Nicki?"

"Enjoying being on the sea. I don't understand any of the racing business."

"My mother would be more than happy to explain but…" He laughed. "Veronica's taking care of her. So, let's see how our champion gets on." He glanced at his watch, a hefty gleaming affair, probably a Rolex or some such thing costing thousands. Instinctively, I glanced at my own. Twelve pounds fifty from the local market. Interestingly, they both gave the same time. One thirty. "Any moment now, I think."

Sure enough, a pistol shot rang out and a distant cluster of surfboards with wings surged forward. I had no idea where Cal Junior was in that mêlée, or whether Gareth Hughes was among them. All the boats looked the same, and the sailors in their buoyancy jackets, straining out over the waves, were indistinguishable.

"A clean start," said Oliver. "Good."

"Yes! There he goes!" roared Eastermann in my ear.

Oliver raised his binoculars to focus on the front of the pack. "Nicely positioned."

"Come on, boy!" Eastermann was taking it extremely seriously. "Concentrate! He'll have to tack away or lock himself out. Yes! Good boy."

I sidled closer to Willow and she gave me a little nudge. I looked down at the phone in her hand. *2992*. I smiled. "Any idea how he's doing?"

She shrugged.

"Here," said Oliver at my other side, handing me his binoculars. "If you'd like to get a closer look. There's he is, at the front. 3598."

I peered through the heavy things. Every time I thought I'd got it in focus, the boats had moved. I was still struggling with it as the leaders approached the distant buoy. The number on the sail, that was it. 3598. Yes, that was Cal Junior, but where was Gareth in that mass of straining sails and straining bodies? As the boats swooped round the buoy and came hurtling back, all I could see was utter confusion. One boat capsized and righted, a couple fell way behind. There it was! 2992. Not too far from 3598, but from my angle, I couldn't even work out which one was in front. They were all streaming back at full tilt. Eastermann was still very urgent in his concentration, but everyone else seemed relaxed.

I handed the binoculars back. They were wasted on me. "Can you see who's going to win?" I whispered to Willow.

"I think they go round again," she whispered back.

"My God, can I stand the suspense?" I grabbed another canapé and there was Oliver topping up my glass again.

"Getting the hang of it?"

"Not remotely."

"They'll be through the gate, then tacking into the wind back to the first mark."

"I take it you know all about sailing."

"I have been known to dabble."

"I'm guessing you don't merely dabble in anything."

He laughed, raising the binoculars again. "Cutting across. He's having to hike hard, but he's a strong lad."

"So's that other one," growled Eastermann. "Equal weight, by the look of him. Don't like the way he's closing up."

"I think Gareth's on him," whispered Willow, grabbing my hand.

Once more, the boats zoomed together to skim round the distant buoy and now the tension on the Artemis began to build. More of the guests were watching with increasing excitement.

"Come on, Cal boy! Let 'em have it!" Eastermann's nostrils flared as he shouted. Others took his cue, calling encouragement although there was no possibility of the racers hearing a thing.

"Come on Cal!"

"Keep going, Cal! You can do it!"

"Go, Cal, go!"

"Gareth! Come on, Gareth!" The shout burst out of my daughter and the sound unstopped my own lungs.

"Come on, Gareth!" I roared, feeling people shift away from me. Unrepentant, I shouted again. "Come on, Gareth!" I had no idea what was happening, but who cared?

"There they go," said Oliver, behind me. "Cal's squeezing one of the other boats, tacking, oh! That's got to be a penalty."

"The stupid fool!" raged Eastermann.

"But there's still time for him to make up for it. Ah, no! Surfed off a wave straight into the back of another. And... no, looks as if the other chap has stolen his lead."

Eastermann was seething. My daughter was still yelling "Come on, Gareth!" at the top of her lungs and Alex was watching her with pained displeasure.

I couldn't see how it ended, but others could. The shouting subsided to normal conversation.

"Your Gareth came third," said Oliver, with a polite smile.

"And Cal?"

"Fifth. His own fault." He glanced at Alex and Willow, deeply involved in a quietly forceful exchange. "An interesting outcome."

"Sorry. We weren't very diplomatic, were we?"

Oliver shrugged. "I can't say I welcome Eastermann's nose being put out of joint, but he's a grown man and you're quite entitled to support your own champion. Who is it? Gareth Hughes, by any chance?"

"Yes."

"Well, he sailed a good race. Congratulate him for me."

"Hughes." Fabia was out of her throne and advancing on us, though Veronica was coming behind her, ready to swoop if necessary. "I don't understand how they let him in on the race. His sort shouldn't have been allowed."

"Now, now, Mother." Oliver shook his head over her. "You know everyone's allowed to race. It's not the preserve of minor royalty."

"But…"

"And you are traducing one of the stars of Tregelli. A highly educated engineer with a very bright future."

"But… Hughes!"

"I'm sure I wish him the best of luck," said Eastermann, oozing acid.

"People were cheering him." Fabia wasn't going to let it pass. "They shouldn't have done that, should they, Oliver?"

"Yes, Mother, they should. He sailed a very good race."

Willow, parted from Alex who seemed to be sulking, tugged my arm and whispered in my ear. "Were we bad?"

"No. Why shouldn't we cheer Gareth on? He deserves it. But Alex is jealous, I gather."

"Well… He's a bit funny about Gareth. He liked the idea of Cal being beaten, but Gareth… you know, being Gaynor's brother, and all that. He was really upset by her dumping him. He pretends not to be."

"That's what I thought. I think he's a young man who's experienced a lot of hurt. You will be careful, won't you?"

"I will. We're friends, okay. That's all. Anyway, we're going home soon, aren't we? So…" Her words trailed away as Fabia's excited voice rose again above the babble.

"Oh yes, a lovely girl, Willow, such a charming name, and a little bird tells me her engagement to the son of the Duke of Argyll is about to be announced. Such a delightful match, just as it should be. How many times have I told Oliver, he should have chosen a lady, not that vulgar creature Helena. I had to get rid of her. But dear Willow understands the rank to which she is entitled. Her mother, Lady Nicola, you know her? Dabbles in art, so charming. The daughter of an Earl of course. Her husband is a great friend of Oliver's, comes to him for advice on just about everything. Sir Justin de Winters, you know him? He and Lady Nicola are a delightful couple, often dine here."

Willow's giggle at Fabia's absurdities was cut off by a gasp. She turned to me, her face white with shock and disgust. "She can't say that!"

"No, she can't."

"My dad's not sir something de Winters. Why's she saying that?"

Willow's distress was as deep as my own. Suddenly, the whole charade turned from a joke to a hurtful insult. "I'm not going to listen to this! I don't care what crap she comes up with about earls and dukes, but she has no right to go giving me any sort of husband in place of your father!"

Oliver, who seemed to have been listening to four or five conversations at once, glanced our way, saw our expression of grief-fuelled fury and immediately stepped in to intervene. "Mother, that's enough!"

She looked up at him like a naughty child, not sure what she had done. "But I thought…"

"Veronica, perhaps you would like to escort my mother inside. She needs a nap, don't you think?"

Veronica Erving nodded and guided her bewildered charge away.

Oliver turned back to me. "I am sorry. She doesn't understand how discomforting her notions would be to you."

"Then make her understand!" I hugged my daughter. "I am married to Adam Winters, not some chinless twat with a title. Tell her that. Adam is dead and I can't bring him back, but no one, no one is going to write him out of existence!"

"Yes. Yes, I understand. It was unforgiveable. Come on. Let me take you inside, get you a drink…"

"No! Thanks, but no. I'd rather not." I no longer wanted to be a part of this absurd scene. "In fact, I'd rather just go home. That's all I want."

He hesitated for a second. "Of course. Yes." He half-turned, beckoning Alex who was standing bemused, aware that something was seriously wrong. "Alex, can you run Nicki back to the harbour? Willow, would you prefer…"

"I'm going with Mum," said Willow, gripping my arm firmly. Adam was embracing us both.

"Quite right. Again, Nicki, I am sorry. Everyone knows how my mother's imagination runs wild, but that's no excuse. What can I say? Please tell me she hasn't ruined the day for you."

I forced a deep breath, muttered something meaningless. To everyone else on board, I was probably making a hysterical fuss about nothing, but I just wanted to go. Alex, still not quite aware of what had happened, ushered us through the ship. From a cabin, I heard Fabia.

"Oh, but Lady Nicola…"

"Lady Nicola doesn't like people talking about her husband, Fabia. It's not considered polite and she's a little over-sensitive."

Over-sensitive. Yes. A dark cloud was engulfing me again, my hands shaking as they grasped stair rails, that knot of anger and grief hardening inside me. Why had I come?

"Was it Fibs?" asked Alex, handing me back into the launch, with Willow's support. He looked genuinely concerned, no longer sulking.

"She thinks Mum's married to some…" said Willow, her voice shaking too. "Someone else. Not my father. I don't care if she thinks I'm going to marry a duke or something, but…"

"Oh, for fuck's sake!" Alex started the engine as if firing the first shot of a world war. "Sorry," he added hastily. "Fibs is… she's a joke, except sometimes she's not funny. She doesn't understand when she's hurting someone."

His words passed through me and floated out to sea as we sped across the waves back to the harbour wall. Then they floated back and penetrated my mind as I caught the hint. Had Fabia hurt him too in the past? The boy whose mother walked out on him. The vulgar Helena that Fabia had chased away. His grandmother would have done nothing to ease that pain. I would have felt sorry for him if my own feelings weren't swamping everything else.

16

We were leaving Carregwen. In my current mood, I would have been happy to get straight in the car and leave without a backward glance, but we couldn't do that. We had to tidy up, clean the cottage, pack our cases, say goodbyes.

I could tell Willow was struggling with silent pain again. She had seen so buoyantly recovered these last few weeks, but one silly comment by a daft old lady had set her right back, immersed in grief again. And I was back where I'd started. *You're mine*, said Adam, wrapping his arms around me. *You always will be.* And then he wasn't there and it was all a lie. A hateful heart-rending lie. All the therapy of our summer escape had been wiped out at a stroke. We needed to start again, move on to another phase, Willow's new life at university.

I was sorting out the summerhouse studio, wrapping up pictures too big for the car, to be collected later, when I heard Siân's heavy footsteps approaching. She glanced in, diffidently.

"This is where you've been working then?"

"Yes. On and off."

"And you're off back home now."

"Yes. What with Willow going off to Exeter soon, we need to sort things out."

"Gareth says you've been upset. Willow told him. Said that Fabia bloody Wyatt got under your skin."

"You could say that." I managed a smile, which brought angry tears to my eyes.

"Daft old shit," said Siân. "Come and have a cup of tea."

"Sorry, I should have been offering you one."

"You've got enough to do. But have a break, eh?"

So I followed her back to the cottage and let her make tea. Gareth had come with her and was sitting in the living room with Willow, examining something on her laptop.

"Congratulations on the race," I said, joining them on the sofa and glancing at the screen. Something to do with Exeter University. It was a relief that he seemed bent on keeping her on course.

Gareth grinned, sheepishly. "Well. You know. Only came third."

"But you beat Cal Eastermann."

"Yes. Okay, that was pretty satisfying."

"Pity it wasn't Alex Wyatt," muttered Siân, coming through with a tray.

Gareth shot her a warning glance and she pressed her lips together.

The old resentments, other people's pain – what was I to do with it all? I had no magic powers to put things right. I was leaving, walking away from all this. I walked to the window and stared out, blinking. Adam had died. I could walk and walk and walk, but I couldn't walk away from that.

A creak told me Willow and Gareth were tiptoeing out into the kitchen. I turned to find Siân waiting quietly with a mug of tea.

"Me and my big mouth," she said, pressing the mug into my hands. "Shouldn't be heaping our worries on you."

"Sorry." I took a deep breath. "I'm in a bit of a muddle at the moment."

"Best by far if you go home and dump the lot of us, I reckon. Clean start." She looked round, assessing the cottage. "So, this is what they've done with the place. The MacDonalds. Kept that beam. I remember ham hanging from that. Old lady who lived here when I was a girl. Mary Phillips, that was her name. Here, till the very end. Ninety-eight, she was. Must have been born when Victoria was on the throne. Had a cow and she'd insist on milking it by hand." She sniffed, peering at the wide windowsill. "That dish, now. Earthenware. She had one like that. For the cream, I suppose. We were all busy chucking out our old stuff and getting Tupperware."

She was chatting away, a friendly drone, giving me time to compose myself. Or was she telling me that life carried on, an eternal flow, and everything would pass, even pain?

I pulled myself together. "Thanks for coming, Siân. I would have dropped in to say goodbye, but…"

"You've got enough to do. Got to get that girl of yours ready for uni. I'll be on my way, leave you to it." She eased herself up, glancing back into the kitchen. "Expect Gareth will follow in his own good time. He'll be off soon too. Making a start in Manchester. Not down the road like Cardiff. I'll miss him."

I rose, following her to the door. "I know you will, but he'll always be there for you. Siân, I really do hope you hear from Gaynor soon. She'll be home. One day, you see."

Siân's eyes searched mine, no smile in them though her lips curved. "We'll see. You take care now, fach. Tara." With a last pat of my hand, she was off, striding down our track.

I thought as she disappeared from view, I should have offered her a lift back to the village.

Call yourself a friend? Asked Adam.

"Call yourself a husband?"

That's exactly what I am.

"No, you're not, you're a pile of ashes. You left me, you bastard."

There was no reply. Of course there wasn't. Time I faced up to that. Time to go home and start again. Move on.

PART TWO

1

Pembrokeshire was supposed to have been a break, a sharp slice through the emotional turmoil of grief bound so closely to the time and place of sheer unendurable awfulness. In many ways, despite the sour shadow cast by Fabia Wyatt's hurtful fantasy, our stay in Carregwen had done the job. We were sane again, ready to face new demands, preparations for university, for my exhibition, for sorting out endless paperwork, getting the lawn mown.

But the moment we passed the corner Spar a hundred yard from our home, I was back in a flash. As I turned down our road, all I could think was this is where Denis Anderson came swerving at full speed, drunk as a newt. And when I pulled up outside our house, by the gatepost where Adam had died, there was our front door, emblazoned in red paint with BITCH! LIAR!

Willow rammed her fist to her mouth, sobbing silently.

Mrs Gravell, our neighbour, must have seen our car draw up. She rushed out to greet us. "Oh dear, I am sorry. I didn't realise you'd be back today or I'd have got Bill to clean it off. But it keeps happening so often, it was getting too much of a chore for him."

Bill, behind her, was nodding polite agreement but his eyes told me we were becoming the local nuisance.

"I'm the one who's sorry," I managed to say. "It wasn't your responsibility. You should never have to deal with it at all. I'll sort it out."

God knows how. The sight of the graffiti had knocked the wind out of me. We dumped our luggage in the hall and I bent down to gather up the scattering of mail that awaited us. Flyers, a few stamped letters… and a whole pile of unstamped ones, folded paper stained with felt tip. Was I going to open them and absorb their vitriol?

"Leave them," said Willow, brushing past me, armed with brush and cleaners from under the sink. While I stood there, useless, she was outside, scrubbing the door clean, crying with rage. She came back in, snatched the letters from my hand and took them, unopened, down to the incinerator. Summer had vanished like a dream lost on waking, and we had achieved nothing.

I'm still dead said Adam.

"I know!" I screamed at him, and that night I relived the whole bloody thing.

* * *

My nightmares were back. What was I going to do about it? I couldn't just sink back into the morass of grieving paralysis that had blighted the first couple of months. My daughter needed me. I should be helping her, not making her distraught with worry about me. I saw my GP and he offered to arrange counselling, but he warned me there would be quite a wait. Until then, he prescribed more pills.

Willow was unimpressed. "There's no way I'm going off to Exeter with you still screaming in the night," she warned me.

"Oh God." I looked at my daughter. All the sun of summer had gone from her. "I don't want to wreck things for you." Before I could tear my hair out, the front door rattled. I turned to see another screed of felt-tip. I couldn't cope. I couldn't cope. I couldn't cope. It was Willow who threw the door open and went hurtling out in pursuit of the culprit.

"Willow!"

She was gone. I went out, to the gate, to the place where I didn't want to stand. A distant hooded figure was running, throwing herself around a corner. Willow was charging in pursuit, closing the gap, only paces behind when they disappeared.

What should I do? Follow? Wait? Something, surely? Or nothing.

It was more than an hour later when Willow returned, with a scratch on her face but defiant.

"It's his bloody sister!"

"What?"

"Anderson. The man who murdered Dad. It's his fucking sister!"

"Hush." I drew her in, patting a tissue on the scratch, though she flinched away. "Did she do this?"

"This?" Willow touched her cheek, forgetting the scratch was there. "Yeah. Tried to fight me off. It's nothing to what I'd have done to her, but people got the wrong idea. Thought I was mugging her. Someone called the police."

I was horrified. "You weren't arrested?"

"Nearly. I told them about her, the stalking and all that, and they let me go."

"I should think so!"

"Said we should report it properly and let them deal with it."

Of course we should. I should have reported it when the persecution had first begun. Why hadn't I? Why had it seemed so important to pretend it wasn't happening? Because I couldn't cope with any more reality? "Yes. I will, I promise. But what happened? Did you speak to her? How do you know she's Anderson's sister?"

"She said, didn't she? Said 'You're just trying to destroy my baby brother. It wasn't him. He didn't do anything. You bitches are trying to destroy him.' I mean, how stupid is that?"

"Totally stupid. It's not as if we have anything to do with the prosecution."

"Right. She's just mad. Totally mad. Like Fibs. That must be what happens with old ladies. Don't get old, Mum." Willow realised the import of that joke, and burst into tears, hugging me. "No, no, please grow old, Mum."

"I'll do my best," I whispered. "She's old, is she?"

"Sixty, at least."

"Ah. That's old, is it? She moved fast for a sixty-year-old."

"There's nothing of her. Really thin."

"Ill, maybe."

"I don't care. I hope she is ill. And him. I hope they both die!"

"Don't! Please, Willow. Look, I am going to do what I should have done months ago. I'm going to go to the police. I can show them this letter at least." I opened the latest note.

Bitch. You'll be sorry. I'll kill you.

"Speak to Naomi," said Willow.

* * *

I called my family liaison office, Sergeant Naomi Strong, who had been efficient in keeping me abreast of developments, accompanying me to the inquest, giving me dates of hearings and useful contacts that I hadn't followed up. Now she came round to hear my weary recital of the persecution that had been going on since the day after Adam's death.

"Why didn't you report it before this?" she asked, with obvious exasperation.

All I could do was shrug.

"Well, we'll sort it now." Naomi turned to Willow. "You accosted her, that's right? And she said she was Anderson's sister? Good enough." She took the note as evidence. "You didn't keep any others, I suppose."

"No. Sorry. And our neighbours cleaned off most of the graffiti while we were away."

"I'll have a word with them." She gave me a stern look as she added, "I'll let them know they won't have to deal with it again."

"I shouldn't have put them through it, should I?"

"No accounting for how grief affects people." Sgt Strong was not strong on empathy, but she lived up to her name in other respects. Now that I had seen sense, it took no time at all for the nightmare to be resolved.

Brenda Gough. That was the name of my phantom stalker. Fifty-seven, divorced, alcoholic and, as Willow had deduced, the elder sister of Denis Anderson, drunk driver and killer.

The inexplicable had become explicable. She wasn't just a random apparition of malicious fate. She might have no rational excuse for blaming me for her brother's situation, but rationality didn't come into it. Just as I hadn't been able to cope with Adam's violent, pointless death, so she hadn't been able to cope with Anderson's guilt, or rather its consequences for him.

"Seems their mother died when he was a little lad," Naomi explained, once Brenda Gough had been whisked off to the police station, to be threatened with prosecution for criminal damage and served with an injunction to stay away from us. "His sister brought him up. Obviously got a bit obsessive about protecting him. She's seeing a psychiatrist."

This was an irony not lost on Willow. "You ought to rob a bank, Mum. Then you won't have to wait months for counselling."

"I'd strongly advise against it," said Naomi.

* * *

I began to take control of things again. I had acted. Far too late and only after my daughter had set the example for me, but I had acted, dealt with a problem that should never have been allowed to fester. I was determined that Willow would see I was on top of things and stop worrying herself sick about me. I concentrated on getting her ready for university. Or at least suggesting a string of essential preparations that she explained she had already made.

Finally, Willow agreed that it was safe for her to go and I drove her down to Exeter. Or rather, she drove, and allowed me to see her settled in her student accommodation. Her new world, her new life. I wanted it all for her.

Now I needed to deal with my own life. My forthcoming exhibition. That at least diverted me from dwelling on what lay beyond: Christmas and then the trial.

Christmas without Adam. It would be a nightmare. But maybe we would get through it because my brother Paul had tentatively suggested that we come out to join him and his family in Melbourne for the holiday, to help keep the shadows at bay. I had prevaricated, but now I decided, if Willow agreed, we'd accept his offer.

As for the trial... No, I wasn't ready to think about that yet. Concentrate on the exhibition, immerse myself in work.

After two days of serious painting, I looked out and there she was, my hooded stalker, staring at my house. Not by my gate but across the road. What had the restraining order said? Was she allowed in our street? I could call Naomi to deal with it, but I didn't want the aggro, the bother, the wasted explanations and the unpleasantness. I decided, to hell with her, I was going back to Wales.

The only sensible solution. Carla had said I could have the cottage for as long as I wanted. I wouldn't need to get out and socialise. I could steer clear of Fabia and her fantasies. I could sit it out, all alone, in Carregwen, and immerse myself in painting. It was the obvious thing to do.

2

Tregelli in October. I had left it in bright sun, thronged with holiday crowds. Now it was silent, chill drizzle washing the vibrant colours of summer to a uniform grey. There were only four vehicles in the carpark, and the door of The Bell, which had stood wide throughout the summer, was shut against the weather. There was no one in sight except a man tying up his boat against the quay.

Harry Roberts, who else?

A sharp sea breeze drove fine salt-flavoured rain into my skin like needles when I got out, fresh and clean like healing acupuncture.

"Hello, Harry."

He turned sharply, hands full of rope and did a double take. "Well, Good God! Mrs Winters. You're back then." He squinted into the car. "Willow not with you? No, she's at uni, of course."

"Yes, Exeter. A well-earned break from her neurotic mother."

He sniffed, before breaking into a smile. "You'll find it a bit different now. End of season. Half the houses already shut up."

"Yes, I can see."

"A bit too quiet for you?"

"Quiet is exactly what I'm looking forward to. I'm going to work."

He nodded. "I'll be up then, to connect the gas."

"I'm sure I can manage, but please do come up. Come and have tea. Or something. I've got gin and Scotch."

He touched his cap in acknowledgement and I returned to the wheel, edging the car round the narrow alleys between the quayside cottages to the lane along the inlet. I felt proprietorial as I tackled our track, zigzagging through up to the windswept clifftop, reclaiming every stone and pothole. I wasn't a mere summer visitor. I was here to stay. For a while. Carregwen crouched low in the rabbit-cropped turf, its white walls gleaming through the rain, its windows dark and blank, its ridged grey roof dipping in quiet slumber.

The breeze was more of a gale here, buffeting me as I got out, to the crash and boom of waves. I hurried into the cottage and gazed around with a sigh of satisfaction, drinking in the slight odour of damp.

So here we are at last, said Adam.

"Yes, here we are."

You did the right thing, getting away from the house.

"I know. And I know you're just my imagination telling me what I want to hear."

Does that matter?

"No. Just keep doing it."

I didn't do much to wake the house up. I filled the kettle and switched the storage heaters on. They hadn't been needed when we were there in the summer, and they would take some time to generate a bit of heat.

In the kitchen, the cooker reminded me that it would be useless until the gas was connected. I had no wish to go out in the rain and fuss with spanners. Leave it for now. Drink the tea and then open that bottle of whisky. Medication. That would do.

I had just opened it when Harry arrived. He must have come straight up from the harbour. He looked in through the door. "You done it then?" He nodded round the side of the house.

"Not yet," I admitted, and he marched off, spanner in hand. I pulled my fleece around me and shivered. The place really was cold, not somewhere to entertain. If Harry was going to come in, I needed to create some warmth. Should I attempt to light the wood-burning stove? The open grates of my parents' home had been replaced by gas fires by the time I'd come along. I was kneeling, surveying the empty stove with bemusement, matches in hand, when Harry returned.

"Want me to do it?" he asked, and promptly hunkered down, giving me a skilled demonstration in fire-lighting. In a couple of minutes, the flames were blazing up. He watched for a moment, then added a log, shut the door and straightened up.

"That easy, eh?" I poured two glasses of whisky.

"Keep this here open until it's going strong," He tapped a lever. "You'll soon get the hang of it."

I indicated the sofa and he sat down, spreading himself comfortably. I proffered a glass. "Not offending chapel sensitivities?"

He chuckled, taking the whisky. "I'm teetotal in chapel, not outside. Like the rest of them, to be honest. So." He looked around, studying the interior of Carregwen in detail and then nodded. Whether he was nodding in approval or telling himself 'might have

147

guessed' I wasn't sure. "How long are you back for? Just a weekend, is it?"

"No, longer than that. Maybe till Christmas." I settled myself into an armchair. "Home is… it's not really home at the moment. Too many issues."

"I can imagine."

I wanted to steer him, and myself, off the topic of death, grief and bereavement. "For one thing, we had a spot of bother with a malicious stalker."

Harry frowned. "What, like knocking on your door? Silent phone calls?"

"That sort of thing. Graffiti, vile notes thrust through the letterbox in the middle of the night. Anyway, she's been stopped. Well, in theory. But it was a distraction." I took a hasty gulp of Scotch. If the graffiti started up again in my absence, my neighbours had full permission to call the police this time. "So, with Carla lending me this place, I thought I'd make the most of it. I just want to get this year out of the way. Once we're through the trial…"

"Trial?"

"Denis Anderson. The man who killed my husband. He was drunk, driving like a crazy man. A dozen people witnessed the whole thing besides me, and he's pleading not guilty. Claims some invisible person was driving, not him. I can't believe it. It's just mad. Everything's mad. Anyway." I took another gulp. "The trial's set for early February. It's not as if I'm worried about him getting off. He won't. It's just that until it's all over, I'm stuck in this endless rut, just waiting and waiting and waiting."

Harry sucked through his teeth. "Bad business all round. Having to wait like that."

"So anyway." I forced a smile. "With my little chick flying the nest, here I am again. Ready to paint, I hope."

Harry nodded. "Time and space, that's what you need." He rose and added another log to the stove. The room was almost feeling warm. "And you know where we are. I'll tell Siân you're back, so if you need anything."

I smiled more easily. "I'll be fine. Feeling at home already."

* * *

"Put these here, shall I?" Siân settled on a cupboard in which to stow onions. I had stocked up in the supermarket where she worked and I had offered her a lift home, but she had insisted on coming back to Carregwen with me to help me unpack.

I shut the fridge door, shoved a box of washing powder under the sink and reached for the cafetière as the kettle clicked itself off. "Come on, that will do. Let's make the most of the sun while we've got it."

Siân seemed slightly bemused that anyone would choose damp garden chairs in a brisk breeze when there was perfectly comfortable seating in the warm living room. I was still getting the hang of the wood-burning stove but the storage heaters were doing their stuff and the smell of damp had gone.

"I know." I laughed, leading her out onto the mossy slabs that gave way to rabbit-cropped turf. "I'm mad.

There's a magic here. I've only been back a couple of days and already I feel, well, almost sane. It's the sea air. It feels so clean. I keep thinking, if I can only breathe enough of it, it will wash out all the grit inside me."

She accepted the cushion I offered and nodded. "Harry said you were on edge about the court case."

"Iodine on the wound, that's all. An extra pointless irritant. Why can't he just… Oh, no, don't think about the trial. I am just going to breathe." I sucked in a huge lungful and then ignored my own advice. "That's one of the reasons why I'm so glad Willow's gone to university. She's out of it, all the updates, all the waiting… and the trial itself."

"But you'll miss her though." Siân wriggled to get herself comfortable on the creaking chair sodden with a month of autumn drizzle. "Your girl."

"God, yes. I do already and she's only been gone a week. But I speak to her on Skype. Not every day obviously, but we're keeping in touch. Checking up on each other."

"That's nice," said Siân, her eyes fixed on the ink-blue horizon.

I bit my lip. I was so busy contemplating my own problems that I'd forgotten hers. "Have you heard any more from Gaynor?"

Siân shrugged. "Been messaging Gareth, he tells me. I'm no good with that sort of thing."

"Facebook Messenger you mean?" Perhaps I could make amends of a sort. "Wait here." I rose and, seeing her planted so uncomfortably on that damp chair, I changed my mind. "Better still, come back in. I'll see what I can find."

She rose with alacrity, frowning at the damp patches and green stains on the cushion as she carried it.

"Wasn't such a good idea, was it?" I took her through to the living room and opened my laptop, before sitting beside her on the sofa. "Let's see." Facebook revealed an endless stream of updates, photos and pointless witticisms from my brother in Melbourne, Carla in New York and a handful of friends back home. "Gaynor Hughes," I typed.

There were plenty, but I didn't have to look far down the list to find the right one. Siân's finger shot towards the image of her daughter, then stopped short, as if afraid to approach any closer. I clicked on her smiling profile picture.

She was a busy girl if her Facebook page was anything to go by. Plenty to say that involved a lot of exclamation marks and emojis, but nothing that gave any useful information. Pictures, of course. The usual cute cats. Crowds of friends having a wild time. A couple of selfies, one taken at a theatre door, but I couldn't tell which one. There was a fetching photo of her with a smart-looking young man I wouldn't have trusted an inch. Taken somewhere on the South Bank, I think. Somewhere a world away from Tregelli, though she still had the patchwork bag I remembered from the photograph on Alex's page. One small thing from her past that she'd taken with her. Not all ties cut.

Siân was staring blankly at the page. I thought she'd be eager to see more as I scrolled down, but she kept her emotions to herself.

"Would you like to message her?" I prompted.

She frowned puzzlement.

"I can type a message to her, say it's from her mum. Shall I?"

Siân caught her breath, hesitating on the temptation, then shook her head, folding her arms emphatically. She turned away from the screen. "No."

"Are you sure?"

"Yes. Leave it." She pulled herself up. "I'd best be getting on. You stay there, I'll leave you to it."

"No, I'll drive you home."

"No need. I'll call in at Harry's. You get on with sorting yourself out."

I couldn't dissuade her. She wanted to be gone and I was left staring after her. I'd been so relieved, at the supermarket, that the difficulties of the summer had been brushed aside and we were on our usual friendly terms again. But one glance at a computer screen had brought down the shutters. I didn't understand it. Her daughter's absence distressed her, so why the reluctance to message Gaynor or even respond to her image? Gareth had claimed there'd been no row between mother and daughter, but he'd have been away at college, surely. There must have been a row. More than a row. Words said that could never be unsaid. Words that made Gaynor run for the other side of the country. Words so bitter that Siân still couldn't bring herself to heal the breach.

We were friends, I hoped, but she wasn't willing to share this tragedy with me. I hadn't learned from my futile attempts to help in the summer. I was doing it again. Stop. Siân clearly didn't want me sorting out her hurt for her. She needed to do it for herself, just as I needed to do.

3

I had come to work, and the urge to paint re-ignited the moment I returned to Carregwen. I threw myself into it, letting it consume me. Occasionally I went into the village for fresh milk or bread or eggs and once I stopped for coffee with Siân before she started her cleaning stint. Some of the holiday cottages in the village – which meant most of the houses – were still occupied by visitors seeking the quiet life, and she had the school to deal with. We made anodyne conversation, I took care not to mention Gaynor and we parted on good terms.

Most days I kept to the cottage, or rather the summerhouse, though the light was no longer as bright, and I needed the oil heater. No one came near other than the postman, but I didn't lack company. Adam was there, listening to my ramblings, sometimes answering, sometimes just watching. He was becoming a part of the furniture. Every few days I exchanged drolleries and occasional advice on Skype with Willow, who had plunged enthusiastically into student life. That was enough. Every day, I took solitary walks out to the headland, absorbing the sound of crashing waves and seabirds. I saw Harry once or twice, out on the *Lotte Lenya* with his fishing gear, tourist trips put to bed for the season.

Weather. Back at home, it had been a mere subject of conversation when people didn't have anything to say. Even here, over the summer, it had been nothing but a fringe variable influencing our choices for the day. But now it shook itself into elemental significance, one with the sea and the rock beneath me. I watched the layers of cloud sweep across from the west, casting a ballet of shadows and light across the land, drawing purples, greens, silver from the infinite blues of the sea. I watched the wind clutching foam from the waves and snatching suddenly at the bent trees. I saw dark cascades of rain out at sea and waited, rejoicing, for them to sweep inland and drench me.

I watched the build-up to a storm, the dark clouds on the western horizon banking up and spreading out like crow's wings, advancing, a portent of apocalypse as the wind built steadily and the sea grew black and ominous. Harry called by to advise me that I might want to put up the storm shutters, because we were in for a serious blow. He had to show me how, because I didn't even know I had them. The kitchen and bathroom, facing down to the cliff, were plunged into gloom, as the shutters shook with the force of the gale when it hit in its full force. The cottage echoed with a kettledrum roll of rain. I ventured out just once, clinging to the side of the cottage, to look out to sea and saw spray hurtling up, higher than the cliffs, as the storm waves crashed onto the rocks below. I tasted salt on the knife-sharp wind. It wasn't hard to imagine the ocean, whipped to a fury, overwhelming the land altogether.

But overnight the storm ripped itself apart, stumbling on inland, and I awoke to a pearly morning, the sun rising into a singing, azure sky. Hurrying to take the shutters down, I found them filigreed with a white crust.

I had an overwhelming urge to dance naked on the grass in the storm's wake. Almost overwhelming. The thought that Harry might suddenly emerge from the lane to check on me held me back. Instead, I walked out with bare feet and felt the wetness of the grass drive up between my toes into my legs, into my soul. Water Goddess.

You're getting a bit pantheistic, aren't you? suggested Adam.

"Well maybe. Why not? All is one. You are one with it. That's all right, isn't it?"

It's all all right. That's why I'm here.

"I like to think it's why you're here, even if it's not true."

I'm here for you. So be here for me. Go on, get your kit off.

"But what if Harry turns up? Could he cope with the sight of me playing Isadora Duncan in the nude?"

He'd take it like a man. Go on, you know you're itching to.

"Well…" I was already pulling my T-shirt up.

"Hello? Is someone there?"

The voice, coming out of nowhere, made me jump. I turned, already in flight mode, before I figured out where it was coming from. Someone was standing on the far side of the wall between Carregwen's land and the adjoining pasture. Fabia Wyatt. The stones had tumbled in places and the hedge that topped it had thinned, creating a gap, but even so she was so petite she could barely look over it, her waxed jacket and rain hat swamping her.

"Mrs Wyatt." I adjusted my top and strolled over to the gate. Her silly comments on the yacht had left me wanting to snarl but now, taken by surprise, I was too flustered for anger. "That was some storm we had."

"Oh yes. We do get them on this coast. I just came out to see if the pasture is drying out. Oliver has a new horse. I do love horses, don't you?" It was Fabia and yet not Fabia. Not the batty princess with weirdly antiquated snobbery, but an old lady sounding quite eager to strike up a conversation. It seemed she had spells of normality in between the fantastical delusions. "I'm so glad that you've returned to Tregelli. I see so few people at this time of year."

That's why I like it, I thought. But didn't say it because there was something pathetic in her comment. "Alex is back at Oxford?"

"Yes, yes he's gone. I miss him. And your daughter, busy preparing for her marriage."

I wasn't going to get annoyed that she hadn't been put right. I'd just play it straight. "No, she's gone to university. Exeter."

"Ah. Well, well, Exeter. I'm sure he won't mind. They don't seem to, these days. I'm terribly sorry, am I interrupting? I thought I heard you speaking to someone."

Tempting as it was to say yes, I shook my head. "I had the radio on, that's all."

"Ah then. All alone, like me. You must come round to Cwrt y Frân. I'd love some company. I get so tired of playing rummy with Veronica, and I'm sure she's bored with me. We'd both welcome a new face."

"Doesn't Oliver take you out and about?"

"Oh, my son's never here. Always off somewhere on business. He's in South Africa, I think. Or is it Japan? I can never keep up."

Off on business, leaving Fabia all alone with Veronica Erving in that great house. Housekeeper, carer and gaoler.

Fabia grabbed at her hat as a gust of wind caught it. "I used to travel with Bill, when he was alive but that was just around the Midlands, or Scotland. But Oliver is always on the go, doesn't stay still for a minute. I don't know when he'll be home. Please say you'll visit. I love to entertain."

Did I have to? "I'm here to work really. Nose to the grindstone. I need to finish a dozen more pieces for my exhibition." Not true. I only needed three more to satisfy the gallery, and two were almost done, thanks to the liberation of Carregwen. The third, embodying the storm, was fermenting in my mind, itching to spill out onto the canvas.

"Oh but no need to stay long. Just drop around for tea. Or morning coffee. No need for any warning, just if you're passing by."

That was the trouble perhaps. No one did just pass by Cwrt y Frân. I gave in. "We'll see. If I can make the time."

She clapped her hands. "Oh, please do. It would be lovely."

Behind her, Veronica Erving was marching purposefully towards us across the field, looking distinctly irritated. I was tempted to applaud Fabia for having evaded her gaoler, but it wouldn't do to stir the waters. "I really must get back to work now."

"Of course, of course. But any time."

"Perhaps." I stepped backwards, pace by pace, until I could justifiably turn my back on her.

I could hear Mrs Erving now. "Fabia! What are you doing out here? Get back to the house now!"

Damn. The last thing I'd wanted was a social call on Fabia Wyatt, but this wasn't the woman I'd known in the summer. She was a lonely old lady, imprisoned, slightly confused and in desperate need of company. I was beginning to feel obliged.

You don't have to go, said Adam, as I returned to the kitchen.

"I know I don't have to. But…"

What if she tries to give you a chinless aristo for a husband again? Can't have my wife being fobbed off on the inbred wastrels of the universe.

"I'm not being fobbed off on anyone. Anyway, she doesn't seem so weird now. Just labouring under misapprehensions because no one has put her right. No one to talk to at all, that's the point."

Except the servants. She's got Veronica Erving and probably half a dozen others.

"You're not helping, you know. I don't want to go, but I'll feel bad if I don't."

I'd have to go, for my peace of mind if not for hers. Not today though. Or even tomorrow. I wasn't going to let unreasonable expectations set in. But the following day, I'd get it over with. Duty done, I could get back to work.

4

I was nursing frustration as I rang the bell at Cwrt y Frân. Work was calling me. I hadn't wanted to stop for this.

Veronica Erving opened the door. "Good afternoon, Mrs Winters. Please come in. Mrs Wyatt is expecting you. She'll be very pleased you could find the time."

"How is she?" I asked, as Veronica deposited my coat in the cloakroom.

"Quite well, I'm glad to say." She ushered me into the drawing room. "Lady Nicola is here to see you, Fabia."

I was furious with the woman, using that absurd title, but before I could say anything, Fabia had risen from one of the striped satin sofas, where her toes had only just touched the ground, and was clasping her hands with an air of pathetic excitement, dropping the glass she had been holding. "Oh, you came!"

"Hello, Fabia. I came to tea as I promised." I came forward and offered my hand.

She grasped it. "Please, do sit down. It's so sweet of you to think of me. Are you still alone or has your husband…"

"I'll bring some tea," said Veronica, quietly picking up the glass and gathering a tray of medication from a side table. "Why don't you show Lady Nicola your jigsaw?" She addressed her like a child and Fabia responded like one.

"Yes, yes, Lady Nicola, what do you think?"

"Fabia, I'm Nicki, okay. Please drop the Lady Nicola thing." I gazed at the unfinished jigsaw of birds of paradise, half the pieces obviously in the wrong place and pitied, even more, the desolation of Fabia's life. "You've made a good start."

"Yes, yes… I used to be good at these things, but now…" Fabia picked up a piece, her lips working. She looked from the jigsaw to me and back again and I had the feeling she was beginning to feel slightly disorientated and anxious with it, so I turned away, searching for a different topic.

"You have some lovely pieces here. I can see you're an avid collector." It was my chance to examine the artwork more closely.

"Yes. I… yes. Oliver has taught me so much. My husband Bill… William. Sir William. He preferred the old style. Oh, but you are an artist, of course!" A memory had slotted into place. "Nicki Bryce. Yes, we have a few of your paintings. Have you come here to work on some more?"

"That's right. Is that a new vase? I don't think I saw it last time." In the style of Clarice Cliff or possibly genuine.

"Yes!" She sounded surprised to see it there. "Yes, yes I don't think… I don't know. But this one." She led me to a picture on the far wall. "This one is by you."

"That's right."

"Oliver was very taken with it." Her fingers were working compulsively. "Lady Nicola."

"Actually…"

"Here's tea," said Veronica, returning with a tray of fine china.

"Oh lovely." Fabia returned to her sofa, as Veronica arranged the cups. She paused, her hands hovering over two teapots. "Now then. Earl Grey or Darjeeling? Milk? Lemon?"

"Earl Grey with lemon," I said. I didn't want Earl Grey with lemon but I decided that a snap answer was best.

Veronica passed me a cup.

"It's very quiet at this time of year," said Fabia. "We must find some entertainment for you. I know! There's a Schubert concert at Bethesda."

"We went to that last week," said Veronica, handing her a cup.

"Did we? Oh. There'll be a shoot. Do you shoot?"

"No, I don't," I said. Less sentimentality, more the memory of picking endless lead shot out of a rabbit a poacher friend has presented to my father.

"We have guns. Your husband, maybe..."

"Fabia," said Veronica very softly, demanding the old woman's attention and shaking her head.

"Oh. Oh yes. But you paint. Yes of course you do. We have one."

"You have several," said Veronica.

"That's right!" She was, if anything, becoming more distracted.

I needed to keep something like conversation going. "I imagine you're looking forward to seeing Alex again. Is he coming here this Christmas, or are you all going to Switzerland again?"

"Alex! Oh, I hope they're here over Christmas. Not just for a few days, this time. We must throw a dinner party. Will you be here? No, of course you'll be preparing for your daughter's wedding. Such a wonderful thing. A very grand affair, I'm sure. Perhaps Alex will be invited."

No, I was not going to play that game again. "Fabia, there isn't going to be a wedding. Willow is not getting married."

"Oh, no! It's been called off? How very sad. You must be so disappointed. But…" She paused, suddenly frozen, before fixing her eyes on me with a stiletto brightness. "Will you be here for Christmas, you and your daughter?"

"No, we'll be in Australia this year."

"Ah! Australia. That's good. Very good news." My reply immediately cheered her up. "Now, would you like to see our stables? You ride, of course. We have excellent horses here, don't we, Erving? You must come and ride whenever you wish. I know you're a great horsewoman."

"I'm afraid I don't ride at all," I said, wondering if I could politely take my leave yet. Fabia was slipping more and more into her alternative reality.

"Oh. But you must have had a pony at least, on your estate?"

I hesitated. I'd had a donkey ride once at Blackpool. Did that count? "Only as a girl."

"I had a pony," she said. "When I was a girl."

Mrs Erving glanced at me with the slightest smile of mockery.

I disliked that mockery. "Did you?" I said. "Tell me about it."

"He was a palomino, such a beautiful mane. I rode to hunt when I was just seven and everyone said I looked

163

like a princess on him."

I let her carry on talking about her imaginary horse. She was a child again, lost in a fantasy world. "He was called Morning Star," she said with a sigh.

My lips twitched. In my world, it was the communist party newspaper. "Lovely."

"Every girl dreams of having a pony. I suppose you gave your lovely daughter one? And she's sure to have the very best when she's married to the Duke's son. You must be proud to have settled her so well." She blinked, hesitating suddenly as if a small needle in her brain was trying to remind her she had something wrong there. She gave a shake, then a little laugh, giving up the struggle to work it out. "What we wouldn't do for our children, eh, Lady Nicola?" A cloud crossed her face. No, it was more than a cloud, it was a complete transformation. The sad little girl dreaming of ponies transmogrified into the haughty pantomime duchess. The change was frightening in its suddenness. "We must protect them, must we not? At any cost. That's my business, you know, to prevent my son and my handsome grandson falling gullible victims to the unworthy. Oh yes! It always has been and it always will be." She was a pocket-sized Napoleon ranting on a soapbox.

"I'm sure they're very grateful for all you do," I said.

"Men are weak. They let themselves be led into the most hopeless muddles." Fabia was up and pacing now, as Veronica watched with an enigmatic smile. "There are wicked poisonous traps awaiting them in the world, and they can't see it. We have to be there for them. They're so easily fooled by the sly witches out there, and their siren tricks."

"I'm sure," I said. I'd had enough. When she was like this, she wasn't sad or pathetic, she was just unpleasant. It might be a mental condition, but I didn't want to listen to it. I was going to take my leave as soon as I could get a word in.

Fabia was unquenchable though. "One has to deal with the consequences, pick up the pieces for them. Like that Helena creature. We are descended from Sir Thomas Wyatt, you know. We have a position to maintain. How could I allow a woman of that sort to corrupt our lineage?" She was getting louder, wilder, out of control. Veronica rose, unhurriedly, as Fabia was almost dancing round the room. "It wouldn't do at all. She had to be got rid of. I made Oliver see things clearly. See that he'd been dazzled by a fortune-hunting hussy, no class, no breeding, such a little tramp."

I couldn't keep quiet any longer. "Are you're talking about Alex's mother?"

"If you can call her a mother. Not fit to bring up a child. But fortunately, he had me." Fabia's nostrils pinched with triumph. "And I dealt with her in the end. Oh yes. I disposed of her. She won't be troubling us again." She snorted triumphantly. "Oliver doesn't need any of them."

I'd had enough. "Well, that's very interesting, but I'm afraid I have to go now."

Veronica Erving took the hint. "Ma'am, I'm afraid Lady Nicola has to take her leave."

"Go? Must you? So soon?" Tirade exhausted, Fabia was all graciousness again. "So good of you to call. Do come again."

I bit back the response on my tongue. "Thank you for the tea," I said.

Escorting me back to the front door, Veronica glanced out at gathering clouds, and offered me an umbrella, which I declined. "You mustn't mind Mrs Wyatt," she said. "These little fits come on her occasionally."

"Triggered by what? I don't think it helps when you refer to me as Lady Nicola."

"But I'm afraid that's how she thinks of you."

"Can't you put her right?"

"That's for Mr Wyatt to decide. He feels her make-believe world keeps her happy."

"She didn't seem too happy when talking about fortune-hunting hussies. I don't imagine that's a remotely accurate description of Alex's mother."

"I couldn't say, Mrs Winters. I only came here after she left. But I wouldn't give it any more weight than the idea that Fabia split them up. Mr Wyatt isn't the sort of man to let anyone manage him. Wife or mother."

"Or loyal retainer. Is that how she sees you?"

She smiled. "Very likely. While in reality, I am just an employee paid to humour her."

"Paid well, I imagine."

"Oh, extremely well, Mrs Winters."

Of course. But since Oliver could undoubtedly afford the best, couldn't he find someone more sympathetic than Veronica Erving? I really didn't like the woman.

* * *

I found the antidote the next day, when I bought a few groceries at the village shop and Siân was waiting for me outside.

"Saw you go in. Thought you might have time for a coffee."

"Yes of course. Why not? The tea shop is still open, is it? Everything's been so quiet till now, but suddenly there are people around again."

"School hols. Mind, I could do with a bit of peace and quiet. Café will probably be better than Rhys blasting the house out with his bloody music. Rhiannon will be keeping it going till the end of half-term. After that it will be like we've fallen off the map. All the houses shut up."

"No more cleaning work then?"

"I'll still have the school to do and I'll keep on at the supermarket. There'll be another bit of a flurry at Christmas, I expect."

We had reached the teashop and it wasn't as quiet as Siân might have hoped. A couple of families were making a lot of noise and mess. We found ourselves a corner and Siân ordered two coffees – or I guess that she did. The rest of her brief conversation with teashop owner Rhiannon was in Welsh and lost on me.

"Sorry," said Siân, seeing my bemusement and slipping smoothly back into English. "I forget. Your girl picked it up so quick."

"Willow learned Welsh?"

"Well, you know, Gareth was teaching her a bit. No harm done."

"None at all. She's studying languages so I'm sure she'd have no trouble picking up another. I'm afraid I don't have her ear. I should have made more of an effort."

Siân chuckled. "You don't want to be wasting your time with that. You keep to your painting. Going well, is it?"

"Yes, it's good to be able to concentrate on something so…"

"Unconnected?"

"Yes, that's it. A different universe. I can lose myself."

She nodded as Rhiannon brought our cappuccinos. "Not getting lonely, out there on your own?"

"No, quite the reverse. I mean, I do miss Willow, of course I do, but I'm enjoying the space, the silence, the freedom. To be honest, I wouldn't mind being lonelier still. Fabia Wyatt discovered I was back and I had to pay a social call. Not one I want to repeat. I don't know what to make of that woman. I feel sorry for her, with whatever she's got. Alzheimer's? Schizophrenia maybe? People keep telling me she's harmless and I know she's confused and lonely, but when she starts ranting, she makes my skin crawl."

"You won't catch me calling her harmless. Arrogant, spiteful bitch."

"Isn't that a bit harsh? She's obviously doolally."

"I don't care how doolally she is. She had it in for my Gaynor right from the start. Not good enough for her precious grandson to wipe his feet on." She slammed down her cup.

"She called Willow a slut. Sounds like she had the

same opinion of Oliver's wife."

Siân snorted. "Don't suppose Helena Treece was expecting the mother-in-law from hell when she married her millionaire."

"You knew her?"

"Wouldn't say that. Knew of her. She was a high-flier, his secretary or personal assistant or something. Probably thought she could deal with anything but Fabia made her life a complete misery, from what I heard. You'd have thought a decent man would stand up for his wife, but no, he let them fight it out. Indulges his mother like she's some sort of amusing pet. He's dumped her here as if Tregelli's a playground just for her, and we're supposed to let her do what she wants. Shoplifting. You or I did what she does, we'd be slung in jail, but oh no, Mrs Fabia Wyatt must be allowed to help herself and Oliver pays everyone off. Harmless my eye. You know she fired a shotgun at some boys once?"

"No, I didn't. Seriously?"

"Some of Gareth's friends. They were only larking about, out on the sea for the day and they put in at the Wyatt's landing place. Didn't think about it being private. Mair Davies was doing some cleaning at the big house and she said Guy Masters mentioned he'd seen them and warned them off, but Madam Fabia acted like they'd invaded Poland and off she stormed with a shotgun, down to the quay and started blasting at them. They were out of reach by then, but it scared the daylights out of them. Reported it to the police, but Oliver Wyatt got it all hushed up. As usual." Siân's hands were clasped around her cup as if she wanted to strangle it. "Nothing harmless about that woman. Only luck those boys weren't hurt or even killed."

"Good God. If she comes nosing over my hedge again, I think I might hide. It's even harder now, sympathising with her."

"Save your sympathy for everyone around her, if you ask me. Bloody Wyatts. I wish the lot of them were at the bottom of the Irish Sea."

I understood the bitterness, but that was a minefield that needed to be avoided. "Seems Oliver Wyatt is due here next week so hopefully he'll keep her occupied. Maybe he'll take her off to shoot some pheasants somewhere."

"Shoot some peasants more like."

The subject couldn't be doing Siân's blood pressure any good, so I changed tack again. "How is Gareth doing in Manchester?"

Her frown immediately turned to smile. "Loving it. Loving the work. He tells me about it and I don't understand a word, but never mind. And Willow? Gareth says she's enjoying Exeter."

"Are they keeping in touch? That's good."

"Oh yes, you know, young people, all this, what do you call it, social media lark. Everyone knows what everyone's doing. Well, it's nice, isn't it? Nice that some friendships last, if nothing else does."

"Yes. It's nice." A cold hand stroked my neck, always there, ready to remind me. It wasn't true. Even friendships couldn't last. Death would undo them in the end.

5

I wasn't lonely at Carregwen. Far from it. Maybe it was my visit to Fabia Wyatt that did it, but I began to feel a desperate desire not to see anyone, even Siân. I wanted to shut myself up, disappear into my work and block out the rest of the world.

I hadn't realised how neurotic I was becoming until a Range Rover made its way up Carregwen's rutted track and pulled up outside the cottage. A surge of panic seized me. A man was driving but I could see Fabia Wyatt seated in the back. I ducked down, praying they hadn't noticed me through the window, and I crawled on my belly into my bedroom to hide behind the bed until the knocking and the calls had stopped and the Range Rover had driven away again.

I lay there, thinking, I am hiding behind a bed because I can't bring myself to answer the door to a pathetic old woman. What is wrong with me?

"Am I loopy?"

It's Fabia who's loopy, said Adam.

"I think I'm going the same way."

Are you loopy enough to take pot shots at children?

"No. For God's sake knock me on the head before I get to that stage."

Can't promise.

"No. That's right. You can't promise. You can't do anything! You can't kiss me, you can't put your arms around me and hold me, you can't make love to me.

God, I miss you, I ache for you. You bastard, why did you have to die?"

Don't cry, Nicki.

"Why not?" I rubbed the tears from my cheeks. "Why bloody not?"

* * *

I got a grip. One painting still needed finishing before the end of November. I'd need to get my collection sent off… and then send myself off too, to my exhibition preview, to sip white wine and smile and talk, pretending my high heels didn't hurt. I wasn't looking forward to it, but I'd have to go through with it, just to prove I could.

Locked away, I was aware that something had changed. I couldn't put my finger on it at first, then I realised that the background hum of Tregelli had ceased. Up on the cliffs it was easy to forget that a harbour village existed down there, but in the busy times there was always the faintest vibration of noise, of engines revving, dogs barking, children shrieking, laughter bellowing, buses reversing, kegs clattering – everything imprecise and indistinguishable, but creating a sound patina on the air. Until suddenly it was gone and there was nothing but the noise of the wind and the waves and seabirds, broken only by intermittent sounds so startling in their irregularity that they brought my head up every time they snapped at me. Cows suddenly lowing. A boat chugging out of the harbour. A tractor somewhere in the distance. Half-term was over, the interlopers were gone and the land and sea rose to reclaim their primeval supremacy.

A car. Coming closer. I mocked myself for my infantile response to Fabia's visit, but still I was relieved when I heard its direction change, turning up Bethel Lane. It must be the mighty Boss coming home. At least that meant Fabia would be occupied and I would be left in peace.

Too much to hope for. The next morning the Cwrt y Frân Range Rover turned up again at the cottage. I could hear it from the summerhouse, but no one need know that. I would carry on working, pretending I didn't hear the knock on the door.

But I couldn't pretend not to hear the footsteps approaching. I swallowed my resentment at the intrusion as Oliver Wyatt gave a tap on the open summerhouse door and stood there, filling the space, taking my light.

"Nicki. Veronica told me that you were back in Tregelli. I want to thank you for calling on my mother. It was a generous gesture. She doesn't get much society when I'm not around. I hope you didn't find it too taxing."

"I survived." I was cleaning brushes. I didn't stop.

"You know, I am delighted to find you here. Perfect timing as it happens. I wasn't expecting your return."

"Well, here I am. Like you, making money."

"And art. Money and art." He studied the large canvases stacked against the back wall, head critically cocked. "And as I said, your return is remarkably opportune. I'd like to invite you…"

"I'm afraid I won't be able to spare the time for another dinner party."

He burst out laughing. "No. I wouldn't do that to you. It's quite a different affair I have in mind. I came down with a colleague, Peter Redman. You know him? Art dealer."

"No, I don't think so."

"He knows your work, which won't surprise you. I've been telling him about a couple of local artists I think bear consideration. Dominic Hart?"

"Mm." I had met Dominic Hart once at an exhibition in Bristol. A man totally up himself and I didn't like his work.

My expression clearly showed it, because Oliver laughed again. "He has a market. Anya Garvey, you know her?"

"I know her work. I like it immensely." I laid my brushes down and wiped my hands.

"I do, too. John Patrick? Anyway, my plan was to gather them, invite a couple of other local collectors and set up a small exhibition for Peter's benefit, to demonstrate that the area is not without potential. I hadn't included you in my plans because I assumed you'd be back in Hertfordshire, but since you are here, can I tempt you to attend? Add a little cachet to the gathering."

"Bare-faced flattery, if ever I heard it."

"Not at all. I do, after all, have some of your paintings to add to the exhibition. Seriously, I hope you will consider it. Friday?"

"I don't know. Not sure I am up to making conversation with a host of strangers just now."

"Yvonne Wright isn't a stranger, is she? She'll be there. And..." He pulled a pained face. "My mother won't be, if that makes any difference. Veronica will be taking her to see her medics."

Yes, it did make a difference.

"Friday afternoon then," he said, before I could respond. "Excellent!" He shook my hand, his free hand gripping my shoulder. It was almost a hug. A sudden and unexpected encroachment. "Friday it is then."

I was cornered. I watched him go, annoyed that I'd let it happen. Annoyed too, or rather disturbed, by that near hug. He had no right to be so familiar and yet... God, I ached for a hug.

* * *

On the Friday I found myself actually debating what to wear.

Fuck 'em, said Adam. *Wear what you like. What are they going to do? Throw you out?*

"You're right, damn it. Why should I care?" I pulled on clean jeans and a baggy Fair Isle sweater that had once been Adam's. I added a cagoule as it started to rain just as I was about to set out, along with walking boots to cope with the slippery steps. I put a pair of sandals into my bag to change into – or so I thought, but when I reached Cwrt y Frân, my boots caked with mud, to be greeted by a willowy young woman with immaculately sculptured hair and features fit for a cover of Vogue, I discovered I had forgotten them.

"Natalie Green, Ms Bryce, Mr Wyatt's personal assistant. Please don't worry, I'm sure we can unearth something for you in here." She opened the door to the capacious cloakroom, where raincoats and wax jackets hung like kill after a hunt, some of them dripping onto the quarry tiles. My cagoule joined them. Boots and shoes were stacked under the narrow window. Most of them must have been Fabia's, too tiny for me, but Natalie Green eyed my feet as I struggled out of my boots and handed me a pair of canvas slip-ons.

"Do you think these will fit you?"

They did. A little too roomy, but I wouldn't trip over.

Natalie smiled with satisfaction. "If you don't mind literally stepping into the late Mrs Wyatt's shoes."

"Late!"

"Sorry. A slip of the tongue. I mean Oliver's wife, before she left. I presume she no longer calls herself Mrs Wyatt."

"Oh. I see." Yes, I did mind stepping into Helena Wyatt's shoes, even in a literal sense. I tugged my jumper down as I straightened up, determined to be enveloped by something of Adam's. Those shoes had me irrationally itching with resentment. "Well, where do I go?"

"This way, Ms Bryce." Natalie ushered me to the drawing room, which had been transformed since my tea party with Fabia. Most of the furniture had been moved out, but the number of art works had tripled at least. It had become a small gallery, and the company that had gathered there looked as if galleries were their milieu. Not geriatrics or jetsetters but the art brigade. My world.

I spotted Dominic Hart in a pale pink suit, holding forth by the marble fireplace. John Patrick was the bearded gent in the corner, looking as if he wanted to be somewhere else. I recognised him from a brochure. I guessed that the young woman in dungarees, with a few flecks of titanium white in her green-streaked hair, must be Anya Garvey. The other guests, the ones without paint under their nails, were the collectors presumably.

I should feel more relaxed. This was the world I would be facing again soon, although Carla was flying back from New York just to stand between me and the pack like a bodyguard. I didn't have a bodyguard here.

You've got me, said Adam.

"Stick with me," I said, looking round for Yvonne, and spotting her on the far side of the room, in her usual diaphanous scarfs.

"I beg your pardon?" Natalie handed me a martini and skilfully turned me in the other direction as Oliver who came striding towards me. "Your last guest, Oliver."

"Nicki! Thank you for coming. And thank you, Natalie. You've done an excellent job, as usual. I can always rely on you."

She purred, and it occurred to me that she was the one hoping to step into the late Mrs Wyatt's shoes. He'd married one PA. Why not another? She'd certainly play the part to perfection.

"Nicki, I want you to meet Peter Redman. Peter, this is Nicki Bryce, just as I promised.

"Hi!" The stout Peter Redman was affable and, I suspected, slightly drunk. "Nicki Bryce. A name I certainly know. I had no idea you were a Welsh lass."

"I'm not. Just staying in a friend's cottage for a while."

We chatted. Oliver paraded me occasionally. I found a fellow spirit in Anya Garvey, who was knocking back Martinis to hide her nerves.

"I didn't know it would be this posh. I'm not exactly dressed for it."

"Neither am I. Don't let it worry you. We're the artists. They're dressing for us, not the other way round."

She laughed. "I'm not in your league though."

"Bullshit. Maybe I've sold more, that's all. I love your work. I was having a good look at it in St David's in the summer."

"Oh." She blushed.

I was feeling almost benign as we talked art, though it might have owed as much to the Martinis as the company. This wasn't so bad. I could get through the afternoon without too much pain.

Then…

Oliver was chatting to one of the collectors, pointing me out, when the drawing room doors swung open and Fabia came in. Still wearing coat, hat and gloves, with a handbag on her arm.

A couple of seconds behind her, almost at a trot, came Veronica Erving, directing an apologetic look with Oliver, and an exasperated one at his PA. All three promptly smiled suavely as if Fabia's arrival had been intended all along.

"Mother, I wasn't expecting you finish with the doctors so soon. All well, I hope? You're just in time to join the party. We have been admiring your latest acquisition. Come and say hello to Marian." Oliver swept her up and presented her to one of the collectors, a woman who must have understood the Fabia situation, because she immediately shook hands and started talking.

Oliver stepped aside to hear a whispered explanation from Mrs Erving. He frowned, then looked across at me with an apologetic shrug.

"Is that his mother?" asked Anya. "She looks like a miniature Queen Mother. God, now I really feel under-dressed."

"Oh, don't worry," I said. "Tell her you're minor Balkan royalty and she won't mind if you're wearing a bin bag and sniffing glue."

Anya started giggling, a little too loudly, because Fabia turned to look our way. Her aged face had a questing look, but I couldn't tell, as her eyes settled on me, if she was seeing me as a friendly neighbour or a social trophy. She was caught in a moment of indecision. I made my mind up. Despite the advice I'd given Anya, I'd had enough of Downton Abbey make-believe. No more Lady Nicola.

Fabia unfroze and came towards me, hand extended, chin raised, back stiffened.

"Ah, Lady Nicola, how good of you to come and grace my little soirée."

I briefly touched her hand. "Hello Fabia. It's just Nicki, remember. Not Lady Nicola. Hope all was well at the doctors"?"

"One has these little flutters as one gets older, but nothing serious. How is your father, Lord Bryce, these days?"

"Still dead," I replied, before adding with a forced smile, "As he has been for sixteen years."

Anya snorted in amusement and alarm, but the retort was wasted on Fabia. "Lord Bryce and my late husband Sir William used to hunt together," she explained to anyone and everyone in earshot. "I hope your husband, Sir Justin, has accompanied you today? Oliver and he are old acquaintances."

I felt a dozen pairs of eyes suddenly fixed on me, in surprise and interest, and urgent words were passing between Oliver and Veronica Erving, but I wasn't waiting for their intervention.

"Fabia, listen, will you please stop this. I am not Lady anything, my father wasn't an earl, he never hunted with anyone, and I am not married to some knight of the realm. My father was a trade union official. I grew up on a council estate and I never had a pony. I have no breeding, or class, or whatever else you imagine, and I have no idea why they've let you carry on imagining all this crap. I am the widow of Adam Winters, just plain Mr Winters, and I am proud of who I am and who he was, so please stop this stupid game which is not remotely funny. In fact, it's bloody distasteful." I'd started off gently, rationally, but I couldn't stop the anger taking over. Why hadn't they put her straight long before this? If Oliver wanted to indulge his mother, he had no right to do it at my expense.

Fabia was staring at me, her eyes glazed. Oliver and Veronica Erving were closing in, edging aside the people around us, as I continued to face down Fabia. Her lip quivered, her brows gathered, then a look of horrified fury contorted her face.

"Oliver! Oliver! This woman is an imposter. Get rid of her! Call the police. Throw her out!"

"All right, Mother, calm down now." Oliver had her arm, but she jerked free.

"Get rid of her, get the dogs or I'll take a shotgun to her too! Widow, coming here, making eyes at my son! I know what she's about, the filthy little gold-digger, but she's not having him!" Before I grasped what she intended, she was thrashing at me with her handbag. I jumped back, but the catch caught my cheek.

"Veronica, take my mother..."

A vase flew at me, catching me on the shoulder before smashing on the wall behind me. After that, Oliver and Mrs Erving were frog-marching Fabia from the room. I heard Oliver's voice, raised and angry, snapping something about medication, as I was surrounded by other guests, curious and solicitous, someone mopping a trickle of blood from my cheek.

"Are you all right?" asked Anya, her face shocked.

I was too stunned to respond for a moment. Then I shook myself, rubbing my shoulder. "I'm okay."

An elegantly manicured hand brushed my arm. Natalie, the PA, was satisfying herself that I wasn't concussed. Then like a true pro, she turned to face the company. "Everything's all right, people. A misunderstanding, that's all. Please don't let it spoil your enjoyment. Megan, more martinis?" She turned back to me and gestured to a door. "I am so sorry, Ms Bryce. Come into the library, let me see to that cut. And your shoulder?"

"Bruised, nothing more. No need for a fuss. I'll just take myself home if you don't mind. I don't think I should stay any longer today." I touched Anya's hand in farewell, and marched back to the hall, breathing deeply. It was the first time I'd ever faced physical violence, and it shook me, but at the same time it was slightly cathartic. At least I didn't have to pretend any more.

Natalie followed me out. "Ms Bryce I am terribly sorry. Mrs Wyatt wasn't due home for another hour at least, and no one expected her to behave like that. It's so out of character although, you do appreciate, she has become a little disturbed in recent years and…"

"Disturbed? Look, the whole world knows she's mad as a hatter." I was back in the cloakroom, kicking off the borrowed canvas shoes. "You do know Oliver should be getting her proper psychiatric treatment instead of playing games? He should have put her straight about all this Lady Nicola crap months ago."

"I'm sure Oliver… but please, do stay and speak to him. He'll be distraught if he discovers that I let you go without allowing him to apologise."

"I think Mr Wyatt can cope with being distraught. Sorry, but I've had enough." I pulled on my still damp cagoule.

"Then at least let me call Phillips, to drive you home. I can't let you walk."

"Watch me."

With a sigh, she tapped on a number pad at the front door and opened it. "If you are sure…"

"Absolutely sure." I marched out into light rain, the shock already dissipated and the liberation giving me wings.

Well you managed to be the life and soul of that party, said Adam.

"It wasn't me who shook things up. It was the mad woman in the attic."

Next time, throw something at her.

"I might, too, except that there isn't going to be a next time. She doesn't seriously imagine I'm after her son, does she?" I punched the air to stop the tears flowing. "No, there'll be no more hobnobbing with the Wyatts for me." The ornate gates swung open as I approached. As they bloody well should. "I'm going to work. I'm going to paint and that's it.

Got your blood up?

"You bet."

Atta girl.

6

I walked into Tregelli the next morning, along the coast path, passing Harry's cottage, his garden backing on to the track. He was there, dismantling bean poles, and he looked up with a grin and a wave, coming down to the fence to speak to me.

"You been in the wars then, I hear."

"Word's got round already?"

"Oh, Mrs Wright was all agog with it, apparently. Told Chloe and it's all round the village now. That Fabia Wyatt took an axe to you, that right?"

I laughed. "She swung at me with her handbag. Oh, and threw a pot. I'm glad everyone was entertained."

Harry shook his head. "Sounds like the reception I'd expect at that place." The old family grievance speaking again.

"I don't expect to be asked back. Siân okay? I haven't seen her for a few days."

"She's fine. Bucked up no end at this business."

"Glad something good came out of it, then."

Down in the village, I was heading for the shop but Yvonne must have seen me. She was at the gallery door, beckoning me in.

"Are you all right, Nicki? Not wrapped in bandages? What a to-do, eh?"

"Don't pretend to be shocked. You're loving it."

She grinned. "It's the most exciting thing to happen in Tregelli since Geraint Davies smashed the bridge parapet. We have to get our entertainment where we find it, you know. So, you're out to catch Oliver Wyatt then. A few gob-smacked faces when she said that." She sobered up. "A bloody awful thing to say from your point of view, of course."

"Yes. It was."

"But she really had the bit between her teeth. Best stay clear of her son while she's around or she'll have her knives out for you like she did for his wife."

"She attacked her too?" I followed her into the gallery.

"Well, she certainly let the woman know she wasn't good enough for Oliver. Or for Alex, either. Fabia acts as if she's his mother. Always did. You'd have thought Helena was just some sort of nursemaid tagging along. It was quite shocking, to be honest. Fabia would be shouting Helena down, over what school he'd go to, that sort of thing. All in public. If Oliver intervened, his mother always won. That's why she did it, I suppose. Helena, I mean. Upped and left. No warning, nothing, just disappeared one night. Ran off with a Pakistani according to Fabia. But then that does sound like something Fabia would come up when she's being a daughter of the Raj."

"And Helena didn't take Alex."

"Yes, now that is shocking, isn't it? Maybe she thought she'd already lost him. I remember, a village football match, just a friendly kick-around, you know. Helena turned up to watch with all the other mummies, and at the end, she held out her arms to give Alex a hug, and Fabia popped up out of nowhere, called to Alex and he ran to her instead." Yvonne frowned over the memory. "I've never forgotten the look on Helena's face. Bereaved, that was it. I suppose she thought if she took him, he'd just be screaming to go back to Granny. But still. Apparently, Alex has never once heard from her. Isn't that awful?"

"Yes. Awful. She just upped and went, you say. Did you see her go?"

"No. Left without a word to anyone. You should have heard Fabia crowing about it afterwards. Talk about triumphant."

I bought my shopping and walked home, thinking. The late Mrs Wyatt. A slip of the tongue, Natalie Green had said, but… I kept remembering Fabia's face, snarling with violent rage. *I'll take a shotgun to her too.* I'd thought, if I'd thought about it at all, that she must have been referring to the boys on the boat, but was it a reference to the last woman she had driven away from her son? Helena Wyatt had vanished without a word. She had never even tried to contact her son. Surely Fabia couldn't have actually… No. Someone would have stopped her.

Who was there to stop her? asked Adam. *Oliver? Always away on business?*

"Yes, but even supposing Fabia did shoot Helena… That's absurd, isn't it? What would she have done with the body? A little woman like her, she wouldn't be able to drag a corpse anywhere."

No, but her son could.

"He wouldn't. Not his own wife."

To protect his mother? Doesn't he mop up after her, all the time? Make excuses for her? Let her get away with…?

"Murder! Surely not. No. What would he have done with the body?"

Bury it? Burn it? What did you do with mine?

"Stop it!" I was at the crematorium again, feeling the grief rise up in me like a great wave of suffocating black sludge. "No, no, no!" A bramble brushed against me, snatching with its claws, and the sharp pain slapped my consciousness. What on earth was I thinking, delving into absurdity. Things like that just didn't happen. Wasn't there enough horror and misery in real life, without inventing it?

* * *

Oliver Wyatt was sitting on my doorstep when I got back. Looking almost human in a sweater, not a smart suit. He rose as I approached.

"I saw your car here; thought you must have taken a walk so I decided to wait. How are you? Have you seen a doctor? Can I…"

"I'm fine."

"You're sure? Well then. I've come to apologise, yet again. I don't know what came over my mother. She doesn't usually explode like that. I suppose your blunt explanation…"

"My blunt explanation wouldn't have been necessary if you'd put her right at the start."

"True. You'll probably want to throw things at me if I tell you I didn't just let my mother believe you were daughter of an earl and all the rest. I actively encouraged it."

"Encouraged it! Are you as mad as she is?"

He shrugged apology. "It must seem that way. No, I'm sure you'll have realised that Fabia has a totally irrational jealousy of any woman who comes near her boys, as she calls us. One of her less endearing eccentricities. Friends, colleagues, casual acquaintances – it makes no difference to my mother. She sees them all as a threat."

"How did your wife cope?"

"Badly." His mouth twisted into a rueful smile. "As I'm sure you've heard. It was too much for Helena, and for all the perfectly innocent ladies we chance to meet. It's especially tricky for poor Alex who has had to keep any girlfriend under wraps if he doesn't want her subjected to a barrage of insults. So, we hit upon the idea of inventing non-existent husbands and fiancés for all our female acquaintances. Most of them have found it amusing and played along. You are a widow and that made you a potential threat. I am afraid it made no difference how much you were still grieving, so I invented a husband for you in the city and gave your daughter a fiancé. I let the hint of aristocracy sugar the pill and she built her own fairy tale on that. I was only thinking of saving you both from verbal outrage, without giving enough consideration to the pain such deceit would give you."

"No… you didn't consider. I don't care about your mother's insults. I do care about my life, my loved ones, being turned into someone else's fantasy. I want to be who I am. Why couldn't you just sit her down and explain that I am Mrs Winters and I'm not in the slightest bit interested in becoming the second Mrs Wyatt?"

"I should have done, if I'd realised that you'd be having any contact with her. But there was your daughter, and you'll agree she was interested in Alex. Not seriously, I assume, but I didn't want her becoming the target of my mother's diatribes. For her sake and my son's. You hadn't come to have your summer ruined by a silly old lady. In retrospect, I acknowledge that I got it wrong, and again, I apologise. Profoundly. Which seems to be all I ever do with you. Yesterday was supposed to be an enjoyable experience, for you and everyone, not a bloody battlefield. I am thoroughly ashamed. Which is why I am tentatively offering recompense with a proposal that I swear doesn't involve my mother at all."

"Please, just forget it. I don't want recompense. I'm not really hurt. Not physically, anyway. I think you'd be better off worrying about what to do with Fabia."

"Veronica is taking good care of her."

"Her gaoler."

"That's a little unkind. Veronica used to run a nursing home. She knows how to deal with the elderly and the slightly deranged. Now, please don't brush off my apology until you've heard what I'm suggesting."

"Go on then."

He smiled. "Alex told me you were expecting the Artemis to be a sailing yacht. As it happens, I do have a sailing boat."

"Just the one?"

His smile broadening. "One at your command. Would you allow me to take you out in her? Please? To reassure me that I am not cast into the lowest circles of Hell? Perfect forgiveness, I appreciate, is more than I can hope for."

"Don't be ridiculous."

"I'm not being ridiculous. It's a heartfelt invitation. Natalie has taken Peter back to London. I'll be following myself, in a couple of days, so, while I'm here, let me make amends for what I've put you through. You did want to sail, didn't you?"

"But I don't know the first thing about it." I looked up at the sky. Yesterday's rain had cleared away. White clouds were skimming across pale blue sky. "Isn't it a bit windy?"

"Nothing that I can't handle. You'll be safe in my hands, don't worry. I know what I'm doing."

"I never doubted it." I looked out over the sea, glinting like white fire on the horizon. Glide like an albatross on the wind. It appealed. And what was the alternative? To send Oliver Wyatt packing with a haughty rebuff and sit nursing my anger and hurt? Much better to demonstrate I was immune to his mad mother's assault. It was only an afternoon outing, for God's sake. And no chance of Fabia messing things up.

"Just a pleasant day on the waves," said Oliver.

"Okay. All right. Yes."

Watch it, said Adam, but Oliver was pushing him out. "Excellent. No need to do anything except wrap up warm."

I deposited my groceries and donned a warm fleece, and then I allowed Oliver to hand me into his Range Rover. I was relieved that he turned onto Bethel Lane, rather than heading for the harbour. We wouldn't be observed by the whole village. By Harry and Siân was what I meant. I bit my lip. Was I right to be doing this, if it was already giving me such twinges of guilt?

Oliver mistook my anxiety. "Don't worry, we won't be going into the house. You won't even catch a glimpse of my mother."

"I'm not bothered one way or another about Fabia."

"Good." He smiled warmly at me. "Though I'm afraid I am."

He turned in at Cwrt y Frân, round the house and through the yard, onto a rough track. It led over a gorse-strewn ridge into an unexpected relic of industrial activity. Long-neglected activity – a few ruined workshops, some rusting ironwork and the overgrown slabs of an abandoned quarry.

"What is this place?"

He waved a hand vaguely as he parked up by a shed built against a sheer wall of rock. "There was some attempt at quarrying roadstone at the beginning of the last century. It didn't come to much. There are more productive quarries further along the coast. But they worked it for a few years, blasted out a shoot to send the material down to the sea and built a small quay."

"Yes! I've seen it. Your private harbour."

"Quite so."

I was out of the car before he could play the gentleman and hand me down. He unlocked a padlock on the shed door and opened it with a bow. "After you."

"Lovely!" I stepped inside, expecting oil and machinery, but it was clean and orderly, stacked with assorted boating gear. He picked up a couple of life jackets and opened another door, flicking a light switch.

Beyond the door, steps led down a tunnel cut in the rock. The same tunnel I had seen from below on that early morning in August. It was lit by a string of safety lamps, set against the gleaming rock, but their light, if anything, intensified the gloom of the sloping shaft.

Oliver was already heading down. He stopped, sensing that I was hanging back. I was only on the second step, but I was fighting an urge to go no further, to turn back from a descent into Hades.

"Are you all right? It's steep, I know, but the handrail is quite secure. Not claustrophobic, are you? I should have asked."

August. A seal swimming towards a yawning tunnel mouth in deep shadow. *Into my grave* said Adam, disappearing into darkness.

I shivered. "There's a ghost here."

Oliver looked up at me, his face eerily lit. "What?"

"Sorry. I'm being fanciful."

"It will be the light playing tricks on you."

"Probably. Come on." I hurried down after him, towards the bright daylight, where the rock steps ended.

We were at the iron grill at the bottom. Again he unfastened a padlock and I emerged, with relief, onto the crumbling concrete quay that ran into the mouth of the cave. Water dripped on me from above, and every sound echoed in the black chasm beside us. The dark cliffs of the inlet loomed over us and the two boats tied up there, the Wyatt launch, snug in waterproof coverings, and a sailing boat – a proper boat I could get into, not a skateboard with a sail, but not the huge monstrosity of teak and chrome I was expecting him to flaunt.

"She's an old lady, but still does the job. I bought her, must have been thirty years ago. My first love, you might say." He slipped a life jacket over my head and fastened the straps. That discomforting intimacy again. I looked out across the inlet to the brightly lit headland where I'd sat. An age ago, so long ago that I'd moved on?

No I hadn't. Panic was niggling at me, ready to swell. I shouldn't have accepted this invitation. I shouldn't be here with him. But it would be ridiculous to go haring off up that dark flight of steps now. I pulled myself together and let Oliver help me down into the boat.

Over the summer I'd watched the little sailing boats that vied with kayaks for use of the harbour – watched them being set up with mast and sail and chaotic threading of ropes. This one was already set, the sails just waiting to be raised. Oliver smiled as I settled down, indicating a hamper, ready prepared. He hadn't allowed for the possibility that I might say no. No point being annoyed about it. I had said yes, so why not enjoy it?

I'd enjoy it more if we could just get out of the gloom of the inlet. The chill air of the tunnel and the cave was prickling my neck. *Into my grave.*

"Are you comfortable there?" asked Oliver, busying himself with the sails.

"I'm fine. Do I have to do anything? Heave on something?"

"Just sit back and do nothing. Except duck if I say so. I don't want you brained by the boom if we go about."

"I'll duck."

"Right then."

We were off, gliding from under the overhanging cliffs, along my headland, and out, steered skilfully between rocks looming just below the surface, until we were clear of the land and the sails cracked taut. Out from the shelter of the cliffs, I was grateful that my stomach was as strong as I remembered, and that I had a sweater under my fleece. The waves provided a bucking bronco ride and the breeze, peppered with salt spray, now felt chill and unrelenting, straining to hurtle us onwards, out, far out, to distant horizons, towards a mystery forever out of reach.

"Let's sail to Byzantium," I suggested.

"That's your goal?" asked Oliver, with a smile. "Escape?"

"I suppose it must be. Release? What do you find when you are alone on the sea with no wealthy Americans to woo? Just the elements?"

"What do I find?" Oliver considered, then added "Duck," and as I obediently dropped my head, the sail swung over me and the boat changed course, the wind finding new weak points in my gear. He settled back, relaxed, tiller in hand, coolly, casually in control. "Not escape. I have nothing to escape from."

"No?"

"You're thinking of my mother and her strange ways. Not surprising. You bear the scars, literally. Yes, she is growing more difficult as dementia takes a hold. But with the exception of yesterday's show of aggression, she has always been controllable. I don't usually have any serious worries about her."

"With Mrs Erving in charge. How long has she been with you?"

"Veronica? Since… ten, no, eleven years now."

Since his wife disappeared, in other words. Was that when Oliver decided his mother needed a gaoler? Because of what she'd already done? Oliver wanted me to believe that yesterday's violence had come out of the blue, but she'd already taken a shotgun to boys on a boat. She'd practically boasted about it. I glanced back at the shore, not much more now than a pencil smudge between sky and sea. She couldn't shoot me from there; we were too far out. Just as long as she wasn't waiting for us, fully armed, when we returned.

"Veronica's a dedicated woman. My mother managed to evade her yesterday, but she's done an effective job over the years. What's the alternative? Put Fabia in a home, among the other Alzheimer sufferers?"

"Is that all there is to it, do you think? Alzheimer's?"

"Duck. About." He changed course again and was silent for a moment or two. "No. You're right. I think, looking back on my childhood, she was always slightly unbalanced. I just assumed she was a mother with a lot of imagination. But functioning perfectly well back then. She played an active role in my father's business. I never suspected anything until my father died and her moments of delusion became more obvious. And the shoplifting. She was arrested twice. That's why I decided she'd be better off filching from a village shop that I could compensate rather than being let loose in Harrods. I know she misses the city, but she can queen it here, without any harm. And don't worry, she does see shrinks. She thinks they're cardiologists."

"She cares a great deal about Alex," I said.

"Adores him, you mean. She'd smother him if he'd let her. Fortunately, he's mostly away, at school and now at Oxford, so he hasn't grown to resent it."

"Boarding school of course. Let me guess. Eton?"

He smiled at my challenge. "I'm sorry to disappoint you. Not Eton."

"Harrow? Rugby? Charterhouse? Winchester?"

His smile broadened. "Possibly one of those. Because I can afford it. Are you going to tell me that if you had the money, you wouldn't give your child the best education you could afford?"

"By best, you mean one that inculcates a sense of entitlement and a disdain for others?"

"You'd prefer a state school that inculcates a disdain for work, property and the law. About!"

I ducked on command. "I wonder how my daughter survived at such a school."

He laughed. "Her mother's fighting genes no doubt." He was enjoying this. "You won't find me apologising for investing in my son's future."

"He's not destined to take over the family empire though. Haven't you got a career in politics lined up for him?"

"Alex is a bright boy and he has a lot of charm, but he doesn't have the killer instinct needed for business. He'll do far better in politics."

"Controlling the world, one way or the other. Don't you need a killer instinct for politics too? Or is it just a case of knowing the right people?"

"Maybe it's more a case of knowing how to know who the right people are."

"Very astute."

"I am. And I only attended a very minor public school."

"Poor you. How you have risen from the gutter. A proper Bounderby."

He rocked with laughter, then sighed, inhaling the sharp breeze deeply. "Had enough of the class war, for now?" He gently guided the boat around, and suddenly the wind seemed to drop out of the sails. They hung limp, fluttering lightly. "How about some lunch?"

"Lobster and champagne, I hope."

"I wasn't quite that well prepared. But beef sandwiches, a Pié d'Angloys from the local supermarket, and a decent Burgundy. Are you willing to slum it?"

"If I must."

"A truce then." He opened the hamper and set about uncorking the wine, absent-mindedly sniffing the cork, before pouring me a glass. "Your health, ma'am."

"And yours." I sipped, and took a sandwich, shutting my eyes and enjoying the mere sensation of rising and falling on the waves, the breeze bathing my face and rippling through my hair. When had I last simply enjoyed the sensation of anything? I breathed deeply. Someone floated just out of my vision.

A gust of wind snatched at the sails, rocking the boat alarmingly, but Oliver was master and commander of his ship and he knew what he was doing. I didn't have to worry about anything. Just be in the moment. I leaned over to trail my fingers in the water and turned back to find him refilling our glasses.

"No finer restaurant on Earth."

Best dining room in the world, said Adam, brushing Dorset sand off a hard-boiled egg before handing it to me, his bare toes digging into the heap he and Willow had been digging.

The tannin in the wine was suddenly dry and bitter on my tongue. A sense of loss swept over me, so strong it wrenched a whimper of pain from my lips.

"Nicki?" A hand covered mine, comforting – but it was an alien hand. It had no right to be there. I snatched my hand away.

"I'm sorry. Did I say…?"

"No, sorry, it's me. I forget and then, suddenly I remember and… please, forget it. I'm fine."

"Of course." He shut the hamper and slid back to the tiller. "Enough for one day, do you think? Let's turn for home."

"Please."

We were flying once more, tacking back and forth. He was eying me solicitously, but he didn't speak, except when telling me to duck my head. By the time we were approaching the shore again, I had got the better of the unbearable ache. I turned to look as a seal popped up ahead of us, stared insolently in our direction, then dived from view. Another appeared, and another.

"There'll be pups still on the storm beaches," said Oliver. "Would you like to see some?"

"Of course." I managed a false laugh. "Women and small fluffy things. You know we can't resist."

He chuckled softly. "Let's see. This one I think." He turned us towards a small cove, backed by cliffs and sure enough, on the steep-banked pebbles at the head were a couple of white fluffy bundles. Seals were circling us underwater, streamlined against the current.

"Best not go in any closer. Here." He handed me binoculars and I managed them slightly better than I had at the regatta. I homed in on a sad ageless face and two huge eyes.

"Oh!" I turned to Oliver and caught a look of wincing anticipation. "What?"

"You were about to say 'cute?'"

"But I didn't. Might have thought it, but I didn't say it. Thank you. I'm glad I saw them."

He leaned over and squeezed my shoulder. "Thank *you*. Right. Back to the quay."

We turned out to sea again and headed along the coast. The Cwrt y Frân inlet was in sight, a dark shadowed gash in the jagged parade of cliffs. We were turning towards it and its maw awaited us, shadows ready to engulf us. I shuddered, remembering the seal that had greeted me there in August. Adam, into darkness.

I could see the quay, rising higher out of the water now, with the tide ebbing. A scaffold, waiting for the guilty.

I shook myself. Why was I letting such morbid thoughts spoil the day? There was no cause. I was out for a sail with an apologetic neighbour, that was all. I had no more to feel guilty about than Oliver did.

Than Oliver did?

I was a widow. What was he? Where was his wife?

I could picture the iron grid of the tunnel now, in the darkness of the cave. Prison bars. I had watched Adam drift through them. *Into my grave.* There was a ghost in that tunnel…

A cold realisation gripped me. That was where he must have brought her. Helena Wyatt had vanished without trace, without a word, because Fabia had shot her and to cover up his mother's crime, Oliver had carried his wife's body down those steps, taken her out on the launch and…

"You dumped her in the sea, didn't you?"

I'd said it softly, but I'd said it before I even realised I'd spoken aloud. And then…

There was a flash, the world turned upside down and everything went black.

8

It must only have lasted a moment, that blackness, but the next thing I was aware of, painfully aware, was water, salt and icy cold, engulfing me, closing over my head, my mouth and nose full of brine.

For a moment I was utterly disorientated, not knowing where I was, or how I came to be there, totally possessed by a frantic instinct to kick and splash. My head bobbed free of the waves and I gulped a huge breath, coughing the salt water up, treading water furiously, while I tried to get my bearings.

My amnesia lasted only a second. I was overboard and the boat must be somewhere near. I rose on a wave and saw the sails, the low sleek blue hull gliding away from me. He was leaving me! He'd heard me accusing him and he was leaving me to drown. Was there anyone else around? Another boat? Someone? Anyone? I tried to shout and found myself merely gurgling, coughing up another mouthful of water. Blind panic.

The cold was knifing through me. How far was I from the shore? Could I swim? The sea was icy and though my buoyancy jacket was keeping me afloat, my limbs were freezing, already too numb to move at my command. My lungs were refusing to work. I was going to drown, and I was too paralysed by the cold to do anything about it. I attempted a couple of feeble splashes and gasped. A wave heaved me up and I saw the entrance to the inlet. Too far. I couldn't do it. I was finished, swallowing water again.

And then, beyond all expectation, there it was, the blue hull bearing down on me. It turned into the wind and a hand reached down to grab the straps of my jacket. I had my numb fingers on rope, and my panic subsided. What energy I had went into hauling myself back on board. Oliver strained both to help me and control the boat.

Somehow, with superhuman effort and his brute force, my frozen limbs slid with an ungainly thrashing over the side, and I collapsed in a sodden streaming choking heap. Before I knew what was happening, a blanket was around me, and Oliver's arm was gripping me tight.

"There." He held me as I vomited up salt water. As the retching stopped, he wiped the wet hair from my brow. "My God, woman, you nearly gave me a heart attack. Why didn't you duck? Didn't you hear me say about?"

I shook my head, wiping my mouth. I hadn't heard because I was too busy fantasising about murder. "Sorry," I croaked, beginning to shiver violently.

"That was one hell of a knock you took." He was rubbing my back, my arms, rubbing the warmth back into them, peering into my eyes. "How many fingers am I holding up?"

It took me a moment to focus. "Three."

"Mm. Sit there. Don't move."

I sat there, rocking, my eyes shut. The shock of the cold was fading, but I realised my head was splitting. What had hit me? The boom or a sledgehammer? I raised my shivering fingers to the spot, wincing with the pain, and discovered it wasn't just seawater flowing down my cheek.

Oliver was back beside me, peeling away the now soaked blanket and wrapping another around me. He fussed over my forehead, wiping, applying a plaster. Then he handed me a hip flask. "Here. Have a swig of that."

Brandy slipped through my lips, burning down my throat with divine reviving heat. I felt life creep back into my limbs, though my fingers were still too numb and trembling to hold the flask steady. Oliver had one arm around me as if to pour his own body's warmth into mine. Such intimate physical contact, so divinely comforting, and yet alarming. I took another urgent sip. At least my teeth were no longer chattering.

"I thought you were going to leave me there," I whispered. "You were sailing away."

He gave a strained laugh. "Sails don't come with a handbrake, you know. I couldn't do an emergency halt. I had to take her round to get back to you."

"Yes. Sorry. I just panicked."

"I wouldn't leave you," he whispered, holding me closer.

He hadn't had the threatened heart attack; I could feel his heart beating. And mine pounding with it. We sat there for a moment, then he pulled away, to concentrate on the boat.

"Best get you back to shore as quickly as possible. But keep down, this time. Just stay down."

I curled up, snug and sheltered from the wind that now filled the sails again. As he manoeuvred, he had one eye always on me to confirm that I was at least still conscious.

"Am I ever going to stop apologising to you?" he asked, as I felt the shadow of cliffs enfold us. "I offer you a relaxing day on the water and I finish up driving you to A&E."

"No." I struggled to sit upright as the mainsail came down. "No need for that. Now the chill and panic had subsided, there was only my aching head, but it was a cut and bruise, no more. I didn't have blurred vision, I wasn't giddy, and no longer nauseous. "I'm all right, Oliver, really I am. Just soaking wet, that's all. Don't worry about me. I'll be fine."

"You reckon?" He was watching me, preferring to rely on the evidence of his eyes, so I shook the salt water from my hair, pulled myself up and attempted a laugh.

"Just as soon as I'm warmed up." I towelled myself down vigorously with the blanket. "Please. I don't want to spend six hours in a waiting room."

"We'll see. Let's get you onto dry land first." He guided the boat alongside the quay, moored up, and helped me to my feet. I laughed, blaming my unsteadiness on the rocking of the boat.

"Can you climb?" He helped me to the iron rungs on the concrete. I'd have to heave myself up. I was determined to do it, but he was right behind me, supporting me, almost swamping me in an embrace. Then we were on the quay and he was unlocking the iron gate to the dark stair. Before I was aware what was happening, he had lifted me up, as if I were a child.

I squirmed. "I can walk."

"Not up those steps. Hush."

So I hushed and surrendered. I didn't have the energy to resist. How many steps? I lost count, but he didn't lose breath. We were out, from the stairs, from the shed and he was tucking me into the passenger seat of the Range Rover before he let go of me. I sat back, momentarily lost, my head throbbing again. Then he was beside me, driving me back to the house.

I didn't want Cwrt y Frân. "Carregwen?" I pleaded.

"Sorry. Not an option. You think I'm going to abandon you in that cottage all alone after a knock on the head like that? You're probably still in shock. It's either hospital or you come back to the house until I'm absolutely sure you're okay. Don't worry." He gave a wry smile. "Two head wounds are enough for now. I'll make sure my mother doesn't administer a third."

* * *

"We had a little bit of an accident," said Oliver, peeling the blanket off me and unstrapping my lifejacket, as Veronica Erving greeted us in the hall. "Nicki's had a knock on the head. Not serious, I hope, but I'm keeping her here until I'm sure of that. Can you sort out a room for her?"

"Really, I'm fine," I insisted, stubbornly. "All I need is a shower and some dry clothes."

"Precisely. Go up, have a shower, bath, whatever you want, and Veronica will find you something to wear. I was planning to eat out tonight but, Veronica, I assume the kitchen can rustle something up?"

"I'll see to it," said Veronica, ushering me to the stairs. "I'll show you to the green room."

Oliver was watching, so I made a point of striding up the stairs behind her, ignoring the thumping in my head. Veronica beckoned me along a broad corridor. Further along, a door opened and Fabia appeared, enveloped in a dressing gown.

She stared at me. "What's that woman doing here!"

"Hush now, Fabia. Nothing for you to worry about."

"I don't want her here. Keep her away from my son."

"Don't worry, Fabia. You go back to bed." Veronica shepherded her inside, pulled the door shut and locked it. "She'll be asleep soon. This is your room. I think you'll find everything you want."

What did I want? Not the acre of ankle-deep carpet, the vast wardrobes or the queen-size bed, heaped with satin cushions. I staggered round to the bathroom, twice as big and a thousand times plusher that the lean-to at Carregwen, and I ran a deep foaming bath. I eased gratefully into it, shutting my eyes and soaking up the warmth and comfort until I was in danger of falling asleep. Did it hurt to have a little pampering for once? I couldn't remember when I had last relaxed in a bath like this.

I emerged to find my wet clothes gone and fresh ones laid out for me. Veronica Erving was taller than me and big-boned with it, not fat but amply padded, while I had lost any trace of excess weight in the last few months, so I expected the clothes to hang like sacks on me, but they fitted well, far too glamorous for Ms Erving's no-nonsense elegance. There were satin lounge pants, a long, knitted designer jacket, and a silk camisole embroidered with an H. Helena.

Why hadn't she taken her clothes? The dark imaginings that had led me to blurt out nonsense on the boat came back to me. If Oliver could carry me up those stairs, he could as easily have carried a body down them. The protective son. Would he really have covered up the murder of his own wife? He wouldn't. Would he?

When Fabia's husband had died, she'd retreated into a world of fantastical make-believe. Was the same thing happening to me, another phase of my grieving for Adam? I needed to get a grip.

Oliver was waiting for me downstairs. He eyed me appreciatively but said nothing about the clothes I was wearing. "Come on through." He took me into the drawing room and handed me a glass of brandy. Less of a restorative now, more of a relaxation permit. There was a platter of bruschetta too, interspersed with olives.

"The cook prepared a light supper for my mother and went home, but Veronica tells me there's some chicken and I'm sure she can do something with that."

I didn't doubt it. Veronica Erving looked the sort of woman who could wring a chicken's neck without breaking an elegant fingernail. "I like chicken."

"That's good." He was regarding me with unmistakable admiration, taking in every detail. It must have been the soft sheen of silk. Pointless to feel flattered. "How is the head?"

"A lot better." It was just an occasionally nagging throb now, and I was no longer itching to go home.

I finished my brandy and he offered me his arm, leading me to a room lit by fading evening light, a far cosier affair than the grand dining room. There were four chairs at the modest table but only two places set. As he held a chair for me, Veronica appeared with the dishes she had whipped up while I was in the bath. She smiled her supercilious smile at us both and withdrew.

"She's not joining us for dinner?" I asked.

"Veronica? No, of course not."

Thank God for that. "She's not exactly a servant though, is she?"

"Let's call her my mother's companion. She'll be sitting with her this evening. Unless you'd like Fabia to join us?" He smiled, pouring me a glass of chilled wine.

"Let's keep things as they are." I removed covers from the dishes. Chicken with cream and morels, braised celery hearts, fondant potatoes... just a little something Mrs Erving had whipped up on the spur of the moment. A cheeseboard with grapes and pears was laid on the sideboard, to follow. I laughed and Oliver laughed with me. Why not just relax? We chatted lethargically over the meal and drank the wine. I wasn't rushing anywhere; no need to stagger home in the dark so why hold back?

Excellent wine. A second bottle. Wine to warm me and wash all worries away.

We returned to the drawing room and Oliver put on some music. Something soothing and sensuous, and I found myself not exactly dancing, but drifting to it. With Oliver. His arms around me. Fortunate, because the day's trauma had drained some of the strength from my legs. I shut my eyes and swayed with him, round and round the room. Except that our feet were barely moving and, with my eyes shut, it seemed more like the room swaying round and round me. I opened them again with a start and staggered to the sofa.

I stirred awake to find my head on Oliver's shoulder, as he smiled benignly down on me. Such nice lips.

"Go up to bed," said Oliver, raising me to my feet and guiding me gently towards the stairs. Up the stairs. With his help I floated up them. "Sleep well." His lips brushed my neck as he relinquished me at my room. "I shall be next door if you need me."

With the door closed, I groped my way to the bed and languidly stripped, donning the satin pyjamas left ready. Soft on my warm skin. Sea-green satin cushions bobbed around me like waves. How drunk was I? It might be concussion. Did I look ill? I regarded myself in the dressing table mirror. Was that actually me? No, it was someone else entirely. Not me, but someone imaginary, free to do imaginary things. There was someone behind her, someone... no there wasn't. But there should be. There needed to be. She needed someone, this woman.

She staggered up and out into the corridor. The dim light wavered as she knocked on Oliver's door.

If he had taken longer to answer – but he didn't. He was at the door, bare feet, shirt unbuttoned.

If he had only looked surprised, alarmed - but he didn't. He looked suffused with joy, as he drew her into his arms.

9

White marble, gold taps, reflective glass. The en-suite bathroom had mirrors on every wall. No escape. Wherever I turned, there was my reflection. Mine. Where was that other woman who had drifted away from me? Vanished, leaving me naked with the truth. Get me back to the cottage, I thought. Carregwen's bathroom had one small shaving mirror that I could swivel out of harm's way, so I wouldn't have to face myself. And I did not want to face myself.

No choice. I couldn't keep my gaze fixed on the carpet forever. Forcing myself, I raised my eyes. Bruised, wrecked, hung over and riddled with shame. Dear God, I had danced, inebriated, into a Mills and Boon romance, and emerged as a haggard old tart. My eyes blurred and in their place were Adam's, confronting me with accusation. Betrayal.

I doubled up, convulsing over the toilet bowl. Chicken, morels, wine, the lot. So much wine. I knelt, head in my hands, waiting for the heaving to cease. I couldn't afford to shut my eyes. If I did, the spinning would begin again.

Gradually the shakes stopped. I pulled myself up, ransacked a cupboard and poured myself some mouthwash. Better, marginally. What I really needed was coffee. Strong, black, a gallon of it, washing down some serious painkillers. And I needed to be sensible. Forget silly thoughts of a shameful woman taken in adultery. My husband was dead, it was sex, that's all, there was no betrayal. Just inebriated soothing of a perpetual ache.

With Oliver Wyatt.

There was a gleam of pale light through the window. The wind was catching the boughs of the cedar. I wanted to feel it, a cold blast cutting through my boiling brain. No point in lingering to prolong the embarrassment of early morning reality. Silently, without putting the light on, I pulled on the pyjamas I had briefly donned the night before. Before they had slid off again.

Oliver was lying asleep, naked arms and chest free of the crumpled bedding, breathing gently, rhythmically.

A passionate man. However blurred my recollections of the night, it had been undeniably pleasurable at the time. The ache had been well and truly soothed, I could remember that much.

A demon whispered in my ear that I could slip back between the covers with him now. No need to go anywhere. But it was drowned, instantly, by a returning wave of guilt and humiliation, tears prickling my eyes. How had I let it happen? Flee, now.

I tiptoed out onto the landing, closing the door gently with barely a whisper of a click, and I dared to breathe more deeply. My own clothes, freshly laundered, were laid on a table outside my own door. Veronica Erving's work, or some skivvy kept below stairs for just such a service? I carried them down to the chill dark hall and redressed, fumbling with fastenings. I had to go, that was all that mattered. Go before Oliver could wake and urge me to stay. Before he could touch me again and sweep away my resistance.

I padded to the front door, tried the handle. It wouldn't shift. Nothing as quaint as bolts securing it, just the number pad to one side. I'd seen Oliver's PA tap the code in but I hadn't been paying attention. I tried numbers at random but nothing clicked.

I peered into room after room. The French windows in the drawing room were secured in the same way as the front door. On, stumbling over things in the darkness, I found my way to the kitchen at last, a cavern of a place, fitted out in gleaming steel. Another exterior door, with yet another number pad, but this time someone had noted down the code on a post-it slip and stuck it on the door frame. The cook, it seemed, had a poor memory for numbers. I risked a light for long enough to read the number 2598 and tapped it in. The door clicked and I hurried out, through an arch, onto the paved terrace behind the house. The lawns spilled down in wide steps, grey with dew, the surrounding trees heavy with shadow. A magpie swooped low and landed on the grass, looking at me knowingly. Too knowingly.

Time to go. A path led round the side of the house, through the cobbled yard. A few more paces and I would be out in front of the house, marching down the gravel drive. I shrank from the thought of such a brazen exit. I wanted to creep round under the cover of the rhododendrons down that long open expanse, unseen by prying eyes.

But no, I wouldn't make an exhibition of my shame. What was I afraid of? I'd walk down there in the open, head high. Which I did, only to find the gates as securely shut as the front door had been. Should I buzz to have them opened? By whom? Oliver? Too humiliating. Climb over? Probably electrified and anyway, it would be unthinkable, transgression upon transgression.

Then I recalled Fabia speaking to me, over the wall that surrounded Carregwen's land. My cottage was only three small fields away. I walked back towards the house, searching among the shrubs on the eastern side of the drive. Sure enough, a break revealed a five-bar gate. I clambered over it, grateful that the house was virtually out of sight now that the light was strengthening. Another gate, another sloping irregular field, another gate. I nearly tumbled over that one, reaching out to save myself and clutching at long sharp grass. I felt the sting as it sliced into the flesh at the base of my fingers. I nursed my hand as I looked around. The last field was bordered by crumbling stone walls and tangled hedges and there it was, the gentle glow of whitewash through the overgrown hawthorn branches. Carregwen.

I ran to find the place where Fabia had hailed me. Higher this side than on Carregwen's. It must be easy to climb over.

Easy enough to scramble up the stones, despite the readiness of some to tilt or come loose. Not so easy to struggle through the thorns and brambles that topped it, unwilling to yield. I dropped back down. It was impossible.

My hand still stung. I looked at it and an electric shock ran through me. The grass cut had bled, seeping out to trickle round my finger. A perfect ring of blood. We had never bothered with rings of gold, but this – this was my wedding ring.

Shame and desperation whipped through me. Adam was behind me, his hands on my back, pushing me on, and I was up the wall again, thrashing at thorny shackles, fighting my way through. I had to do it. How could I go back and face Oliver now?

I tumbled down into withered nettles, scrambled up again and stumbled to the sanctuary of my cottage.

On Oliver's advice, I had gone with him taking nothing but the key in a zipped pocket in my jeans. I groped. Yes! It had survived my near-drowning and the laundering. It turned in the lock and I was in.

I put the kettle on and while it boiled, I concentrated on cleaning and plastering the worst of the scratches I'd sustained. The sting kept me focussed. I kept the blood ring. I made a pot of coffee and drank it, one mug, then two.

It all gave me time to think and to decide. I had to go. I couldn't stay on at Carregwen with Oliver next door. I couldn't risk a repeat of what had happened last night. It wasn't enough to say I wouldn't let it happen again. I wasn't the only player in this game. How did Oliver regard it? Since our first meeting, we had been politely fencing with each other, driven not by antagonism but by attraction.

I didn't want to admit it, but what was the point of denial? Oliver Wyatt was everything I wanted to dislike, and Siân's friendship should have intensified my dislike. But it hadn't worked out like that. I'd let myself be drawn to him. It wasn't as cheap as the allure of power and money. He was attractive. He was charming. He was witty. Again and again, he had shown a human side, caring, concerned for me, for his mother. He'd never demonstrated the sort of arrogant indifference that would have repelled me. And I was nursing a numbing sense of loss and abandonment. That was why I had let myself be drawn in.

But what had been driving Oliver? It was clear to me now that he had been attracted to me from the start. Clear to his mother too, or why else had her psychotic jealousy made her take so irrationally against me? Had he been hoping that this would happen? Was he thinking that last night was merely the start of our relationship? I couldn't let him carry on nursing that illusion. It had gone too far and it had to stop.

"Where were you, last night?" I demanded as I swilled out my mug.

Forgotten by you, said Adam.

"Why do you haunt me all the time, but as soon as I need you to be there…"

You didn't want me there. You had him instead.

"But I want you. I only want you. Not a substitute. That's all he was."

You wanted him. You practically seduced him.

"I didn't mean to. If you'd just spoken to me, touched me, anything, I'd never…"

You betrayed me.

"No! No. I've got to go. I've got to go, before it can happen again."

Are you so weak?

"Yes! Yes, yes, yes. I'm going." I was emptying the fridge, shoving milk, butter, salad, into a carrier bag. I emptied wardrobe and drawers, stuffing everything, willy-nilly into case and holdall. Then my pictures. I couldn't wait around for a courier to collect them. They'd have to come in the car with me and risk damage. I hurried out to the summerhouse, flinching every time I caught the faint growl of a car's engine, but nothing came rumbling up to Carregwen while I struggled to wrap and stow three canvases on stretchers into a hatchback far too small for the job. Slamming the boot down, something crunched but too bad. Oliver must be up and about by now, and I needed to be on my way before he turned up to stop me.

I took a deep breath and started the engine. My head was still splitting, but all I had to do was drive along the creek and through Tregelli and I'd be safe. It meant passing the entrance to Bethel Lane. My heart was pounding as I edged past, expecting Oliver's Land Rover, or his Jaguar to be lurking there, waiting to pursue me, demanding to know why I was leaving him?

No sign of him. I breathed easier. Through the village now. A different guilt began to nag me as I threaded down the narrow streets, through the harbourside square and up the valley. I should at least stop to say goodbye to Siân. What would she think to me, driving off without a word? But what could I say? What sort of lame excuse could I offer? The one thing I couldn't possibly tell her was the truth. I would never be able to look her in the eye.

I drove out of Tregelli and away.

10

Carla hugged me. "Nicki, you're looking..." She searched for a word and then opted for the truth. "Not as great as I was hoping. Still far too peaky. I'd hoped Carregwen would do the trick." She was back in England briefly, for my exhibition. "At least it seems to have got you painting again though. I was getting seriously worried about that, but these new pieces are fabulous. So how are things at home?"

"Quiet," I said. "Willow's still in Exeter, so I'm all alone." Not entirely true. No sign of Denis Anderson's sister, lurking outside again, but inside, Adam was present all the time. Rubbing in my guilt. Looking betrayed. "Carregwen did work some sort of magic. We had a lovely time there, over the summer. Willow really benefited from it. As soon as her term finishes, we're flying out to stay with Paul for Christmas, thank God."

"Yes, oh God yes, you don't want... Great idea going to Paul's. You don't want to be at home, not this year."

"No."

"That's why I thought a change of scene at Carregwen would help. How was October out there for you? You didn't stay long. Too lonely?"

"No. No, not at all."

Carla, adjusting a scarf round my neck, eyed me suspiciously. "Do I sense a wee bit of caginess creeping in?"

"No. Why do you think that?"

"Something happen?"

"No. Maybe. No, it was nothing."

"Okay, this isn't just creeping caginess. It's galloping, darling. Obviously something happened. Something upset you."

"No. Yes. Yes, all right. I had a... I don't know what to call it. Hardly an affair, but... There was a... I got drunk and it happened. Just the once."

"Oh God, you mean you had a tipsy one-night stand. Is that so bad?"

"Yes!"

"Why? Come on, now. Do you really think Adam would want you to spend the rest of your life celibate, in mourning for him? He'd want you to be alive and kicking, Nicki. Don't hang it round your neck like a millstone."

I pulled away, fiddling with the scarf. "Easier said than done."

"Look, Nicki, everyone needs a bit of comfort now and again, - especially in your situation. Where's the harm? It wasn't date rape or anything, was it? Did you like the guy?"

"No, it wasn't rape, and yes, I liked him. Sort of. Wished I didn't, but yes."

"Anyone I know? Can't think of that many men in Tregelli who'd get me hot and bothered. A visitor maybe. A holiday fling. Was that it?"

I was silent.

"Go on, tell me."

"It was Oliver Wyatt. All right?"

Carla's jaw dropped. "Oh. My. God. Okay." She blew out her cheeks. "Right. I'm..."

"Surprised? Appalled?"

"No, no… er. I mean, I can see the appeal. But, just take… Has he been in touch since?"

"No." I was relieved. Mostly relieved. A tiny treacherous part of me was resentful that he hadn't made any attempt to do so. A man like him would have been able to find out my number or address easily enough. But then, I had walked out on him without a word, so maybe he was justifiably stung.

"Well then." Carla was fussing needlessly with my hair, her mind obviously on other things. "Forget it then. It was just a passing thing that happened, for both of you, that's all."

"Did you know his wife?"

"Helena? Yes, she was okay. A bit of a dipso, but not surprising, given what she was up against. Did you get to meet Fabia Wyatt?"

"I certainly did. I understand what you mean by up against."

"So you know what you'd be dealing with, if you got any deeper involved with her son."

"I won't be. Were you there when Helena Wyatt disappeared?"

"Disappeared? Sounds a bit dramatic. Ran off with a lover, I heard, and I don't blame her. But no, I wasn't there, so I don't know all the juicy details, but I'm sure Yvonne or Chloe do. Look, I can see this business with Wyatt has got you in a frazzle. Don't let it. Some time or another you're going to be making a new start. It's not a sin to think about it. Now, are you ready? Let's get out there and wow them."

PART THREE

1

Christmas in Melbourne. We didn't have dinner on the beach, as Willow had hoped, but it was in the garden. It was so utterly different to Christmases we had known that the worst of the pain was alleviated. Not that we didn't shed copious tears and repeatedly share comforting hugs, but we survived.

Back at the airport, my brother took me aside and offered to fly over for the trial to support me, but I whispered assurance that I'd cope. I thought Willow, chatting to her cousins, hadn't heard, but as soon as we settled into our seats on the plane, she said "Only a month now."

"Yes."

"What do you think will happen?"

"He'll be convicted. How can he not be?"

"Will he go to prison?"

"I would think so."

"For how long?"

"I don't know. Longer than if he'd pleaded guilty."

"Someone said fourteen years."

"That's the maximum, I think."

"It's not long enough. I hope he dies in prison."

I squeezed her hand. "I know, I know. But it doesn't matter how long they lock him up or what they do to him. It still won't bring… it won't undo anything."

"I wish it was over."

"So do I."

* * *

Willow returned to university. I sat alone at home, waiting and waiting, growing more and more numb by the day, Sgt Naomi Strong did her best to support me.

"If he had an ounce of humanity, he'd have pleaded guilty and we wouldn't be having this farce. There'd just be the sentencing. But it's his prerogative to plead not guilty. We've got more than enough to establish the facts, so we won't need to call you as a witness. That means you won't have to go through it all again."

I laughed, hysterically. "I've been doing just that ever since it happened, every time I shut my eyes."

"You really should be seeing someone about that. I'll get those contacts again for you. But first, let's get through this trial. I'm afraid you'll be listening to all his pathetic lies again. Are you sure you want to go? It will be very painful."

"It will! But I have to be there, for Adam. As for Denis Anderson, I can't begin to define what I think about him."

Naomi patted my arm. "Don't worry, no chance he'll walk out a free man. It will be a prison sentence."

"It already is."

"Yes, well, see how you feel after Tuesday. You've done your victim impact statement, haven't you?"

"Yes. Such as it is. I wrote a lot of words, probably every word in the Agony section of the thesaurus, and none of them mean anything. What I feel isn't something that I could ever put down in a statement. It makes it all so phoney. But Willow wanted me to do it. I'm sure hers will be much better."

* * *

The evening before the trial, I considered taking a sleeping pill. What if I overslept, on that day of all days? I was still debating it when the front door rattled and my stomach turned over. I'd seen no sign of Brenda Gough since the new year, but the eve of her brother's trial was precisely when she would decide to defy the injunction. I wasn't having it, not this time. I charged to the door and threw it open.

"If you think…" I gaped. There was my daughter, struggling with key, bag and backpack on the doorstep. "Willow, why didn't you tell me you were coming?"

She dropped her luggage and threw her arms around me. "Because you'd have got in a state, telling me not to."

"I'd much rather you weren't here for this."

"I'm not a kid, Mum. I had to come."

"Aren't you missing lectures?"

"I cleared it with them. They understand. Look, Mum, I want to be there to see that bastard convicted." She burst into tears. So did I.

"Never a tissue when I want one."

2

I didn't take a pill, and I didn't sleep. At least it meant no nightmares. I lay all night, numb, waiting for an ending that I couldn't grasp. The next morning we were at the Crown Court, being greeted at the glass doors by Sgt Strong.

"Anderson's the first case of the day, so you won't have to hang around, waiting for it to begin."

Willow was peering across the lobby. "Is that Mrs Proctor?"

"One of our witnesses, yes."

Mrs Procter who lived almost opposite, looked desperately nervous. Next to her, Gerald Armstrong, three doors down, was bristling with importance.

A young man joined my neighbours as they were hustled off to a private room. A young man who would have looked fit and athletic, but for the crutches. Ewan Davis, the cyclist that Denis Anderson had knocked off his bike before swerving on to hit Adam. Still crippled by it. This was everyone's drama, about to reach fulfilment. I was a mere spectator. Just as I'd been that day, unable to do anything. Utterly impotent.

"Here you are," said Naomi, shepherding us into court number one. "Phones off, remember."

"It's like a lecture hall," said Willow. "I thought it would be more sort of dark and Gothic."

"More like Ikea. It's not exactly the Old Bailey, is it?" I steadied my breathing, as we took our seats in what was apparently the public gallery. A solitary reporter was settling himself but there was no one else yet in our part of the courtroom. I looked out across a blur of blonde wood and blue upholstery, seeing and not seeing. I didn't want to see it. I stared at my hands in my lap. An elderly couple arrived and sat next to us. The woman was fat and wheezing. Interested parties or idle passers-by? I didn't trust myself to make eye contact.

"Are you okay?" whispered Willow.

"No, I feel sick."

"Oh God, do you want to go out?"

"I'll be all right."

More people were taking up seats around us, behind us. Others were gathering in the body of the court, black gowns, silly wigs.

Then he came in. Denis Anderson, with a prison officer. The one person I didn't want to see, but I couldn't stop myself staring at him, feeling the blood drain from my face. The nausea doubled.

I don't know exactly what he had become in my imagination over the last months. Something monstrous. On the day of the accident, I had barely registered him except as the focus of something bewildering going on down the street. My stunned, heart-pounding attention had all been for Adam as I had crouched by him. I'd seen Anderson at the committal hearing, briefly, in and out, but I had been too distraught to take anything in. Since then he had grown in my imagination into a sneering, slimy version of Bill Sykes. But now here he was, in the flesh, a non-descript little man, running to flab and going bald, uncomfortably twitching in his best suit, his face grey, shiny with sweat, his eyes blinking with sheer terror.

He'd killed my husband and for a moment I felt almost sorry for him. Willow squeezed my fingers brutally and I could hear her breathing, hard and angry.

His eyes wandered around the courtroom, found the public gallery and fixed on someone, behind me and to my left. Instinctively I turned to look. A middle-aged woman, drawn and anxious, dark rings round her eyes despite an attempt to put on brave makeup. And next to her a girl, couldn't have been more than sixteen. Too young to be watching this, surely. She shrank back in her seat and I saw, beyond her, my stalker, Brenda Gough. She looked so old, so desperate, her gaunt face a mask of anger, mouthing words at Anderson and ready to charge into the court to carry him off.

At least she wasn't looking at me. My eyes returned to Anderson and met his. He had found me, recognised me, and his face seemed to melt. His mouth opened and closed like a fish yanked out of water.

Everything was swimming. I was seeing Adam again, blood spraying from his mouth, his eyes glazing over.

Willow's hand was at my elbow, bringing me to my feet. Through the roaring in my ears I caught the words "His Honour Judge Gravely." There was a clown in court, a man in a wig and a lavender gown and a red sash and how could any of this be taken seriously? I had a manic desire to laugh. To collapse laughing. Stop it. Get a grip. Along with everyone else I sank back into my seat, the nausea rising again. Rustling. Fidgeting. The clerk was talking. I tried to listen but the roaring wouldn't stop.

"Denis Percy Anderson, you are charged..."

Percy? Pinky and Perky. All I could think was, why did his parents give him a name like that? Why did we give our daughter the name of a tree? Adam's idea. Naiads and Dryads. Blood on his lips. I couldn't breathe.

"March 29th last, you did cause the death..." It seemed to go on and on and on, as I bit my lip hard enough to draw blood. Why put it into so many words, so much babble, dangerous driving, under the influence, serious injury. He killed my husband, wasn't that enough?

Then, "How do you plead?"

The roaring stopped. Everything was silent. Any misplaced compassion I had felt for the man in the dock turned back to ice-cold bitter anger as I waited for him to say not guilty.

"Guilty."

A second more of silence and then a hubbub of murmurings like a giant swarm of bees, and one shriek of "No!" from somewhere behind me.

* * *

It was a long day. It lasted at least three hundred years, though the clock claimed it was only a few hours. Naomi pressed pre-packed sandwiches on us in a cafeteria, but neither Willow nor I could face them. Food was too solid for the unreality of the day. Then we were back in court for the sentencing. Denis Anderson had been the only one nursing any delusion about his guilt, so there was no need for a lengthy adjournment. I watched his face. No fear and guilt now. Just relief.

At last we were free. Naomi bustled us out of the courtroom. "Are you both okay? I know, I know, it doesn't seem nearly enough, does, it? Six years for Adam's death. But I'm afraid..."

"It's all right, Naomi. It doesn't matter."

"I expect you'd have wanted him to be given..."

"Seriously! It doesn't matter how many years he serves. Adam is still dead. Can't we all just get out of here?"

"Yes, all right, come on then."

I turned towards the doors.

Brenda Gough was before me, in my face, snarling. "Satisfied now, you fucking bitch? I hope you burn in Hell!"

I had a split second to realise that she was trying to strike me, but hands were gripping her arms, pulling her back. Naomi stepped in, amidst a hubbub of shock and indignation, anger and sympathy. All I could see was Brenda Gough, straining to get at me. She couldn't claw my eyes out, so she gathered herself and spat. I felt it run down my cheek. Then she was gone, dragged away, and someone was dabbing at my cheek and hair with a tissue. I was too stunned to respond. Shaking myself at last, I looked round for Willow and found her rigid, weeping tears of sheer anger.

I grabbed her hand. "I'm all right. Come on, let's go home."

3

I had a long deep bath to clean away the pollution of the court. I needed silence, a moment of peace to try and come to terms with my own response to the day. Forget Brenda Gough's assault. The day had been about the trial of the man who had killed my husband. Something I'd longed for, and dreaded, for months. Now it was over. He had admitted his guilt, and he was on his way to gaol. What was I supposed to feel? Triumph in revenge? Satisfaction that justice was done? Dissatisfaction at the inadequacy of the punishment? In reality, I felt nothing. Was this what was meant by closure? The cauterising of a problematic nerve ending. Time to move on.

I dressed and went downstairs. Willow, wet from her shower, was busy on her phone.

"I'd better think up something for dinner," I suggested. Then I froze at the sound of a rap on the front door.

Willow leaped up. "If it's her, I'll kill her."

I put out a hand to reassure her, determined to resist paranoia. "It will be Naomi, I expect. Stay there. I'll answer it."

She didn't stay, of course. She followed me as I opened the front door. It was the girl from the court, shivering on the doorstep like a frightened rabbit.

We stared at each other for what seemed like an age before I collected myself. "It's you."

Denis Anderson's daughter, white-faced and desperately trying to dredge up her deepest resources of courage. "Mrs Winters. I just…"

"Come in." I couldn't leave her standing there on the doorstep in the rain. She was soaking.

Nervously, she followed me into the sitting room. Willow watched in stony silence.

The girl swallowed, her lip quivering. "I just wanted to say me and Mum are so sorry about everything. About what Aunty Bren did, I mean, and Dad. I know it's… I just…" She looked up from the carpet to me, to see if I were about to hit her. I hadn't moved so she took a deep breath and plunged in at double speed. "I'm so sorry. That's all. We tried to stop her, but she's, like, you know, a bit mental. She always has been a bit, sort of. Mum says stressed. She drinks. She was like his mother, see – Dad's, I mean. She's older than him and their mum died when he was little so she brought him up and she's always been, like, she's always defending him and if he does something stupid, it's always, you know, someone else's fault." She paused for breath, realising the point she'd reached, and her lip quivered again. "Like the accident. It was awful. I don't know why he didn't just admit it. It was Aunty Brenda telling him to shut up…"

"No." I interrupted her. "Stop." I took her hand and guided her to a sofa. "Sit down."

She perched on the edge, pulling her wet cagoule around her. I drew up a chair in front of her. "What's your name?"

"Bryony Anderson."

"All right, Bryony. First of all, there's no need for you to be apologising for your father or your aunt. What they did is on their conscience, not yours. You and your mother have done nothing wrong."

She chewed her lip. "Mum's gone to bed. She says she'll never dare show her face again."

"I understand how she feels. I understand how you feel. I understand a lot, I think. You thought your father wasn't admitting anything because your aunt was telling him to lie. Yes, she probably was. I think we all realise your aunt is more than a little mixed up. She can't cope, so she gets defensive and blames everyone else in the world if something goes wrong. Just like she blamed me for your father's arrest, as if I had something to do with it and he had nothing."

"I'm so sorry, we didn't know what she was doing, writing on your house and all that. Not till the police came."

"Yes, I'm sure you didn't. But I saw your father in court."

Her head hung low. I glanced at Willow, who was at her most enigmatic, not hostile, not sympathetic, just reserving judgement.

"Listen, Bryony. I saw him and I didn't know what to think. I tried to work out what was going on in his mind and while I sat there in court it made no sense, but I think I understand now."

I'd heard the reports on Denis Anderson along with the victim impact statements. I knew now what tiny links had made up the chain that finally killed Adam.

Anderson had been prosecuted for drink-driving three years earlier, which lost him his license and his job with it. He'd gone steadily downhill in a futile search for employment, until he finally landed a position with a firm that, a month later, was bought out and downsized. He was back to square one, the explanation for him being dead drunk, maybe even suicidal, as he sped down our road and struck Adam. I didn't excuse him. I would never forgive him. But at least everything had stopped being a meaningless maelstrom without cause or reason.

And now, remembering him in court, I understood what had been going on in his mind.

"I think your father refused to admit his guilt because he couldn't believe what he had done. There must have been someone else driving. In a way, I suppose there was. He couldn't accept that he had just killed a man, injured another. And once he'd denied it in his own head, he didn't know how to take the lie back. Especially not with your aunt egging him on. When he came into court today, he was terrified. I could see that. I thought he was terrified of punishment, but it wasn't that. He was just terrified of being forced to confront the truth. When he saw me and my daughter, he did confront it. Later, you know, when the judge handed down the sentence, he wasn't scared any more. He was ashamed, yes, but not terrified. He'd faced the truth and he was free from that hell."

Bryony raised her eyes to mine, searching for a clue. Was I glad that he was free from that hell? Or would I like him to burn in it forever? It wasn't until that moment that I knew it myself. I was glad. Otherwise, there was no point in anything.

"The law is punishing him, Bryony, and I think he's actually grateful for that. I don't know whether the punishment makes sense or not, but at least everyone accepts the truth now and that's what matters to me. I don't suppose he'll be in prison for the full six years. You'll visit him, won't you?"

She hesitated before nodding.

"How old are you, Bryony?"

"Fifteen. Nearly."

"How are you going to manage while your father's in gaol? Does your mother work?"

"Yeah. She says she'll need to get extra so we don't lose the house, but I can get a Saturday job. And then I'll finish school in a year and I can get a proper one."

"At sixteen? That won't be a proper job. What sort of thing did you want to do?"

She shrugged. "Dunno."

"Well, no reason why you should at fifteen. But think about it. Whatever you want your life to be, go for it. Be an astronaut, or a rap artist, or a doctor or a ballet dancer. Whatever it is you dream of, don't let this terrible thing slam the door in your face. We are all losers here, every one of us. There are no winners. Adam is dead. I've lost my husband and best friend. My daughter's lost her father, your aunt's lost her sanity, your father's lost his liberty and any prospects that he might have had, you've had your family wrecked. It's overwhelmed us all. But we have to struggle back to the surface, those of us who can, and start swimming again. Don't let it drown you."

She bit her lip.

"Come on." I held out my hand and helped her to her feet. "You are the strong one in your family. I know that because you had to be incredibly brave to come here today like this. If you can do this, you can do anything."

She mouthed "Thank you," as I led her to the door. I watched her walk away, head higher now.

I turned back to face my daughter. "Was I wrong?"

Willow shrugged.

"I'm not forgiving him, you know," I said. "A part of me would still like to see him boiled in oil. But I realise something about justice now. It can be about putting things right, but that can never happen in this case. Or it can be about punishment, but that's just revenge, isn't it? Sheer vindictiveness. The only justice that really matters is the truth. What do you think?"

My daughter pulled a face and twisted a hank of hair between her fingers. "I think…" She shrugged. "I hope she becomes an astronaut."

I smiled.

"Right, so." Willow clapped her hands. "I'm going to make the dinner. Thai, okay?"

"Thai is fine."

We had survived the day.

* * *

Willow was returning to Exeter the next day. She wandered around, toast in one hand, repacking her bags with different clothes and considerately leaving me with dirty ones. Her phone was left on the table. She'd been thumbing it all the previous evening, just as I'd been passing on the news to Carla and Paul.

I picked up the phone and glanced down the names listed on Willow's messages. There was a message from Gareth Hughes. *You ok? Must have been tough.* A gushing message full of OMG and emojis from someone called FluffyBun. Alex Wyatt... she was still in contact with him then. *I know it must have been shit but at least you know your Dad didn't want to leave you.* Not the blasé comment of an urbane Oxford student but the cry of a little boy hurting.

"You sneaking a look at my phone? That's private, you know." Willow had slid silently back downstairs with her bulging backpack.

"Sorry. I was just looking at the message from Alex Wyatt."

"Yeah." She took the phone, rereading the message, her face serious. "Shit, isn't it? I mean, for him, never hearing from his Mum, not knowing where she is. Or even if... She might be dead and he wouldn't know. That's awful."

"Yes. It is. Poor boy."

She pocketed the phone and then we were off, to the station. As her train doors opened, I gave her a last hug to reassure myself that she had come through it all intact. She was fine.

I walked back to the car, and sat in it, thinking. Thinking about Alex's message and rethinking what I had said about truth being the only justice that mattered. Had I got that right? Was ignorance bliss, or a sort of hell?

I was still thinking about it when I got home to find Carla urgently calling me.

"Sorry, darling, sorry, sorry, sorry. If we hadn't had that bloody meeting fixed up, you know I'd have been there to support you. I got your message. Six years! Not nearly enough..."

"It's all right, Carla. It's over, now."

"But tell me all about it."

So I did, and just by telling her everything, the trial slipped effortlessly into the past. Over. For me and for Willow it was over.

"If there's anything I can do?" said Carla.

"Do you know anything about tracing people?"

"Um... in what context?"

"To find out if they're still alive?"

Since I had been dealing with Adam's death for the last eleven months, it was hardly surprising that Carla was instantly alarmed. "Nicki, what do you mean?"

"If someone had been murdered, there'd be no further trace of them, would there?"

"Murdered! Who's been murdered?"

"Helena Wyatt?"

"What? What? Who said she was murdered? Why on earth do you think that?"

"She just vanished, didn't she? And never once got in contact with her son, afterwards."

"Are you sure about that?"

"He's really hurt by it."

"Oh dear, poor boy. But seriously, Nicki, just because a woman walks out, it doesn't mean she's been murdered. Any sane woman would walk out on Fabia Wyatt."

"I know, but I just want to be certain. I want everyone to know the truth about everything."

"Be careful what you wish for, darling. Most of us would rather not know the truth half the time. Is this something to do with your little fling with Oliver?"

"No! No, it isn't. I just feel sorry for Alex, that's all. Forget it."

4

If Carla had forgotten it, so, probably, would I. But she didn't. I must have alarmed her into a spot of efficient on-line investigation. A couple of days later I had a text from her. No chat, no chiding, no told you so, just names and an address. Enough to prove that I had been totally wrong.

Which was why I was sitting in my car, looking at an architect's house, all plate glass and oak timbers, nestling under the South Downs, surrounded by shrubs and lawns and an area of chaos designed for children. I gazed in through the open gates, hesitating before taking the plunge. Not from cowardice, but because I knew I might be making a monumental mistake. I'd interfered in other people's family problems before and achieved nothing more than ill will. But that message from Alex Wyatt haunted me. *At least you know your Dad didn't want to leave you.* I could understand Helena Wyatt wanting to leave her mother-in-law, husband even. But walk out on her son, without a word? Why?

I could at least ask. She might slam the door in my face, she might call her partner and have me picked up and thrown out. But I was going to do it. Whether or not it was closure, the trial had moved me on somehow, nursing a pious belief that the Truth would make all things right.

When I rang the bell, I was met with a cacophony of over-excited yapping and a woman shouting "No! No! Bad dog. In your basket. No, in your basket." She was pointing sternly with one hand as she opened the door with the other, before turning to face me. "Yes?" Abrupt but not hostile.

"Helena Treece?" I needed to be sure. She didn't look as I had imagined Oliver's wife. My age or thereabouts, slim, classical features fit for a model if made up with care and attention, but she wasn't made up. She was wearing jeans and a baggy sweatshirt and her fair hair was knotted up in ramshackle fashion with a chiffon scarf. She looked like a busy, slightly harassed mother. No wedding ring.

"I'm Helena Treece."

"You were married to Oliver Wyatt?"

"Why? Who are you?" Her eyes narrowed with suspicion. "Did Oliver send you here?"

"No. I know your son, that's all. Or rather, my daughter knows him."

She was still gripping the door, barring my way. Her free hand rose to her throat. "Alex?"

"Yes. We were staying in Tregelli over the summer and they became friends. I'm Nicki Bryce and my daughter…"

"Nicki Bryce? The artist? Of course he'll have collected you." She stood summing me up for a moment longer, while I wondered if my cheeks were burning as much as I imagined. What did she imply by *collecting me*? Nothing too offensive, it seemed, because she stepped back. "You'd better come in."

I followed her into a central hall open to the roof rafters two floors above, with light pouring in from all sides. She indicated an alcove housing a couple of sofas and a cabinet. "Sit down then." She opened the cabinet and produced a bottle of wine and a couple of glasses. "How is he?"

"Alex? Healthy. Handsome. Confident. Charming."

"Like his father, you mean."

"I suppose so. He's at Oxford, did you know that?"

She filled the glasses, her hand shaking. "Yes, of course, he would be. Twenty." She shook her head. It was clear she wanted to talk about him and at the same time didn't want to. "I imagine he's forgotten all about me. She'll have seen to that."

"Fabia? I'm sure she tried, but he hasn't forgotten you." I accepted the glass she proffered and took a polite sip before setting it down. "He pretends not to care, but he does. He's hurt. Angry that you left him."

She said nothing but took a large swig of her wine.

"Why did you do it?" I asked. "Walk out and leave him?"

She flared up. "Do you think I wanted to? And who the hell are you to interrogate me like this? It's none of your damn business."

"I know it isn't. But I've been through a lot this last year. My husband was killed and healing has been hard-going, but it's coming. I just wanted to spread some of it around, help Alex heal a little too."

She turned away, her hand over her face, breathing heavily. Then she took another deep gulp. "I'm sorry. About your husband, I mean. But Alex and me, Oliver and me, Fabia and me… it's all way too complicated to explain. I thought she'd have told him I was dead."

"No, she didn't, although I half-suspected it myself. I was told you'd vanished suddenly and I thought maybe Fabia…" Looking back, the idea was so fanciful I was too embarrassed to spell it out.

"You thought she'd done me in?" Helena gave a humourless laugh. "Wouldn't have put it past her. She's quite capable of it, evil cow. She had me in her sights way before we were married, when I was Oliver's PA." She glanced at me sidelong and shrugged. "Yes, all right, I was more than that. His mistress. You have to say that, don't you? Oliver Wyatt's mistress. If he'd been a milkman or a plumber, I'd have been his girlfriend, his partner, his lover, but Oliver's a tycoon so that made me his mistress. I organised his business and slept with him. I travelled the world with him. I was his match in some ways, you know. Arrogant, ambitious, I loved the thrill.

"It was fine, except that we'd go to see his damned mother, and she'd be circling round me like a lioness defending her cub. She wanted me to sleep in the servant's wing, eat in the kitchen. I thought it was a joke at first, she didn't understand who I was, but then it became irritating, her jealousy, her possessiveness, it was pathetic. Didn't want the noble lineage polluted. You know she claims they're descended from the poet, Thomas Wyatt?"

"Anne Boleyn's lover? Yes, she told me."

"Total bull. The family name was really Cannell. Victorian blacksmith, came to Birmingham for work, married the foundry owner's daughter and agreed to take her name, but she died in childbirth and he married again, so there's not a drop of real Wyatt blood in Oliver's veins."

"As I supposed."

"But dare to challenge her… Oliver just said 'Indulge her.' I hated it. That's why we got married, his peace offering to make amends, when we were out in Japan. I thought 'What are you going to do about it now, Mrs Fabia bloody Wyatt.' I could be as bloody-minded as her, give as good as I got, so she had to learn to shut up, at least while Oliver was in the room. She just pretended I didn't exist."

She took another swig of wine. "It wasn't so bad while I could escape, but then Alex was on the way. Not exactly planned, but Oliver was delighted. I thought I was, too, until I realised he didn't want a pregnant wife cruising round the world with him. He took on a new PA and I was dumped at Tregelli with Fabia and then there was no end to it. I was a cheap little whore, a fortune-hunting hussy and he'd find out what I was before too long and throw me back in the gutter where he'd found me. It wears you down, you know."

"I can imagine."

"And then Alex. If I thought she was possessive with Oliver… It was even worse with my son. It didn't help that I had a bout of post-natal depression. Maybe it was lingering resentment or simple biology, I don't know, but I didn't really bond with him for months. I was just knocked out, mentally, and that allowed Fabia to take over. She had a nursery set up in the room next to hers, and she kept the key. She made all the decisions. When

I finally tried to assert myself again, it always finished up with Alex howling in distress. She was an expert at making that happen. It was all nasty Mummy's fault. She accused me of drinking too much. I did. That's how you survive, in a psychopath's household. She never held back, never stopped insinuating that I wasn't a fit mother, that I couldn't be trusted with him. If I tucked him up at night and told him stories until he dozed off, she'd wake him up again, so that she'd be the one reading him to sleep."

"And Oliver didn't intervene?"

"When he was there, you mean? No, he couldn't see what all the fuss was about. Wasn't Fabia being the perfect grandma? That was the shit thing, of course. She really was, loving, firm, encouraging, the perfect mother that I wasn't. Oliver said I should be grateful that she was taking on so much of the burden. I should indulge her. Like I said, life with a psychopath, there's nowhere to turn. Just indulge her is all he'd say."

"He's still saying it."

"Yes, he would." Helena refilled her glass. "He was never there to see his mother slap me, or stab me with her umbrella, or kick me. She's built like a fairy but she kicks like a mule. If I'd stayed, I would be dead, you know. She'd have killed me or I'd have done it for her. I stuck it out for, how long? God knows, it felt like a lifetime and I was that close to…" She sighed and tugged the scarf from her hair. It flowed down free, a metaphor for her thoughts. "But then Sandy came on the scene. You know… well you must, if you found me."

Yes. I knew she was living with Sandun Da Silva, architect. Sri Lankan not Pakistani, though it was probably all the same to Fabia. Thanks to Carla, I knew that she and Sandun had two daughters aged nine and six. I nodded.

"He was taken on by Oliver for some project and he came to stay. We fell in love. God, that sounds so corny, doesn't it? But it happened. It was only when I met Sandy that I realised what a sham my marriage was. I was just a showcase wife, imprisoned in Purgatory, while Oliver lived his life elsewhere. Sandy was all for taking me and Alex and heading off into the sunset, but I… Jesus, why didn't I just go? I had this stupid idea that I should face the beast, be honest, tell them what I was doing. So when Sandy had gone, I did just that.

"Fabia exploded, of course, screaming that I was an adulterous slut, an irresponsible alcoholic and she'd call in the social services, the police, anyone, demand that I lose custody of my own son. Oliver didn't even raise his voice, just said 'You're not taking my son anywhere.' He called Alex and whisked him off, to some shoot or something. Calm as you like, as if nothing had happened. When they came back, Fabia took charge of him, wouldn't let me near.

"I wasn't giving up though. The next day, Oliver drove off to a meeting. Fabia was watching me like a hawk at first, so I shut myself in my room, until I heard her talking to someone from the stables. A horse was lame so she went to see, and I seized my chance. I called for a taxi and went to find Alex. He was in bed. Mid-morning and fast asleep. I didn't get it at first, but then, when I couldn't wake him, I realised she must have drugged him. That did it. I wasn't going to bother with anything else. I picked him up and carried him downstairs. He was a big boy, then. A lot to carry. But I made it. I wouldn't wait for the taxi to come to the door. I carried him down the drive. Made it as far as the gate before I heard Fabia screeching, back at the house, coming after me. Thank God the taxi had just arrived. I had to waste time persuading the driver I was the mother and not a kidnapper. He wasn't too happy about it, but when Fabia caught up with us and started beating on the boot, screaming filthy things at him, he drove off.

"I asked him to take us to Swansea station. I thought we'd be safe there. Far enough away. But the London train wasn't due to leave for half an hour. Why didn't I get on the first train out of there and find my way to London later? I was so stupid to wait there like a sitting duck. The train arrived and once we were allowed to board I had to manhandle Alex onto the damn thing. He still wasn't properly awake, lolling around like a rag doll. I don't blame the suspicious looks we were getting. I was still trying to get him up the step when they turned up, Fabia and Oliver and one of his men.

"Not good, making a scene in public. Guards were about to call the police. I said 'Come on Alex, please, for Mummy, get onto the train,' but he was staring around, no idea where he was or what was happening. Then Fabia called out 'Alex darling, come to Granny.'" Helena was almost sobbing. "'We won't let that nasty woman hurt you. Come to Granny Fabia.'

"And he went, like a well-trained puppy, before I could stop him. Oliver grabbed my arm, I shook myself free and – God, I know, I know. I should have run after

Alex, but I didn't. I just stepped onto the train. I stood there, facing Oliver down, as the doors closed, and he shrugged. That's all. He shrugged, and the train pulled out. Why did I do it? I've been asking myself that, ever since. Anger, I suppose. Sheer rage. It hurt so much that Alex had gone to her. And I wanted to salvage enough pride to defy Oliver for once. I regretted it before the train was out of the station but it was too late.

"I don't suppose Alex remembers a thing about that day. God knows what Fabia told him. I've never seen him since."

"Didn't you ever go back to Tregelli, try to contact him?"

"Of course I did. What do you think I am? I went back to the house a couple of times but I never managed to get in. They'd changed the security codes. I tried his school, but they'd taken him out, sent him to a new one and the staff wouldn't tell me where. I tried to phone, but my calls were barred. I wrote, but I doubt if any of my letters were even opened, let alone shown to Alex. I tried contacting other people, staff, neighbours, but they couldn't help, or wouldn't. The landlady at the Bell, is she still there? Knows everything about everyone, but she thought Alex was off to Eton. He was down for it but he never went there. They told me Mr Wyatt had changed his mind. Sandy said I should apply to the courts for custody, or at least for contact, but I thought, by then, what was the point? Sandy was struggling to keep afloat because Oliver had ended the contract and was doing everything he could to undermine him. We didn't have the money to take on the legal machine that Oliver could conjure up with a snap of his fingers."

"Did you never ask for a divorce? A settlement?"

"No! I wanted to prove I wasn't the fortune hunter Fabia liked to claim. I didn't want Oliver's money, though I bloody deserved it. I was too proud. Too stupid. And he'd have fought me over a divorce, with the best lawyers money could buy, just as he would over Alex. What would that have done to my son? A vicious custody battle? Fabia had been weening him from me from the day he was born and she'd have pumped him full of poison against me by now. If I tore him away from his home, he'd probably hate me. So, I decided to leave it. It wasn't just the futility; it was the shame. Guilt at having left him in the first place. I decided to walk away. I told myself that if I found him when he was an adult and free of them, I'd tell him the truth. He'd still hate me but there was nothing I could do about that. I'd wait."

"He's an adult now."

"Yes. I suppose." She hesitated. "He's at Oxford, you say."

"I have his mobile number." I produced a folded sheet of paper. "His college, his digs, social media accounts. It's all there. My daughter gave me the lot."

She took the paper, unfolded it, stared at it, folded it again. "I don't know. I've left it so long. It's too late now to undo the damage."

I stood up. "My husband will never be able to speak to his daughter again. You still have the chance. It's never too late while you're still breathing."

She followed me to the door. "I'm sorry about your husband, but this isn't the same. I'd just be opening old wounds. Alex has a life without me, and I have a new life here. A new partner, children, a new home, new career. Do I really want to risk shipwreck for the lot of us?"

I could only look at her in response. It was up to her now. Surely she'd make contact. She wouldn't be able to resist. I walked away in a golden glow of smug righteousness. How good was I, healing the world?

* * *

Not as good as I fancied, it seemed. Willow skyped me on a day when we were both determined to be upbeat with each other.

"You'll never guess who turned up at Alex Wyatt's door on Sunday. Only his mother! You know, the woman who dumped him when he was a kid."

"Oh. Helena. That's…" I swallowed. "What happened?"

"What do you think? He told her to get lost, of course. I mean, just turning up like that, as if nothing had happened!" Willow laughed, but there was an edge to her laughter that disturbed me.

"It's my fault. I saw her. I gave her his address. She said it would be a mistake but I persuaded her. Have I ruined everything?"

She ignored the question, bursting out, "I told him he was so fucking stupid! What would I give…?" She was crying.

"Willow, I know, I know."

"I told him!"

"Yes, of course. Darling, don't cry. You're so far away."

247

"I'm not crying!" She sniffed, turned away, rubbing her eyes with her sleeve, and when she turned back she had a forced smile. "I'm fine, really. How about you? What are you going to do tomorrow? Not sit at home on your own?"

"No, I'm going to London for the day. Treating myself, going to visit all my favourite galleries. What about you?"

"Oh, you know, going out with the guys. There's a band we're going to hear."

"That's good. Great. You enjoy yourself."
She smiled. As if. Both of us were going to struggle to enjoy ourselves the next day. March 29th. The anniversary of Adam's death.

* * *

I did go to London, not because I was eager to wander round the Tate Modern or any other gallery. Just because I didn't want to be sitting at home, staring out of the window at my gatepost, reliving the accident in glorious technicolour. I went. I looked at a lot of art. I drank a lot of coffee. Being in London didn't keep the ghosts at bay. They crept up on me every time I stood still, so I kept walking. I crossed the Millennium bridge, walked round St Paul's, through the city and back across Tower Bridge. For a moment I paused there, gazing out over a capital that was buzzing, rushing, churning with business, and utterly indifferent to the life or demise of Adam Winters, deceased. Then I gazed down at the water, rushing, churning beneath. Was it just as indifferent, or did it know it all? Adam's death, my pain. It could embrace me more effectively than the city. I could sink down into its depths and drown all memories.

What I realised though, was that I didn't want to sink down and drown. Not anymore. I wanted to move on, trailing the pain and the grief but also the happiness and joy.

I caught a late train home, so late that I didn't arrive at my doorstep until long after midnight. That was all right. It was no longer the 29th March. I had no memory at all of the 30th.

5

It was Willow's idea to go back to Carregwen for Easter. I could hardly explain that it had become a scene of embarrassing humiliation. If our drunken orgy had meant anything to Oliver, he would surely have tried to contact me since, and he never had. I had no wish to seem like a woman begging for more.

No. That was ridiculous. I would return as indifferent as he was. Besides, I did want to see Siân again. Why should I be chased away from her? The chances were that Oliver Wyatt would be far away on the other side of the world.

So as soon as Willow came home from Exeter, we piled luggage back into the car and headed off. At least I could be confident our poor neighbours wouldn't be scrubbing graffiti away in our absence. Brenda Gough was receiving counselling and medication. Court order. I knew this because her niece had come to tell me.

"Bryony has decided to stay on at school," I said, as we headed for the motorway.

"Is she going to be an astronaut?" asked Willow.

I laughed. "No. A nurse."

"Yeah." Willow thought about it. "That's okay. Making things better. She'll be good at that. So, looking forward to seeing people in Tregelli again?"

I concentrated on driving. "Siân, yes."

"Gareth's coming, in a few days," said Willow. "But not Alex." She glanced across at me with an arch look. "Guess where he is."

"South of France? New York?"

"No!" She lowered her voice, although there was no one else in the car. "You're not to tell anyone, you know, but he's gone to stay with his mother."

I said nothing but let out a deep sigh of relief. At least I hadn't totally messed up that situation.

"It's good, isn't it? I think it was the shock, that first time. But she wrote him a long letter and he went down to Brighton to meet her, and they, like, made it up, you know."

"Oh God, I hope it goes well," I said, fervently. "I don't suppose it will be easy for either of them, but at least they can start to get to know each other again."

"Don't tell anyone though." Willow was earnest. "Fabia thinks he's visiting friends."

"I'm not planning to see Fabia Wyatt if I can help it, let alone tell her anything."

"No, well." Willow grinned and punched my arm. "See, it worked out."

"I'm glad, but can you not punch me while I'm overtaking a tanker?"

* * *

Carregwen was waiting for us in a golden glow of early spring sunshine. The clamour of seabirds washed over us in raucous greeting. The cottage had grown chillier and damper than ever over the winter, but now at least I knew how to bring the wood-burner to life. Willow was seriously impressed. In her world, even striking a match was a novelty.

"So have you heard any more from Alex, other than he's gone to stay with his mother?"

Willow put her arm around me. "He's fine. Bit weird having a couple of sisters suddenly. Well, it would be, wouldn't it?"

I nodded. "Two siblings to cope with. And a stepfather. Any hint of tension?"

"No. Not with them. But he's sort of cagey. I think he's really angry about stuff, you know, like not being told about things. Angry with his Dad and Gran."

"I can imagine…" I stopped. It wouldn't do to discuss my thoughts of our neighbour with my daughter. "I can imagine Fabia hiding Helena's letters and blocking her calls. Thank God they've got round her at last."

Willow chewed her lip. "He thanked me."

"For what?"

"For nagging him to go and see his mother. So you see, you did okay, telling her about him and all that."

"Result?"

"Yeah, result!"

I had helped to heal a fracture in the world. When we walked down to the coast path to head into the village and found a rainbow garden of thrift, squill, vetches, bluebells, campion, daisies and blackthorn blossom, nature seemed to be unfurling a banner to confirm my success. The precipitous cliffs were white with screaming birds, stacking themselves onto every ledge and cranny and applauding me.

"Wow," said Willow, taking a million photos on her phone. She was smiling.

She'll be all right, said Adam.

"Yes," I said. "We both will."

Tregelli was waking up for a new season as if the intervening winter hadn't happened. While Willow chatted with Harry Roberts, presumably negotiating a couple of weeks of employment on the Lotte Lenya, I took myself off to see Siân. I'd warned her we were coming back, but I still had to account for my abrupt departure in the autumn.

"I had a sudden panic attack about the exhibition," I explained. "I had to get home for it then and there. Stupid because I didn't arrange a courier and one of the paintings needed a repair job when I got it home." I was talking too much.

Siân nodded without pressing the subject and I wondered why I'd bothered with the lie. My sailing expedition with Oliver Wyatt was probably common knowledge in the village, along with the fact that I hadn't returned to Carregwen until the following morning. Veronica Erving would never have stooped to gossip about her employer's affairs, business or otherwise, but the village had eyes everywhere.

"So, anyway." Siân proffered the biscuits. "You got through the trial. Six years, Gareth said. Not much, is it, for taking a life?"

I sighed. "What would anyone gain from more lives being wrecked?"

"No. Well. If I'd been you, I know what I'd have wanted done to him. If there was any justice in this world. Which there isn't."

I smiled sympathetically and swallowed my tea. Willow and I had come through our most terrible year and had reached some sort of resolution, so I could afford to put bitterness aside, but Siân was still nursing hers. Did I even dare to mention Gaynor?

"Willow says Gareth will be home for Easter."

"Tomorrow he says! Can't wait to see him."

"Oh good. And Rhys? Still driving you mad with his music?"

She laughed. "Alun Bowen has let them use the old village hall for their practice. Mind, I can still hear them when they really get going."

"Well, they call Wales a land of song."

She winced, chuckling. "There's song and there's song."

"And… Gaynor. Have you heard from her at all?"

"No." Her lips snapped shut, her fists clenching. "You want some more tea in that mug?"

"Thanks, I'm fine."

I'd put so much effort, so many miles, into bringing Alex and his mother back together. Why hadn't I put in at least as much into healing the rift in the Hughes family? My attempts in the summer had been woefully ham-fisted, but I couldn't simply give up. I owed Siân far more than I owed Alex Wyatt. As I strode back to the harbour to join Willow, I determined that I would bring mother and daughter together again if it killed me. I'd consult Carla and I would track Gaynor down. If I had to, I'd go to London and trawl around every theatre and suspect joint until I found her.

To make a start, as soon as we were back at the cottage, I pulled up her social media pages again. Still the pictures of merry friends, amusing cats and the hints and emojis with nothing specific. But the posts had become more and more infrequent. City life must be keeping her busy. The last post, more than two months earlier, had a cryptic comment about adopting a stage name. That really wouldn't help. If she started up a new account, under a glamorous nom de theatre, I wouldn't know where to start. Ah well. It could wait until we went home. For now, we were going to enjoy Easter.

Since Willow had slotted herself back into Tregelli life with perfect ease, I settled down to work in my summerhouse studio. It kept me busy for a couple of days, but then I found myself short of a cadmium yellow and the gallery stocked a small selection of art materials, so I strolled down to the village.

Yvonne was bright and breezy as usual, her gallery well-stocked for the new season. My paintings had gone and she welcomed the small offering I brought with me.

"Lovely. The grapevine says your London exhibition went very well."

"Yes. Carla's pleased, at any rate, and I have a couple more lined up as a result."

"So I can't expect your exclusive attention, then. A pity, what with such a keen collector on our doorstep."

I responded to Yvonne's coy amusement with studied sangfroid. "Oliver Wyatt, you mean? The collector who actually pays, not his mother who just pockets things."

Yvonne chuckled. "Daft as a brush, but harmless…" She stopped, remembering the events of last autumn. "Well, not always harmless, of course. No permanent scars, I hope, from when she went for you."

"None. Not even emotional. But I certainly don't want to run into her again. Is she still at Cwrt y Frân?"

"Yes, all alone. No Alex this Easter, I gather. He's visiting friends in Italy. Lucky for some. I do rather pity her, though, marooned out there."

"I don't." I had pitied Fabia, but not anymore, not once I'd heard Helena's account. "Oliver not in residence, then?"

"He was here, when was it now, more than a month ago, took her out to dinner, but no, he's off again. Let's hope he's back soon, to snap up this little beauty. Not that it won't sell anyway."

"Then I'd best get on and produce some more," I said, pocketing my paint. I was relieved that Oliver wasn't around – mostly relieved. The guilt of last autumn had subsided with the passing of months and more significant milestones. Reason was in control and Carla was right, it was just a passing thing that happened, nothing significant for either of us. It didn't matter because I wasn't going to run into him or his mother.

I slipped into the village shop to buy some fresh bread and then I returned to the harbour. The Lotte Lenya was at the quay, ready for its next cruise, and a group of tourists were gathering, but there was a palpable air of alarm about them – enjoyable shock and alarm, just short of schadenfreude I decided, as I drew closer, wondering what had stirred them up. One of Harry's stories?

Then I saw Harry and I was no longer mildly curious. It was my turn to be alarmed. He had his arm around Willow who was shaking, her fists clenched, her eyes wet with unshed tears, her cheeks red. Harry was talking to her, calming her down, but he let her loose as I rushed up.

"Willow, what's happened?"

"Nothing!" She almost shouted, then stamped a foot and smacked her fists together, every muscle taut. "Stupid bloody woman!"

"Who?"

"No one! It doesn't matter."

"Yes, it does. What woman?"

"Mrs Wyatt," said Harry, softly. "Things got a bit heated. Come on, girl. Gareth's on his way, we'll manage this trip. You go with your mother. No need to let that daft woman upset you."

"I'm all right!" insisted Willow.

"Yes, but why not leave Gareth to manage this run," I said firmly, taking her arm and leading her towards the Bell, mouthing a thank you to Harry.

Willow was still shaking when I guided her to a corner table, away from prying eyes, but I could tell that it was more from anger than distress. "What happened?"

"That stupid woman. I wasn't doing anything, just waiting on the quay, and she saw me. She was with that creepy Erving creature. I sort of waved, because I thought, well, she's Alex's gran, after all, and she just came at me. Started screaming that I was… I was a little tart and she knew my sort and all that crap, and I wasn't going to get my hands on her grandson."

Chloe, the landlady, was hovering over us, with a look of knowing sympathy. "Went berserk," she whispered. "We all saw it. I had half a mind to call the police, but well…"

Willow pushed her hair back with both hands, grimacing. It wasn't just anger. It was some sort of remorse.

"What did you do?" I asked, keeping my own temper under control.

"Told her to fuck off, didn't I?"

"Only reasonable."

"Well she was trying to hit me with her bag. Only the Erving woman was stopping her. She said... oh shit, I've really messed things up, Mum."

"Why? How? None of this was your fault."

"Yeah, but she kept going on. She said I might as well clear out, there was no point me hanging around because Alex was safe out of my reach in Italy, and..." Willow looked up at me, guiltily. "I said 'That's what you think.'"

"Ah."

"I mean, I was just mad. She was out of order, right?"

"Totally," I said, as Chloe nodded agreement. "Look, don't worry about it. Chloe, do you think we could have a couple of coffees."

"Absolutely!" Chloe trotted away to the crowd at the bar, ears twitching.

I lowered my voice. "I don't suppose Fabia even took it in."

"She did though. She said "what do you mean, you lying little tart?" And Mrs Erving was looking at me like she was going to investigate or something."

"Did she say anything?"

"No. Not to me, just to Fabia. You know, like, 'Come along, Lady Wyatt, we don't want to be undignified, do we?' She pulled her away and then Harry was there, and it was just as well they went because Harry looked as if he might punch her."

"Well, I don't suppose Alex can keep his visit to his mother secret for long, so don't beat yourself up about it."

She merely swilled her coffee while I drained mine. "I shouldn't have said it."

"Right." My mind was made up.

"It's like I betrayed him."

"No, Willow, it isn't you who betrayed him. Stop worrying about what you said. It's what that woman said, and did or tried to do, that is the issue here. I know she's obviously got psychiatric problems…"

"Like Brenda Gough."

"The world's full of them and they've all got it in for me and mine, it seems." I said it as a joke, but she wasn't smiling. "All right, yes, like Brenda Gough. I let that situation get out of hand by not dealing with it."

"How could you? Dad had died. We were all upset."

"Yes. I wasn't really thinking straight. But I should have done something, right at the start, and got it sorted. So I'm going to do something now. I'm going to go round there and have it out."

"Oh no! Please! Don't! That would be awful. You can't. It would make it worse."

"But someone has to deal with Fabia Wyatt. It's not just a case of nasty words, is it, darling? She's violent. She tried to hit you, and last year…" I hesitated.

"What?"

"I heard that she'd fired a shotgun at some boys. She's not safe to be on the loose. I wonder how many times she's attacked Mrs Erving. I'm sure Veronica can look after herself – but she's clearly not managing to look after Fabia when a fit of jealousy comes on her."

"Yeah but…" Willow heaved a heavy sigh of frustration. "I don't want you to go."

"When I saw Alex's mother, she said she'd spent years living with a psychopath and I thought that was probably just resentment talking, but it's true. The woman is violent. She needs to be locked up."

"Oh right, so you're going to tell her that, are you? And you say she's a psycho? What if she attacks you?"

I tutted away her fears. "I'm going to see Veronica Erving. She's the one in charge there. She's got to make Oliver see that his mother needs professional help in a secure environment. It's ridiculous treating the whole of Tregelli like a private lunatic asylum. And yes, I do want to speak to Fabia and make it absolutely plain that I am not after her son, you are not after her grandson and even if we were, it would be none of her business."

"No. No. Please don't do it, Mum. Don't say a word, please."

Willow was so distressed that I realised I was just making it worse for her. Something did have to be done, but I needed to let it rest for now.

That evening, Gareth turned up on our doorstep and Willow was in high spirits, totally recovered from the incident. I decided, watching them laugh as they headed off for the pub, that maybe it would be better if Fabia's assault was just ignored. But when Willow returned, long after eleven, she was moody and uncommunicative.

"Everything all right?"

She shrugged, heading for the kitchen.

"Haven't had a row with Gareth, have you?"

"No." She returned with a glass of water. "I'm tired, okay? Going to bed. Got things to think about."

"All right." I didn't press it, but there could only be one thing preying on her mind. She hadn't got over it, after all. I made my mind up. The next day I was definitely going to sort things out with our mad neighbour.

6

In the morning, I strolled down to the village, on the pretence of picking up groceries, but really to confirm that Willow would be out on the boat with Harry. She was talking with Gareth on the quay, while the Lotte Lenya was being prepared, but there was no laughter this time. They still looked grave, greeting passengers, as I returned from the shop. I made no comment but I gave them a wave and headed for home, along the road for once, rather than the coastal path. Willow's low spirits reinforced my determination. I turned up Bethel Lane, left my shopping on the muddy steps to our cottage and geared myself up for a major confrontation. Time to clear the air.

The sky was mirroring my thoughts, clouds piling up in the west, churning over a darkening sea, with a threat of possible thunder to come. A good strike of electricity, that was what was needed, to clear the atmosphere.

I reached the gates of Cwrt y Frân and pressed the button, snapping my name at the intercom. The gates swung open and I marched down the long gravel drive.

Veronica Erving was waiting for me at the door. "Please, come in, Mrs Winters. I expect you have come about yesterday's unfortunate incident."

At least she didn't beat about the bush.

"Yes." I stepped over the threshold, wiping my feet.

"Unfortunate incident is a mild way of putting it. If you hadn't managed to hold Fabia back, she'd be on a charge of assault."

"She would hardly have done much harm, you know. She's such a small delicate thing."

"I know how much harm she can do. I still have the scars. But that's beside the point. She can't go around attacking people because she has delusions they are trying to bed her boys."

"Not entirely delusions, Mrs Winters."

"What's that supposed to mean?"

She raised innocent eyebrows. "Your daughter was seeing a great deal of Alex last summer. Most people thought they seemed quite attached."

"And what if they were? What if they were cavorting naked on the beach? What if they got married? How would anything they decided to do entitle Mrs Wyatt to insult them in public or start throwing punches?"

Veronica smiled, like a headmistress being tolerant with a whining pupil. "Naturally she has to be watched diligently. Won't you come into the drawing room, Mrs Winters? Let us have tea." She rang a bell that stood on a console table before ushering me further in. A head appeared round a door. "Could we have some tea, please, Megan? Mrs Winters?" She held open the drawing room door.

As there seemed to be nothing gained by me haranguing her in the hall, I went through and took possession of an armchair, my arms crossed pugnaciously.

Veronica perched elegantly on a sofa opposite. "I understand your sense of outrage. You feel your daughter was insulted and as a mother…"

263

"Yes, I feel outraged as a mother, but that's not the point. Fabia Wyatt, your charge, clearly has mental issues that are making her speak and act in totally irrational ways. Ways likely to result in physical harm. She's violent and from what I've heard, she's been violent for years. Taking a shotgun to some boys?"

"That certainly was a very distressing incident, because of regrettable carelessness on several fronts. I shouldn't have taken my eye off her. Masters shouldn't have talked about trespassers in front of her. And the shotgun shouldn't have been left unguarded for a few moments in the hall. It will never happen again. All the guns are now kept securely locked up in the offices, where she can't get at them."

"Yes, but that's not the point!" I repeated. "The point is that she was willing to use it. What if there's a kitchen knife, or a rolling pin to hand? She'll be willing to use them instead. She's dangerous. Oliver may have managed to sweet-talk the police on that occasion, but is he going to cover up for her if she actually stabs someone?"

"It won't come to that," said Veronica firmly.

"It could have done, yesterday, if she'd had a knife." I turned cold, thinking of it.

She rose with a nod and a smile as a young woman brought in the tray of tea. "Thank you, Megan." She poured two cups. "Earl Grey, I believe, for you, Mrs Winters?"

I took the proffered cup and saucer and set it down, refusing to be diverted. "Well?"

"You know, Mrs Winters, that incident yesterday was partly your fault." She actually sounded amused.

"How?"

"Mr Wyatt had given his mother a story that would have kept her quite content with the situation, but you did insist on spelling out the truth. Fabia was bound to react badly. Had you been content to indulge her little…"

"Bullshit! Is the whole world expected to live a lie in order to indulge her? It's not indulgence. It's just a refusal to acknowledge the truth, on your part as much as hers. She needs professional help, not a diet of silly fairy-tales."

"That is for Mr Wyatt to decide."

"Then tell him. He employs you to care for her, doesn't he? You're a professional, he says. So be professional and tell him what care she needs."

"Mr Wyatt isn't here at the moment."

"Then it's for you to act on his behalf. Get her medical help."

"She's having it. The doctor is with her now." Veronica glanced up at the ceiling, as if to prove the point.

"Well. Good." The wind was taken out of my sails.

"I called him yesterday as she was so distressed. I'm sure she'll be settled very soon."

As if on cue, heavy footsteps descended the stairs. Veronica rose and stepped out into the hall, pulling the door to behind her, but not quite closing it. I could just make out their muffled exchange.

"Well, I've upped the dosage, and that should calm her down."

"Thank you, Neil."

"But Oliver isn't going to want her kept permanently under sedation. You need to watch what else you're giving her. Perhaps a change of scene might be something to think about."

"I'll suggest it to him."

"Well then. Ah! Just look at that rain. I'll use the side door, if you don't mind. Closer to my car."

"Of course. Please. This way."

Their voices receded. I was feeling guilty now. Something did need to be done about Fabia and her behaviour was a danger to others, but was the solution really to keep her doped up on sedatives? Maybe the drugs that were supposed to calm her were actually part of the problem. What else was Veronica giving her, using her authority as a qualified nurse?

No, it would be nice to be able to blame Veronica since I didn't like the woman, but Fabia had been violent long before Veronica arrived. She's been violent against Helena. Something had to be done, but it seemed Veronica Erving wasn't going to lift a finger to change things without the express command of the Boss. Maybe I should write to him. Address it to where, though? I didn't have his email and if I left a letter there, I doubted it would reach him. I needed to work out a plan.

I was on my feet when Veronica returned. "I'd best go. You need to get back to your charge."

She nodded graciously, following me back into the hall. "I'm sure everything will work out, Mrs Winters. You don't have a coat."

"No." I realised that the skies had opened like Noah's flood. The rain was thundering down, flooding the gravel, the distant gates lost in a thick furious veil of grey. All I had was a hooded fleece, which would be soaked in seconds. I sighed. So be it.

"Let me find you something," suggested Veronica, opening the door to the cloakroom.

Reluctantly I agreed to wait, while she rummaged. She produced a pair of Wellingtons. While I pulled them on, she spread apart a forest of coats to unhook a hooded raincoat.

I saw…

"I believe this will fit you."

"What? Oh. Yes. I'm sure it will."

I'd seen… Is it the case with all minds, even the most rational, that they can split in two, fix on one issue and yet, at a deeper level, absorb another that takes a moment to work its way to the top? For the moment I merely felt disturbed that something was out of kilter. It was only when I'd donned the coat, braced myself, and stepped out into the seething, stinging rain, that I properly took on board what I had seen.

A bag.

A shoulder bag of patchwork leather with a fringe.

It was wrong. Wrong because it shouldn't be there. It should be in London, with Gaynor Hughes.

7

I strode through the rain, barely noticing it except as an irritant slowing me down while I wanted to race. I needed my brain at least to speed up. Why was Gaynor's bag at Cwrt y Frân? Did it mean that she'd returned here since leaving home? Without letting her mother know? She must have done. Why? To see Alex again? Willow would have heard about that, surely.

Was it actually Gaynor's bag? There must be thousands similar. Hundreds identical. Maybe she'd seen it here, admired it and bought herself one. An obvious answer. But…

Back at the cottage, I stripped off the boots and the sodden coat, towelled my hands and face dry and sat down with my phone. Once more, I summoned up Gaynor's Facebook page. There it was, that picture of her, standing on the South Bank, with some gorgeous hunk's arm around her. The bag on her shoulder.

I tried to recapture an image of the bag in the cloakroom at Cwrt y Frân. My brain had registered only a snapshot. Was it the same? There was a silver charm dangling on one thread of the fringe. On this picture and on the bag in the cloakroom. I was certain of it. Almost.

It was wrong, creeping me out as Willow would say.

The picture was wrong too. A part of my mind was telling me it was wrong and I couldn't pinpoint why. Unless…

I needed to see another. I conjured up Alex Wyatt's Instagram page, but most of his pictures seemed to have been archived. Frustrated, I checked his Twitter and Facebook account, but there had been a similar tidying. I was not on his list of friends, entitled to view everything. A car engine interrupted me and I looked up to see Gareth's elderly Astra pulling up. Willow climbed out, raising her hood and hunching against the rain to wave goodbye, before running for the house.

I put my phone down as she came in.

"Yuck, Harry said it would be a wet one. And rough. We had to turn back. They cancelled the kayaking in the harbour."

"Here." I helped her out of her dripping cagoule and shook the worst of the water out of the door, while she struggled out of her squelching trainers. "I'll make you a cup of tea to warm you up. Do you want a towel?"

"Please."

I threw her one from the kitchen, then put the kettle on. When I returned to the living room with a couple of mugs, she was on the sofa, peering at my phone.

"What have you been looking for?"

"Nothing especially."

"Alex Wyatt. Why were you checking on him? He won't have posted pictures of his mum anywhere."

"No. I don't suppose he would." I didn't want to share my growing unease with her, but she was the key to finding what I wanted. "Can you log in to Facebook? As his friend? I just wanted to find an old picture."

She looked up at me, oddly, an expression I hadn't seen on her before. Watchful. Cautious. Deadly serious.

"What picture?"

"The one of him and Gaynor Hughes."

She was silent for a moment. Then she fished in her bag for her own phone. "No need. I've got it. Gareth saved it." She flicked the screen, then proffered her phone and I took it gingerly, anxious to see it but fearful at the same time. Two couples, one of them Alex and Gaynor. I took a deep breath. It was what I was both expecting and dreading.

Willow was still looking at me with that curious, anticipatory expression. I bit my lip and brought up Gaynor's Facebook page again. There was no possible doubt. It wasn't just the same girl. It was the same clothes, the same stance, the same light and shadows, the same smile, the same hair flicked by the breeze, the same patchwork bag with the silver charm on the fringe. But another man instead of Alex, and a different backdrop, of London and the Thames, not a pub somewhere in Pembrokeshire. For some reason she had photoshopped the original. Someone had photoshopped it. Why? She was so desperate to disappear that she created a false ID with clues leading up garden paths? Or…

My stomach was chilling. I handed Willow's phone back. She was waiting to see, what? To see if I had realised what she and Gareth had already figured out? I didn't want to voice my suspicions. Not yet. I'd nurtured too many false ones about Alex's mother. I plucked the car keys from their hook. "I'm going to see Siân."

Willow could have asked why. She could have argued, pointed out that in this weather it would make more sense to phone. But she didn't. She said nothing.

The rain was already easing as I drove into the village and headed up to Maes Waun. Siân let me in.

"Terrible weather," I said, because I didn't have the first idea how to begin.

"Well don't just stand there. Come in." She frowned as I hurried over the threshold, a little too eagerly. "You're looking flushed. Not taking ill, are you? I've got some Paracetamol."

"I'm all right, really."

"I'll put the kettle on, anyway."

I almost stopped her, but I needed a free moment alone in her sitting room.

"They'll have cancelled the boat trip, I expect." She was calling from the kitchen. "Willow got a soaking?"

"Yes. Drenched." I called back as I crossed to the fireplace and pulled free the two postcards from Gaynor. I read the messages again. *Dear Mum. Don't worry, everything's fine... Dear Mum. I'm doing well. I've got a great job...*

It had been there in front of me, all the time, the falseness of it all. Gaynor Hughes would never have written these. This was not how she would have written to her mother. Why hadn't I realised that at once? I turned the cards over again. The second one, the view of the city from Tower Bridge, at night – I had been standing on that spot only a short while ago, looking at that view. Except that now it was a completely different view. Where were the skyscrapers, the Gherkin, the Cheesegrater or the hideous Walkie-Talkie, beyond the Tower? This was an old postcard. Why would Gaynor have bought it? Did she buy it, or was it plucked from a store of trivia filched years before by a kleptomaniac?

It was all a lie, from start to finish. And that could only mean one thing. I was trembling as I tried to slip the postcards back behind the mirror. I caught sight of my own reflection, white as a ghost, and I caught Siân too, standing in the doorway behind me. I turned, my heart thumping, wondering what on earth I was supposed to say. What could I possibly tell her?

She was standing silent, her face stony, her eyes pinning me down. Challenging me with the truth, just as Willow's had been. I didn't need to tell her anything.

"You knew," I managed to say, my voice barely more than a whisper.

"What? That Gaynor's dead?" She crossed the room and retrieved the postcards before they dropped out of their precarious perch. "Yes, I knew. I've always known."

She must have known, the moment she'd received postcards written in English. A family that spoke only Welsh with each other.

I swallowed. "Does it look like her handwriting?"

"Seems so. Not that you can tell, it's such a scrawl."

I sank onto the arm of the sofa. Writing that began as a seemingly nervous scribble and got stronger. Got more confident as someone mastered her hand. Gaynor couldn't have written them because she was already dead. She had gone to Cwrt y Frân, pregnant with Alex's child, and how would Fabia have reacted to that news? With a shotgun, how else? Or if not a shotgun, with whatever else came to hand.

But if Fabia had murdered her… I thought back on the account Oliver had given me, of how he had paid the girl off, driven her to London, set her up with a new life. He couldn't have done any of that. Instead, he'd pulled out all the stops to cover up the murder his mother had committed, even down to forging these postcards.

Siân was staring at them, taut with bitterness. "Wrong postcode, see. M, not N. You think Gaynor didn't remember her own postcode? Postmen know us, though. Don't need the codes round here."

I was feeling sick. "Why didn't you go to the police?"

She turned on me, her face contorted with despairing fury. "Course I went to the police! Reported her missing. Gareth came with me. Told them she'd gone to the Wyatt house and never came back. They said they'd ask, and what do you imagine he told them? He was there by then, Oliver almighty Wyatt. Spun them some tale. Then we got the postcards and the police said, there you are then. They said the handwriting was genuine, experts said so. I wouldn't have it. I tried to make them see she wouldn't have written like that to me. God, I made a fuss but no, I was just a crazy woman. Seems Oliver Wyatt had given them an address in London, and a policeman had called round and Gaynor was there and she'd told him she was fine but she didn't want her family knowing where she was, so they couldn't tell me the address, not without her permission. What was I supposed to do? I didn't want to let it rest, but then the hints began. The police kept saying "Mr Wyatt is your landlord. Are you having trouble with your rent, is that it? Do you really want to antagonise your landlord? Your landlord this. Your landlord that. Then we get a letter from his solicitor, saying action will be taken if we don't stop making slanderous insinuations."

She sat down wearily, the cards creasing in her clutch. "What was I supposed to do? I've got Rhys to think about. And Gareth, how's he supposed to get along in his career if the likes of Oliver Wyatt take against him? Blacklist him."

"You can't let it rest though."

"Do you think I want to? But what am I supposed to do? Who's going to believe me?"

Me, I thought, but she hadn't been able to share her thoughts with me, because I was suddenly a great pal of the Wyatts, taking tea with the woman who'd killed her daughter, taking yacht trips with the man who'd covered it all up. Hearing their side of the story and balancing it against hers. No wonder she'd been so resistant to looking at Gaynor's fake Facebook page. No wonder she'd refused to send a message.

"I'm sorry," I said. "I am so sorry."

"So am I," she said, dully.

"Gareth knows then?"

"Oh yes, he saw through it all from the first. But…" She shrugged. "And Harry, of course. But not Rhys. I don't know if he suspects. I don't want him mixed up in any of it."

"No, of course not. But for fuck's sake, the rest of the bloody world ought to know!" I was on my feet again, fired up with rage.

Siân put a hand on my shoulder. "What's the point? Mind you, your girl knows, I think. I reckon Gareth told her last night, after that business with Fabia Wyatt. They're very close."

"She came home upset."

"See, it just gets people worked up, but it doesn't achieve anything. You can't beat them."

I took a deep breath. "I'm not a tenant of the Wyatts. They can't turn me out of Carregwen if I make trouble."

"Don't waste your time, Nicki. What can you do? Go to the police with the same story I've told them? It's all just supposition. You haven't got any proof to offer them."

"I saw her bag," I said.

Siân frowned.

"Gaynor's bag. The one in the photo on her Facebook page. The one she's supposed to be flaunting around London. It's hanging in the cloakroom of Cwrt y Frân."

Siân's jaw dropped. Her eyes widened. But even while a flame of hope ignited within her, it was snuffed out in me. I'd seen the bag and I must have been distracted enough to alert Veronica. She would have seen it too and realised that it shouldn't be there. Because if Oliver had been covering up for his mother, Veronica Erving would have been aiding and abetting him. The patchwork bag would be a heap of ashes in an incinerator by now. I could picture myself turning up at the house with a police escort only to be confronted by Fabia screaming that I was a conniving whore and Mrs Erving expressing complete surprise at my accusations, with a quiet hint in the appropriate ear that I'd had an affair with Mr Wyatt and was now a woman scorned.

Siân must have read my doubt in my face. Her eyes dulled again and she sighed. "You can't fight them. They've got all the cards."

"Maybe. Maybe. I need to think. Siân…"

"Don't fuss yourself over it. Don't get involved. You've had enough to cope with, in your own life. Don't get tangled in ours."

I didn't reply. I just hugged her.

I drove home at a loss what to do. Of course I was going to get involved. How could I not? How could the killing of Siân's daughter be allowed to go unrecognised, unrecorded, let alone unpunished? How could Fabia be left to roam around the village after this? Something had to be done.

Willow was still at the cottage, hugging her knees on the sofa. She looked up, waiting for me to speak.

"I've talked with Siân."

"Yeah."

"You've talked with Gareth."

"Yeah." She sighed. "He sorted of hinted about it before, I think, but… Last night, I was going on about Fabia, stupid cow, and he told me, spelled it out, what they thought had happened. What did happen. It's obvious, isn't it." She was pulling threads on her jumper. It was going to start unravelling soon. She looked up suddenly. "Not Alex! I don't think he had anything to do with it."

"No. I don't think so, either. He's been lied to, like everyone else."

"He thinks she dumped him."

"I know."

"You saw the text messages she was supposed to have sent? To Gareth."

"Yes, but I couldn't understand them. They were in…" I paused. Of course. The cards were written in

English, but the text messages were in Welsh. Because Gareth had texted her in Welsh. As a test, of course. And someone had realised they'd better reply in the same language.

"Crap Welsh." Willow shook her head. "Like, not what she'd have said, really, but like someone was using Google Translate."

"Natalia Green, I imagine. Oliver's P.A." Who else would have posed as Gaynor at the London address Oliver had given the police? Who else would have spent an amusing year concocting fake Facebook entries for a phantom woman, at her employer's request?"

"I don't know what to do," I said.

"Don't do anything," said Willow, alarmed. "Gareth says he'll get the truth out of them, one day. He'll find a way."

The truth. That was what I'd claimed the only real justice to be, when I was bestowing my benediction on Denis Anderson's daughter. It was precisely what was being denied here. At least Anderson's refusal to acknowledge it had been born out of fear and panic. The lies in this case had been engineered with such cool precision. I understood Oliver's desire to protect his mother, but did he even begin to understand what excruciating agony all this fabrication was causing to Gaynor's family on top of the sheer grief of loss?

I didn't know what to do, but I couldn't clear this from my mind. Gaynor, that poor girl. That poor pregnant girl. Fabia had killed her own great grandchild too.

Gareth called round and exchanged meaningful looks but few words with me before Willow took him off. Left alone, I skyped Carla in New York. She, at least, would know the people I was talking about. I caught her a few minutes before she was due to go out, so she warned me it was going to be a short one.

I kept it short. "Carla, I am one hundred percent certain that Fabia Wyatt has killed a girl in the village, and Oliver covered it up."

Her response was equally short. "Nicki, stop it!"

"I know I got it wrong about Helena, but…"

"Yes, you did. Totally wrong. What is it with you and these murder fantasies? I'm getting seriously worried about you."

"I'm not insane. Please, Carla. I mean it, this time."

"You're a hundred percent certain? What's that mean? You've seen the body? Fabia's fingerprints? She confessed?"

"No, all right. Ninety-nine percent certain. I saw a bag, where it shouldn't be, although it's probably not there now, and messages that should have been in Welsh but weren't, and… anyway, enough for me to be sure the girl is dead, and other people know it too."

"But you don't actually know Fabia killed her."

"Don't I?"

"Listen to me, Nicki. Whatever you're imagining, leave this well alone. You do not take on people like the Wyatts. If something has happened, the police will deal with it. Don't get involved."

"I am involved."

"Just because you had a moment of passion with Oliver…"

"No, not because of that! Because a girl is dead."

"Leave it, Nicki. You can't cope with another tragedy, even if it's true. Listen, my cab's here. Don't do anything. Don't even think about it. Promise. We'll talk about it tomorrow."

I didn't press her further. Discussing it with her made it sound so fanciful, but it wasn't. I couldn't sleep that night, tossing and turning as I struggled with the issue. My husband had been killed in an accident, a fatal collision of circumstances, and the law had swung into action, pursuing its version of justice to the bitter end. Here a girl had been killed, not accidentally but maliciously, and the law was doing nothing. How was I to force it to act?

You can't, said Adam.

"That's not what I want to hear. Where's the justice in this?"

There's no such thing as justice.

"There is. There has to be or nothing makes any sense."

She'll still be dead, like me. You can't bring us back.

"No. No I can't. But surely I can stop her being airbrushed out as if she never mattered."

Then try. Try. Try.

8

I would try, if I could just see how. The only action that occurred to me was to visit Siân again, talk it all through once more to anchor it in reality and establish it, not as a supposition or a suspicion, but as the truth.

But Siân was out at work, and I could say nothing to Rhys, who was largely occupying the living room with guitars and a drum kit. I wandered gloomily around the village for an hour, then tried Siân again, only to realise that it was her day at the supermarket. She wouldn't be home until late. I returned to the harbour, frustrated.

Willow and Gareth were immersed in bleak conversation. They looked up as I approached. Looks were exchanged, looks conveying a shared consciousness of the hopeless tragedy, but all we said was "All right?"

"Yup. You okay?"

"Fine."

"Well, I'd best…" I stopped because Gareth's expression had changed, hardened, his eyes fixed on something behind me.

I turned and saw a gleaming black Jaguar slip around the harbour, heading for the lane along the creek. It slowed just enough for me to recognise the driver. Oliver Wyatt was home, then.

I took a deep breath.

"You're not going to see him," said Willow.

"I don't know," I said, which was true.

"It won't do any good."

I sighed. "Maybe. I don't know."

"Don't go," she said.

I shrugged and watched as the Lotte Lenya came chugging into the harbour. Willow and Gareth braced themselves for the afternoon run.

"I'm going back to the studio," I said. "See if I can dredge up some inspiration."

"Okay."

I did walk back to Carregwen, but not to paint. I stood on the stile at the end of our paddock, watching the waves crash on the rocks far below, watching the wind whip up foam on the waves, watching the clouds heave and part and gather again. Eventually watching the Lotte Lenya, heading out to sea with a cargo of tourists. I was watching for some sign to tell me what to do, and no sign came. Unless you count the sign of Oliver returning.

I sat there for more than an hour, summoning up my courage. Yes, I had thought instantly of going to see Oliver, but it wasn't just Willow's pleading that held me back. It was embarrassment at the thought of another meeting. Embarrassment at the memory of that night, and of the lies he'd told me about Gaynor, that I had been so ready to believe.

But it was those lies that made another meeting essential now. He might not have pulled the trigger or wielded the knife, but he was the one who'd created the pain of not knowing, who'd concealed, lied, plotted, and made Siân's agony far worse. The caring son had cared nothing for anyone other than his mother. Did he appreciate the hurt he'd caused?

I had to go, if only to make him see that Fabia couldn't remain at home like a muddled old darling to be indulged. She needed to be placed somewhere secure. She wouldn't be charged with murder. She'd be deemed unfit to plead, but at least she couldn't kill anyone else. Oliver would probably be able to buy his way out of any legal retribution for his part in the cover-up, but Gaynor's death had to be acknowledged. It was time to act. No point putting it off until the morning.

So I went. I gathered up the loaned coat and Wellingtons and set off, striding down the steps to Bethel Lane before I could change my mind. The gates of Cwrt y Fran opened when I gave my name and I marched up the drive, my heart beating faster with every step.

Veronica Erving was waiting for me, a gracious smile on her lips. "Mrs Winters, how good of you to return the rainwear. There was no rush, but please, do come in. Let me take them from you." She threw open the cloakroom door and pushed back other coats to make way for the one I'd returned.

She was making a point of showing me there was no longer a bag hanging there. I made a point of not batting an eyelid. "I believe Oliver is home."

"He's been spending some time with his mother, but she's resting now, so I'm sure he can spare you a moment if you are anxious to speak with him."

"Yes, I am anxious to speak with him. I'll wait here, shall I, while you fetch him?" I didn't want to be shepherded around by her, so I marched into the drawing room and threw myself into an armchair.

"Certainly. I'll ask Megan to bring you some tea."

"No need. I don't want tea."

"As you wish." She must have told Oliver about my last visit, and Fabia's attack on Willow. Maybe that was what had brought him home, so he had better spare me considerably more than a moment.

He came in, all smiles, arms open wide. "Nicki, I had no idea you'd be back in the area. Wonderful. I felt matters faded out somewhat without proper resolution last year, but here you are, and I'll be very glad to resume where our acquaintance left off."

I said nothing, made no move in response. His arms dropped and he grew serious.

"Sorry. That was inane. I know why you've come. Veronica told me all about the incident at the harbour and you want a proper apology. And an assurance that it won't happen again. Which I will willingly give you. Believe me, she really is…"

"Shut up, Oliver. You're going to say she really is harmless, aren't you? Isn't that the line everyone has to spout? Except everyone knows it's not true."

"She didn't actually succeed in hitting your daughter, Veronica tells me, and last October…"

"Never mind last October. I can overlook her taking swipes at me or even Willow, but you know, we both know, it's far more than that."

"If you mean that shotgun incident…"

"I mean Gaynor Hughes."

He had begun to pace, impatient with my interruptions, but he stopped dead and turned to face me full on, the shock visible for a split second before he shook his head in innocent surprise. "Who? Alex's ex-girlfriend, you mean? What is she claiming now?"

I met his eye without flinching. "She's claiming that she's dead."

"Really? How? A traffic accident, maybe? I know how much that would upset you."

"She's claiming that she never left this house alive."

He frowned. "Sorry, I don't understand what you mean. I told you, I drove her to London where to the best of my knowledge, she's living now."

"The fake Gaynor that you created."

"I created?"

"Please stop it, Oliver. I know what you did. Forging those stupid postcards, getting your PA to pretend to be her when the police came to check, taking over her Facebook account."

"This is absurd," he said coolly, but his breath was catching.

"I know why you did it. You'll do anything to cover up your mother's misdemeanours. But shoplifting is one thing, killing someone is another. That's what happened, isn't it? She killed Gaynor and instead of reporting it, instead of calling the police, or even a doctor, you just covered it up."

I could see him struggling between barefaced denial and surrender. Then he gave in. He drew a de Profundis sigh and sank down on a sofa, his head in his hands.

"How did you know?"

"Lots of things. Little things that built up. Her photograph on Facebook for one thing. Photoshopped from a picture of her and Alex. On her phone, was it?"

He sighed again. "As I recall. I left it all to Natalie. She liked the challenge."

"Helps her boss cover up many murders, does she?"

"God, what do you think I am? Or what she is? She has no idea the girl's dead. Just thinks she's providing cover for some passing fancy I wanted to set up away from her family."

"That's been known, has it?"

He almost smiled. "Maybe."

"Then there were the postcards. Written in English."

"Yes!" He almost hissed the word. "A stupid mistake I realised as soon we picked up a text from her brother on her phone. In Welsh of course. Natalie said she'd manage it."

"By using Google Translate? That was another mistake."

He rolled his eyes. "Doubtless."

"As was putting the wrong postcode on the postcards."

"I did?" His eyes flashed for a second. "Well, well. The wrong postcode. I should have checked, shouldn't I?"

"You're asking me how you could have done it better? Seriously? The real question is why you did it at all."

"You know why."

"To save your mother."

"Yes, yes, yes." He ran fingers through his hair. "I was already on my way here when Veronica phoned me in a panic. She'd found the girl dead on the floor. God knows how it happened. For all I know, she could have just slipped and hit her head. But my mother, God bless her, was insisting that she'd done it. Wanting to take the credit for having saved her grandson from a fate worse than death. Hardly credible to believe she'd have the strength to tackle a healthy young woman, but there she was, boasting that she'd killed her with a poker. She wanted to tell the whole world. What was I to do? My mother. You tell me. Go on, Nicki, you tell me what you would have done if it had been your mother. Someone you loved? Are you going to tell me you'd have called the police and watched while she was carted away? Well?"

He was right, I probably wouldn't have done that, but neither would I have done all that he did do. "So you got rid of the body. Where?"

"Out at sea," he said, wearily.

"So simple. And then you set to work on all this elaborate fabrication so that no one would look for her here."

"Yes. We found her phone in her bag, with photos and contacts and so forth."

"So you sent the phone to London. But not the bag, which was left hanging in your cloakroom. Careless."

"Ah."

"Don't worry, Ms Erving disposed of it after I recognised it."

He smiled ruefully. "Veronica's loyalty knows no bounds."

"She helped with the cover-up, I suppose?"

"Oh yes, her duty is to protect and restrain. The restraint failed in that case because she'd left Fabia unattended while she saw to household business. She was hardly to know that the girl was going to turn up on our doorstep claiming to be pregnant. At least that's my mother's version of her visit. It's possible, or it might have been another of my mother's flights of fancy. Either way, the girl was dead, along with anything she was carrying. Tragic, but I couldn't bring her back to life, so all that remained was to protect my mother."

"And did you give the slightest thought to what Gaynor's family have been through?"

"I gave them a story that should have put their minds at rest. What more was I supposed to do? They didn't make it easy for me, you know. If they hadn't started flinging wild accusations around, I wouldn't have had to carry on the pantomime for so long. If they'd just let it go..."

"You'd do that, would you? If Alex vanished, you'd just let it go?"

"People have to face reality."

"I thought that was precisely what you didn't want them to do."

He tutted his irritation. "Now you're just being awkward, Nicki. I ask you again, what would you have done, to protect your mother? Your child? Your husband?"

I swallowed. "It's what you are going to do now that's the issue. Keep your mother on here? Keep indulging her? Keep telling people she's harmless?"

He got up, walked to the French windows, looked out, hands clasped behind his back. At last, he turned back to me. "You're right, of course. It's gone on too long. There have been more and more aggressive incidents recently, and since the only solution seems to be to keep her under permanent sedation, she probably would be better off in a home. I suppose I shall have to bow to the inevitable. I'll see to it."

"And the rest?"

"What rest?"

"Acknowledging that Gaynor is dead."

"What good will that do?"

"Can you really not see?"

"Oliver? I heard voices." The door flew open and Fabia came in. She looked dishevelled, wrapped in a dressing gown. She stared at me, then screamed, "What's that slut doing here? You keep away from my son, you hear, you hussy!"

She came at me, but Veronica, looking almost frazzled, came running in behind her, grabbing Fabia's shoulders and mouthing earnest apologies at Oliver.

He had sprung forward to shoo Fabia back. "You're supposed to be having a nap, mother. Didn't you take your pills?"

But Fabia wasn't to be diverted. "Get her out of this house, Oliver. She's a lying tart, I know her sort. Bitch! Bitch! Get out of my house. I know what you're after, and you're not having him."

"What I'm after," I retorted, "is your proper care in a safe environment where you can't go round killing people."

"You want me locked up so you can get your claws into him. I know!"

"Mother!" Oliver was trying to turn her without using obvious force, but she was stronger than she looked. So much for being too weak to kill.

"I want you locked up so you don't kill anyone else," I said, ignoring Oliver's glare. I wasn't going to help him pacify his mother, not after what she'd done.

"Kill? Kill? What are you talking about? You liar!"

"You killed Gaynor Hughes, didn't you? The girl who was carrying your great-grandchild?"

Her eyes widened and what I saw in them was genuine horror. Oliver was using more force now, dragging Fabia out of the room with Veronica's help, but still she screamed at me. "Liar, liar! Nobody killed her. She's not dead, you stupid woman. Oliver took her to London. Didn't you, Oliver? You told me you'd take her baby for me. You told me!" They were hustling her into another room, while I was left standing there.

Standing there. Cold.

Colder and colder.

9

My ears were still ringing with Fabia's shrieks. Shrieks of denial. I clenched my fists, my skin crawling. Shadows in my head were rearranging themselves. I strode to the windows, needing fresh air, but they wouldn't budge. The curtains concealed another security lock with a number pad and no handy note by it. Damn.

Fabia didn't do it. Just that once, I'd seen the truth in her face. She believed that Oliver had taken Gaynor to London. So, if she hadn't killed the girl…

My phone vibrated in my pocket and I groped clumsily for it. My daughter calling. I managed to say "Willow."

"Mum? Where are you? You're not at the Wyatt place, are you?"

"Yes. I am."

"No. You mustn't stay there. Come home now. Alex is here."

"He is? I thought…"

"I told him what we'd figured out about Gaynor and you saying his gran was a psycho and she said no you'd got it wrong."

"Who said?"

"His mum. She's come. She said she didn't mean Fabia was the psycho. Mum…"

"Not now!" I hissed a reply and slid my phone hastily into my pocket as Oliver came back into the room. It hadn't occurred to me that there would be any danger in coming here, but now sirens were blaring in my head. I needed to act as casually as I could, and not give a hint of my new terrible suspicions. "My daughter," I said, nonchalantly. "Just letting her know I'll be home soon."

"Absolutely. Are you okay after that little scene, Nicki?" He too was acting as if nothing meaningful had been said. For a second I wondered if I'd got it wrong, but as he talked, I was sure once more. "I'm sorry about all that. God knows how my mother managed to stagger out of bed and come downstairs. She'd been dosed up to the eyeballs. I thought she'd sleep till morning. Please. Sit down again. She's under control now. Let me pour you a drink."

"I'd better not, thanks."

"No? I need one if you don't. It can really take it out of me, dealing with her. Of course, you're quite right. She's beyond home care now. I'll start making arrangements to have her settled somewhere, and at least you won't have to listen to any more of her delusions."

"No, that's good." I wasn't sounding nonchalant enough. My words rang with doubt. I'd never been convincing in am-dram.

Oliver was busy pouring himself a drink, but not too busy to glance sidelong at me. His lips twitched into a smile as he turned to face me, swilling the whisky in his glass. "This game really isn't worth continuing, is it, Nicki?"

"Pardon?" I licked my lips, which were suddenly dry as sawdust. "Game?"

"The game of pretending you haven't been busy adding two and two and jumping to unfortunate conclusions."

A game. That's exactly what it was to him, and what was the point of playing it if he saw straight through me. "What conclusions? That just for once your mother was telling what she genuinely thought to be the truth?"

Oliver examined the label on the bottle of scotch. "You think that. Would others though? Everyone knows my mother lost the ability to distinguish between truth and fantasy a long time ago."

"You said she boasted of killing Gaynor and yet she's convinced you took the girl to London." I felt the fear inside me turn to anger. "I don't know how I've been so stupid."

He smiled again, that smile that had once seemed charming and now seemed merely sardonic. "Don't you? I suspect it comes quite easily. But at last you've decided to be clever. A pity. I thought you were so susceptible to persuasion, you'd believe anything."

"Gullible, you mean."

"Quite. Now what are we going to do?"

My heart was thumping. I'd challenged him with the truth and he'd risen to it, because I could do nothing to hurt him and he knew it. I might just as well play the only hand malign fate had dealt me. I'd make him tell me the truth. I'd probably be the only one who'd ever hear it - briefly, before he decided how to dispose of me.

"What really happened to Gaynor? You killed her. Say it."

He merely continued to smile.

"Why?"

"Why do you think? To protect my son's interests. Just as you try to protect your child, in your arty liberal way. Your ambition, let me guess, is for her to be happy. Mine is more meaningful. Alex is going to have a future among the movers and shakers, and I'm going to ensure that nothing stands in his way. He's too young to see the consequences of youthful indiscretions, but I can. The number of times I've had to delete his careless posts. I can hardly stop him messing around with local girls, he's red-blooded enough, after all, but I've warned him to take care and this time he obviously failed to listen. He managed to get the little tart pregnant. It was something she'd be able to hold against him. Not now, maybe, but in the future. My son's future lies in government. Maybe, if we play it right, at the pinnacle of government. It might be more convenient if we were a military dictatorship and he could just manoeuvre to take charge, but being stuck with a namby-pamby democracy, we have play public opinion. The higher you rise in politics here, the more your enemies dig for dirt. The last thing Alex will need is some little bitch popping up in ten, twenty years times, claiming to have his bastard."

I sat down because my legs wouldn't support me. "You killed her because of that? My God, she was right when she said you were a psychopath. I just assumed she meant Fabia, but of course she meant you."

"She? Who?"

"Your wife. Who knows you better?"

"Ha!" He scowled disgust. "I might have guessed you'd go hunting for Helena. Can't leave well alone, can you? So, how is that lover of hers? Da Silva? Finding the odd job and managing to keep his head above water, is he?"

"From the look of their house, he's doing very well."

"Is he? I'll have to do something about that."

"Jesus, you are sick."

"Not at all, Nicki. I like to win, that's all. That's how nature made me. A winner, and that's all that counts. Psychopath, she says, does she? I think you'll find that every winner, in war, in politics or in business, has that particular gene. Tender-hearted morality is for losers."

"And what's your son?"

"A good question. I am afraid I failed to pass on that ruthless gene. One of my very few failures, but I work with what I have, which is why I need to help him on his way, by removing every impediment for him, before it can do any damage."

"Gaynor Hughes wasn't an impediment. She was a living, breathing human being, with her own future before her. She was no threat to you."

He nodded, as if engaging in a perfectly reasonable discussion. "I agree, she wasn't actively making any threats. In fact, I don't think she was even expecting to find anyone here. Veronica had taken my mother to see her consultant, and I had only just called in briefly to check on Masters. The girl expected to hand over a letter to be forwarded to Alex because she didn't have his Oxford address. I guessed what it would be about. Girls text or phone, they don't write letters unless it's something serious that needs the formality of a pen, and what else could it be? I took the letter from her and opened it, just to see if it confirmed my suspicions. She was furious at that."

"She would be." I wished now that I'd accepted a whisky. Several whiskies. I must not tremble. I must not throw up.

He shrugged. "Not quite the hysterical demands I'd expected, but there it was. She was pregnant. Thanks to one frolic too many in those three days at Christmas before we headed for St Moritz. She wrote that Alex wasn't to worry about it, she would cope on her own, she didn't want to hold him to anything, he was to finish at Oxford etc, etc."

"Well then!"

"Oh, she'd say that now, so sweet and generous. But how generous would she be when he was on his way to the top? That's when she'd crawl out from under her stone to sell her story to the gutter press."

"What if she had? Do you seriously think a thing like that would damage your son's prospects in this day and age? I thought today's politicians are expected to sow their seed far and wide, discarding women as they go."

"Possibly. If they've already established a colourful reputation as naughty charming scamps. Alex, though… I can see him developing into a thoroughly decent chap with a loving wife, two golden-haired babes and an affectionate Labrador. A hostage to fortune if ever there was one."

"So, because of this notion that in twenty years' time, just as Alex is patting his Labrador on the steps of Number Ten, Gaynor Hughes might suddenly appear with a juicy story for the tabloids, you decided to kill her."

"I don't resort to violence that easily, Nicki. Did I foresee the possibility? Yes. I told you, I'm a winner. Winners see all the possibilities and move the pieces accordingly. They don't just sit back and hope for the best. They don't rely on the goodness of human nature, they act. I saw the danger to my son's prospects and I acted. I offered to make all the arrangements for an abortion, quick, clean and private. That would have solved everything. She could have walked away and we wouldn't be having this conversation. But no, she insisted she was going to keep the brat. She didn't want money. She didn't want support." He whined mockingly. "She just thought it only fair that Alex should know."

"Why shouldn't he know? Why not let him have the chance to stand by her? Gaynor could have been that loving wife and mother of the golden-haired kids."

"A girl from Tregelli? Daughter of a cleaning lady?"

I laughed, despite the taste of bile in my mouth. "What are you, then? Tsar of all the Russias? Your mother's delusions are getting to you."

"My son's had the best so far. He'll continue to have the best."

"He had the best with Gaynor. He loved her. That's why he's so hurt now. Was that your aim, perhaps? To harden him by hurting him?"

"He'll get over it."

"I suppose you regard love as a weakness to be rooted out on the road to success."

"His love, as you call it, was just a physical itch that needed scratching. There are plenty more women willing to act as scratching posts and it isn't hard to bring them along. Just assess their foibles and their weak points – a vulnerable grieving widow, for example, desperate for a shoulder to cry on and a good fuck. Not difficult to coax into bed."

I felt the blood rise in my cheeks, the resentful fury begin to boil. I wouldn't let it. I knew what he was doing and I wasn't going to rise to it, because this wasn't about anything he'd done to me. It was about what he'd done to Gaynor, nothing else.

"So Alex can have his women, but if he gets them pregnant, you'll kill them."

"If they won't agree to get rid of the problem, yes. If they won't be reasonable. If they are too bolshy for their own good. You know, Nicki, that girl had a lot in common with you. More spirit than I was expecting. When she flatly refused a termination, I offered to get her a position, set her up somewhere abroad…"

"I bet. Somewhere from which there was no return?"

"I hadn't decided. If she hadn't had a hissy fit, telling me to get lost, I might have had to think it through, but it didn't arise. She had this notion of flouncing out with an arrogant toss of her head, after which I'm sure she'd have stormed off to Oxford, found Alex and had him round her little finger before I could intervene. I decided not to let her go. She left me no choice." He smiled. "You know you are quite wrong about me forging the postcards. She wrote them herself. I realised that I'd have to have an explanation for her disappearance. Any number of people might know that she was coming to Cwrt y Frân, so there would have to be evidence that she'd left, too. For London, where there'd be no chance of anyone tracing her. It seemed an excellent idea to make her provide the evidence herself. My mother had a stash of postcards in her bureau, so I made her write a couple."

"Made her?"

"A shotgun to the head usually does the trick. I dictated the words. She was so terrified she could barely hold the pen for the first one, but then she calmed down. I thought she was trying to appease me. She must have realised what I intended, but the slightest glimmer of hope leads desperate people to do anything to buy themselves a moment more time. She added a line to the last one, something about never coming home. I noticed it later and nearly tore it up, but then I decided it made no difference. I suppose she intended it as a clue? Hardly necessary since I hadn't reckoned on English being about as clear a clue as she could have wanted. And putting the wrong postcode. I didn't know about that. Cunning little bitch. Not that it did her any good. Her family may have spotted the anomalies, but the police weren't impressed."

He topped up his glass, happy to give me a detailed explanation of his cleverness, since it would never go beyond the room.

Cunning little bitch. That's how he saw Gaynor. What I was seeing, horribly clearly, was a girl too terrified to write steadily, but then, knowing what he intended, finding the courage to foil him as best she could. She'd known exactly what was going to happen and she'd faced it.

I also knew what was going to happen. Could I face it like her? I wasn't sure that I would have the strength to write clearly, or the presence of mind to make a mistake in a postcode, but like her, I would not be a passive victim.

He was between me and the drawing room doors. I couldn't hope to lunge past him. What about the French windows then? I couldn't unlock them, but maybe I could just throw myself through? No, not a chance. The glass was probably bullet-proof, in keeping with his other security measures. The light was fading out there and my chances were fading with it. All I could do for now was talk.

"A couple of months ago, I saw a man sent to prison for accidentally killing someone. A man racked with guilt, his world destroyed. You have no guilt, do you?

"None. A waste of time."

"What did you do, then? Shoot her?"

"That was my intention – eventually. Strangulation always strikes me as somewhat Neanderthal. But I wasn't going to kill her here in the house. No, I intended to take her out on the launch and dump her where there'd never be any trace of her. And would you believe it, she figured it out. I ordered her to move and she wouldn't budge, not even with the shotgun to her head. She said she wasn't going to help me cover up her murder. I could shoot her then and there and forensics would discover something, sooner or later.

My heart swelled with pride for Gaynor Hughes. "How disobliging of her."

He shrugged again. "So I turned the gun round and knocked her out. I carried her to the car and drove over

299

to the quarry. Hauled her into the shed, had to put her down to open the door to the steps and she came round while I was doing so. She'd probably been pretending to be unconscious for a while. Anyway, she tried to make a run for it, we struggled, she actually bit me, little bitch. I hit her. She fell backwards down the steps. Broke her neck." He actually laughed. "Strictly speaking, I didn't kill her, it was an accident."

"Only a totally twisted mind could think that." I rose, hugging myself, remembering those stairs. I remembered shivering, telling him there was a ghost there, and his sharp reaction. Remembered voicing aloud my suspicion that he'd dumped a body in the sea, followed by my near-drowning. Had he intended to drown me? What changed his mind? Probably the realisation that I could never be any threat to him, whatever allegations I made, so why waste the opportunity to get me drunk and into bed? He was a quick thinker; I'd grant him that. Quick decisions, no hesitation.

"You dumped her out at sea and you were back in time to have tea with Mummy, when she came home."

"Precisely. Fabia knew nothing about it. Not until the girl's family started making trouble and the police came round. I told her I'd driven the girl to London, where she was going to have the baby for Fabia to raise. She was furious that the bitch had dared to come here, but delighted with the idea that she'd get the child. I had to spin a tale for Alex too. I had her phone and he would keep texting her. I told Natalie to take charge of it, to dump him by text as brutally as she liked, de-friend him on Facebook and the rest, give the girl a new boyfriend in London and rub it in. He was upset, of course. I had to go and see him in Oxford, to calm him down, so I told him she'd come demanding money for an abortion and threatening to make all manner of trouble. I'd paid her off so that he could be rid of her. He didn't like it but it seemed to do the trick."

I moved while he talked. Maybe I could work my way closer to the door. "A trick. That's all it was to you. Do you actually have any affection for your son, or is he just another person to serve your needs?"

"He's my heir. I've invested everything in him and with my guidance he'll repay me by doing great things. That's more meaningful than cuddles and kisses."

"Yes, I thought so. You have no idea what affection is. You certainly don't have any for your mother, since you were happy to let her take the blame for your crime. If the caring son act is just a pretence, why set her up here with a house and a minder? What's that about? You're entertained by the havoc she creates?"

"An added bonus. For Veronica's entertainment too, you understand. She has a knack for triggering responses in my mother, while appearing to be keeping her under control. No, the truth is, when my father was still alive, my mother was a partner in the firm, in practice if not in law. She kept poking her nose in, even when I joined him in the firm. Always siding with me, of course, when disagreements arose. I had a more ambitious vision than my father, and it sometimes involved pushing boundaries beyond what the law allowed. It meant that she knew where all the bodies were buried." He laughed. "Not literally. When my father died and her mind went walk-abouts, she became too loose-lipped for comfort, so I shipped her out here, where no one would have any idea what she was talking about. I expected my wife to keep an eye on her, but of course she just ran rings round Helena. Useless woman. Not that it wasn't amusing, watching them fight like cats in a bag. When my wife walked out, I searched for a useful minder and Veronica Erving had just been released from prison."

"She hadn't been running a nursing home, then. Another lie."

"Oh no, she had. Until she was sent down for abusing patients, misuse of prescribed drugs, liberal use of illegal ones. She'd only narrowly missed a conviction for manslaughter. I've found her invaluable."

"In torturing your mother. What did Fabia do to you to deserve that?"

"Drove me demented through my childhood with her lower middle-class pretensions to gentility. Her obsession with napkin rings and terms of address."

"I see. Etiquette is the cause of the sick defects in your character?"

"Very amusing. That's what I like about you, Nicki. No fawning. Such a genuine little shrew. Do sit down, woman. You'll make yourself giddy wandering around."

He was an unspeakable murdering bastard, but he was no fool. Whichever way I moved, he was always between me and the door. I gave up, though I refused to sit.

"That's what I like to see. A woman who when she knows she's beaten."

"I bet you do."

"And since I can predict everything you're likely to do, you might as well not waste your energy."

I was going to die. The thought should have had me collapsing in panic, but it was strangely calming. Adam was standing behind me. I would die and I would be with him, that was all. Except that I really needed to be with my daughter. How could I abandon her? Could I get myself out of this? "What's your plan for me then? Same as for Gaynor? Because you wouldn't want any messy evidence on these carpets, would you? And bleach would wreak havoc on all that lovely silk wallpaper."

"Well guessed. No, we don't want any unpleasantness here."

"Plenty of people know I've come here, so what's the story going to be? You can't say I've gone to London to be an actress. That one's already been tried. It proved how little you understood Gaynor."

"I understood her type well enough. But you are jumping ahead of yourself, Nicki. Do I actually need to do anything with you at all? What will you do? Go to the police and repeat everything I've said? How will they take it? Spiteful rejected lover? I'll feel obliged to reveal our history. Or deranged widow obsessed with the idea of violent death? Don't charge her with wasting police time, I'll say. She just needs psychiatric help. But on the other hand, they'll probably make certain by going round to question Gaynor again in her London digs, and Natalie will be kept busy maintaining the pretence, which is getting to be a nuisance. So maybe it would make more sense to deal with the problem of Nicki Bryce decisively, here and now. Let's see. The tragic widow again, still crippled with grief, suicidal even. I expect you've thought of it. Maybe you've had psychiatric treatment? Counselling? And then a brief affair last year, and you've come back to fling yourself at me in search of comfort in your despair. My rejection is the last straw. When you're found at the bottom of the cliffs, I shall, of course, be crucified with guilt. If only I'd realised. The poor woman. Alas. I shall be almost embarrassed to find that your pictures, my investments, will have shot up in value." He held his hands wide. "I like that idea. What do you think? No opinion. Take your time mulling it over while we take a little walk out to the cliffs."

"I'm not walking anywhere."

"Don't be tiresome, Nicki. Use your head. Walk with me now and who knows, you might be able to make a run for it. Never give up hope." He held out a hand, like a true gentleman and then, as I stepped back disdainfully, he grabbed my arm, twisting it and nearly dislocating it.

I squealed with pain as he pulled me forward. Now that the crunch had come, I wasn't going to keep quiet and reasonable any longer. We weren't alone in the house. I'd seen servants, office staff. Surely, they would intervene. He was an employer, not a feudal overlord. I opened my mouth to scream as he dragged me to the door, but his other hand clamped over my mouth before I could utter a sound. I tried to bite, but he was pressing too hard. His body had me clamped in the doorway, pinioned and muzzled.

I struggled to reach for my pocket, but he was there before me. He pulled out my phone. "I'll take charge of that, I think." He glanced at it and laughed. "No, keep it. It's dead. It will be more convincing if it's found on you." He slipped it back in my pocket, then he coolly called "Mrs Erving, come here, please."

A door opened, and Veronica Erving stepped out, totally unfazed. I might have been a rag doll for all the attention she paid me. "Yes Mr Wyatt?"

"Is my mother settled?"

"I gave her extra diazepam. She's drowsing over an album of hunting prints."

"Good. Mrs Winters is a little reluctant to do as she's told, so I'm going to fetch a means of more forceful persuasion. Would you mind taking care of her here for a moment?"

"Certainly, Mr Wyatt."

Veronica's hands replaced his, but her grip couldn't be as strong, surely. The moment he disappeared through a door into the staff quarters, I tried to hurl myself sideways, back into the drawing room. If I could slam the door on her, I'd find a means of escape somehow, up the chimney if necessary. But she must have anticipated my move, because as I pulled one way, she jerked me the other, out into the hall, and she was every bit as powerful as Oliver. She pushed me back, nearly breaking my neck, until my shins were pressed against the lowest tread of the staircase, hemmed in by the elaborately carved banister. With a smirk, she removed her hand from my mouth.

I screamed. Not very effectively. I hadn't had time to draw breath. I screamed again, louder.

She wasn't in the least worried. "The staff are quite accustomed to screams, Mrs Winters. They'll think it's Mrs Wyatt having another of her tantrums, so feel free."

I screamed louder. Nothing happened. She was right, so I gave up. It wasn't worth the effort. "Does he really pay you well or is this just a hobby?"

"Both, perhaps."

"I can see you enjoy your work." I tried another sudden struggle, hoping to catch her off guard, but her grip on my arm didn't alter. I tried to punch at her with my other hand, the left, ineffectually. She batted it away without blinking.

"Let's just wait for Mr Wyatt to return with the shotgun."

I screamed again, in sheer fury.

Then Fabia appeared, drifting in a daze from the room where she'd been stashed. "Veronica? Veronica, why is she still here? I don't want her here." She clung to Veronica's arm, tugging at her. "Where's Oliver? I want Oliver." It was enough to take Veronica's eyes off me and loosen her grip just enough for me to twist my arm free. She grabbed at me again, but Fabia was pushing between us, getting in her way.

"I don't want you here, you slut." Fabia was hitting at me, but I ignored the blows. I took a step back, onto the first tread of the stair to allow her room to come between us, then I heaved her up, still beating at me, and threw her back into Veronica's arms. It worked better than I could have hoped. Overbalanced, Veronica toppled backwards, with Fabia on top of her. I turned and raced, up the stairs, two, three at a time. It was the only route open to me. No point trying to leap over the two of them to a front door that I couldn't open.

Now it was Veronica's turn to scream, or rather screech, but this time the fact that screams were commonplace worked in my favour. No one came running. She was bellowing for Oliver, and I heard a door open, but by then I was already up the stairs and into a corridor, gloomy in the evening light. I could hear Oliver furiously snapping at his underling as I raced along. I threw open a door at random in a vague attempt to mislead him, then I ran on, round a corner. Another door, to my right, with an antique key in it. I grabbed the key, forcing it out of a lock that it didn't want to leave, then I opened the door and hurtled in, slamming it behind me, to find myself in complete darkness. Stupid woman, no window, what use was this? Too late to choose another. Oliver would already be coming up the stairs. I groped for the keyhole, inserted the key, terrified that I'd drop it in my panic. It turned. At least I was safe for a moment or two.

10

I was safe in my very own dungeon. Where the hell was I? I felt around. There was a light switch by the door. The urge to flick it was almost overwhelming, but the merest chink of light under the door would give me away. I left it, felt further. Slatted shelves on both sides, one above another and no more than three feet between them. A linen closet? Brilliant. What now? Keep silent and hope he wouldn't work out where I was.

I stood still, trying to fight off an instinctive fear of the dark. Listening. I heard his voice, muffled by the door, call, "She's not there. Window's locked. Silly bitch."

I held my breath. He was trying doors, each one in turn, going in to see, closing it again. Getting closer and closer. Then he tried mine. The handle turned. The door shook. Shook harder as he put his shoulder to it, but it was solid Victorian hardwood, not a flimsy modern piece of faux veneer. It refused to shift.

"Mrs Winters." His voice was clearer now, right outside. "Not the brightest place to hide. Do you plan to stay in there and starve to death? Come out now, save yourself a lot of bother."

I bit my lip. I was not going to reply. Let him at least have a moment of doubt.

"Don't be stupid, woman. Do you want me to have to shoot my way in and drag you out?"

He could do it. Even solid oak wouldn't hold out against shotgun blasts. I was lost.

Don't let him win, said Adam. *Don't give in. Let him wreck the place and alert the whole neighbourhood. If you're going to join me, let your death send him to Hell!*

"Yes!" I whispered. There was no point in hiding my presence now and I wasn't going to cower in the dark any longer. I groped for the light switch and flicked it. A dim unshaded bulb came to life and it was as I supposed, a coffin of a linen cupboard. Nothing on the tall shelves but a few linen cloths and a moth-eaten blanket. It couldn't have been used for years, hence the key left to rust in the lock.

"So you are in there," said Oliver. "Does this mean you're seeing sense and coming out? No? I will use the gun if you don't."

No! Don't listen, said Adam. *You don't wait for him, you go, now!* Because I had seen my escape route. No window, maybe, but there was a small hatch in the ceiling. That or nothing. I didn't hesitate, but I had to be quiet. No point in letting Oliver know what I was attempting. I climbed as silently as I could, using the shelves as a ladder, until the hatch was in reach. The catch was stiff, refusing to budge until I nearly broke my fingers. Then it slid free. I climbed another shelf higher to push the hatch up. It wanted to shift but it was wedged in place, with paint or years of dust. I braced myself and heaved. It came free.

Had he heard? He was still talking, calmly persuasive. I blocked out the words. Why didn't he just blast the door in? Because there were people in the house, and screams might be ignored, but the roar of a shotgun would be another matter. It would be his last resort. He'd keep talking for now, waiting for me to realise the hopelessness of my situation.

But it was no longer hopeless. Not quite. I seized both sides of the hatch frame and hauled myself up. I stuck, my legs dangling down, trying to find purchase on a shelf to push myself up. I heaved, wrenching myself through, expecting my pelvis to shatter, and slid forward into a loft. The light from below was enough to reveal joists and lathes and sloping slates on three sides, an upturned V of brickwork on the fourth. There were crates and boxes, thick with dust, piled around me. I dropped the hatch quietly back into place and immediately I was in darkness again. I felt for a crate and dragged it across the hatch, then groped in my pocket for my phone, hoping for a glimmer. But Oliver was right, the battery was dead.

Tough. My eyes were growing accustomed to the gloom anyway, just a hint of twilight seeping in through the slates. I made my way gingerly to the wall and searched, convinced I'd glimpsed a door. There it was. Only three or four feet high, but as long as it wasn't locked…

It wasn't. I crawled through into an attic that seemed bright by comparison, though it was lit only by the lingering gleam of a sun already set, through a skylight high in the sloping ceiling. Dustsheets covered God knows what. I tugged some off, uncovering an ancient rocking horse, a cobwebbed dolls house, an ink-stained school desk, piles of books and boxes. There was a door. I opened it a crack, wide enough to see a dingy corridor and the top of a plain narrow staircase. No point in stepping out. I didn't want to be cornered on the stair by Oliver. There was no key this time, on either side of the lock.

Block it, said Adam.

I shut the door again and pulled boxes across it. They wouldn't keep him out for long, but it would have to do.

Was he still talking down there, or growing impatient with my silence? I could hear, faintly, a car revving up and driving away. Then another. He'd sent the staff away. Nothing to stop him now. I needed to get through that skylight fast. If he was going to kill me, I wanted it out in the open with just a chance that someone would see or hear.

Desk.

"Okay." I pulled the desk under the skylight and climbed up. Like the hatch in the linen cupboard, the catch was sealed solid with rust. I worked at it, till my fingers and palms were raw and bloody, and finally it shifted. The window swung open with a crash, but that was drowned out by a blast from below. Oliver had fired the shotgun at last.

The sound gave me the rush of adrenalin I needed to hoist myself up through the skylight. Onto a steep slate roof. I nearly went flying down it, but I managed to cling on. I shut the window, just as another shot boomed through the house. The door must be matchwood by now and he'd be realising what I'd done. I needed to concentrate on getting off this lethal roof. It ended about six feet directly below me, and I had no idea what was waiting at the bottom. A drop of at least two floors and it wouldn't be onto a feather mattress.

Some way to my left the roof spilled down further, over some single storey scullery or washhouse. If I could edge along to it, at least the drop wouldn't be so great. Not that I had much of a chance. I was probably going to break my neck, but at least Oliver would have to clear up the mess.

Gingerly, I inched across, one hand and foot, then the other, slide my backside along, nearly slipping twice. A bit more. A bit more. I was there, over the longer slope. Now I just had to work my way down.

I must have relaxed. Suddenly my grip went and I was slipping, slithering helplessly down the slates.

Panic took over and then, for a split second, I heard Adam say *bend and roll*, and I was seeing him again, before the parachute jump that was his birthday present, practicing his landing in our living room and nearly smashing the television. *Bend and roll, Nicki*, he said as I shot out into thin air, so, as my feet made contact with something solid, I bent my knees and rolled. And rolled and kept rolling, head over heels, as the ground gave way in front of me. Not level ground but a steep slope. Grass, which was good in theory. In practice, it could have been granite. Did I shriek aloud with pain? I was certainly screaming within as I came to a halt, winded, my shoulder on fire, my neck tingling, and my ankle in agony. I grabbed at it with numb fingers. Foot still attached, no jutting broken bone, but at the very least I had the mother of all sprains.

To hell with the pain. I couldn't stay there moaning. Struggling to recover my breath, I looked around and realised my luck. I'd missed paving slabs on one side and a stone wall with an urn on the other. Either one could have killed me. The garden was terraced in steps and I had rolled down a slope to a lower level. The lamps in the house, which cast pools of pale light across the lawns, left me in comparative darkness for now. Voices were shouting, somewhere in the house, but I couldn't tell if they were still breaking their way into the attic or were already racing down to search the garden. I crawled along in the shadows, or tried to. Every movement made me want to scream and lie still.

You can move, so move. Save your screams for later, said Adam.

"Fuck you," I said, and crawled on. On. On. Keep going. On a bit more. I raised my head. I was past the house. I could try to make it through the office courtyard, but it was lit up with floodlights. I'd be seen at once. No, I'd have to go around, crawling, nose to the ground, pain throbbing through me every inch of the way as I hugged the line of offices to my left until they turned a corner. I turned with them, dragging myself across a rough track, the one that led to the quarry. I remembered the padlocks on door and iron gate: no escape that way. I carried on, past the swimming pool, dim blue lights shimmering in ripples. What I would give, just then, to plunge in. Pain had become so pervasive it no longer had a particular focus; it was all through me. Grit bit into my knees, stinging nettles whipped my hands and cheeks, but finally I was past the last building.

A couple of hundred yards of gravel drive led to the gates. The raised voices were out now, behind the house, Oliver and Veronica calling to each other across the lawns, his voice calm and collected, hers angrier. If I could have done, I'd have taken the chance, while they were at the back, to race down the drive, but I could barely hobble. I was on the wrong side of the drive for the gate into the paddock that would lead eventually to Carregwen, and anyway, I'd never make it all that way. No, it had to be the gate. If I could just get out into the lane, there was a faint chance that someone would pass by and see me.

I'd keep behind the rhododendrons that bordered the drive. They'd conceal me most of the way. Gripping at their tangled boughs and leather leaves, I hauled myself along. Each time I stopped, ready to give up, Adam whispered *Weakling!* in my ear and I'd swear back, anger driving me on.

I was nearly at the end of the rhododendrons. Something was happening at the house. More lights were coming on. Security lights, and I still had fifty yards of open ground to cross before I reached the gates. Then I heard barking. Loud insistent barking. Christ, he was setting dogs on me. Shadows and rhododendrons wouldn't help me now. I broke cover and stumbled as fast as I could across the grass. The gates weren't difficult to find. Like the house, they were illuminated. It took me a moment to realise the light came from outside. From spotlights? Headlights? Something was parked out there. Had he called his men in to block my escape? What could I do?

The dogs were louder now, coming round from the back of the house. They must be on my trail. I'd rather face armed men than snarling dogs. I stumbled on.

And stopped, my mouth gaping, as a roar built up and the lights suddenly merged with the ironwork of the gates, blinding me. I couldn't grasp what was happening, but I heard a thunderous crash, metal screeching and rattling. The ground shook.

"Nicki! Come on! Keep going!"

Gareth? By some inexplicable miracle, Gareth Hughes was calling me.

I stumbled on, out of the dazzling light, and Gareth grabbed me, heaving me up into the cab of a tractor. From the deafening barking of the dogs, I knew they could be only yards behind. Gareth was behind me, pushing me on, kicking as a dog's jaws closed on his trouser leg. Fabric ripped. He was free, slamming the cab door shut as Willow grabbed me on the other side and pulled me out into the lane.

I was bundled into the back seat of a car that stood waiting, its doors open, engine revving.

"Get in quick!" shouted Gareth, pushing Willow in after me, before leaping into the front passenger seat, slamming doors and we were zooming off. I had a second to glance back and see the tractor, a true monster that had made mincemeat of the cast iron, jammed aslant across the gateway, blocking the entrance completely. It took another second for me to realise that I was squashed between my daughter and Helena Treece, both white-faced with horrified shock, and the driver, changing through the gears like a formula one racer, regardless of the tight turns of Bethel Lane, was Alex Wyatt.

I didn't understand any of it. I was free from Cwrt y Frân, but it had happened so fast in the end that I couldn't get my head around it. All I could say was "I thought I was going to die."

"We thought you were going to die!" Willow screamed, before bursting into tears.

I had almost been reconciled to my death – and then there was a way out, and then I was out. It was too much to cope with. My brain reverted to the pain that was engulfing me. "I'm going to be sick."

"Here." Helena offered me a handkerchief and I promptly soiled it.

"Sorry."

"Not to worry." She wound down the window and tossed the handkerchief out.

I wiped my mouth, my teeth chattering. "Thank God you came. Why did you?"

Willow had conquered her tears but not her anger. "Because you were there and he was going to kill you!"

"He would have, too." I couldn't stop myself shaking. "He killed Gaynor."

There was a whimper from Alex and the car slowed a little.

"We know," said Gareth, through his teeth.

"Yes, but he admitted it!"

"Yes. The bastard!" The words were sticking in Helena's throat. She stared out into the darkness, but her hand gripped mine, fiercely.

We were at the end of Bethel Lane and Alex swung out onto the creek road without pausing to see if anything was coming. Not that anything would be, except from Carregwen, the only house further along it.

"Phone the police," I said. "My phone's dead."

"We know," said Gareth. "Don't worry, my mother's called them."

"So did I," said Helena.

"And me," said Willow.

"At least he's blocked in; he won't be able to drive off before they get here," said Gareth, as we hurtled wildly onwards, Alex driving like a maniac now.

No, not a maniac. Like a grieving lover. His father was the maniac, and ice cold with it. I thought of Oliver coolly deciding to kill me, just as he had coolly decided to kill Gaynor and now that plan was foiled, he would simply fall back on the alternative. "You didn't need to block the gates. He won't be driving anywhere. If the police arrive, they'll find him sitting at home, sipping a brandy and expressing complete bewilderment at all the fuss. He'll talk his way out of it, and they'll believe him, because he's Oliver Wyatt. I don't have a scrap of evidence to prove he admitted to anything."

There was a moment of silence as if they all drew breath, then Gareth held up his phone. "But I do."

"What?"

Willow hugged my arm as we swung through the narrow lanes of Tregelli. "I phoned you, Mum, and you didn't switch off. I could hear you, and him. It was all muffled, but I could hear you. All of it until your phone died. Enough to hear him talk about killing Gaynor. Gareth recorded it. We drove up to Cwrt and we couldn't get in, so Gareth drove on to the farm and got a tractor to break the gates down. We've got the recording, Mum. It's enough, isn't it?"

"It's fucking well enough!" said Alex, screeching to a halt in the harbourside carpark, narrowly missing several huddles of people gathered in anticipation of God knows what. Word had evidently spread fast. Alex jerked on the handbrake, then leaned forward over the steering wheel, shaking with sobs. His mother reached forward to stroke his neck.

"My fault," she said, bitterly. "I should have made it clear what Oliver was, years ago. Fabia, wretched woman, is many things, but it's Oliver who's the psychopath."

"He even boasts about it."

"Yes, we heard him. A man without conscience, goes for whatever he wants, like a shark, utterly ruthless. Dear God, and to think I found that exciting once!"

"Let's see how exciting he finds what's coming to him," said Gareth. He jumped out as a gang broke away from one of the huddles and headed for us. Siân, blazing like a fury ready for battle, with Rhys in tow, and Harry, glowering like Judgement day.

11

Willow was out, Alex was out. I wasn't going to be left nursing my wounds. I grabbed Helena as she was about to follow them. "Can you help me?"

"Are you sure? Better stay put and wait for the ambulance. One's on its way."

"No! Later, maybe, but I need to know what's happening."

With her help, and an arm from Willow, I eased myself out. Siân was immediately on me, swamping me with a hug that set me screaming.

"My God, girl, what's he done to you?"

"It's what I did, jumping off a roof. I think I've broken something. But I'm alive. I wasn't expecting to be an hour ago, but I am alive! Dear God, I survived!"

"Yes. Yes!" said Siân, spitting with rage. "Not like my Gaynor!"

"No. Oh Siân, I'm so sorry."

"I always knew it, but now he's said it. We've got the bastard now."

"Yes, we've got him." I glanced round at my rescuers. Willow was standing, hands over her mouth, breathing deeply. Helena was leaning on the car, head in her hands. Alex was thumbing his phone. He raised it to his ear.

"You bastard! You utter fucking bastard! You killed Gaynor! I know you did! It's all recorded, every word, and when the police…"

I grabbed at the phone, knocking it away. "No! Don't tell him!"

He stared at me, too wrapped up in his grief and anger to understand what I was saying.

"He didn't know there was a recording. He'd have stayed there, waiting. But now…"

"He can't drive away," said Gareth.

Helena had raised herself, understanding the implication. "The launch! He'll take the launch."

Alex howled.

Distantly, very distantly, sirens blasted, somewhere inland. Wherever the police were coming from, they were still a long way off, negotiating the single lane roads.

"He'll be halfway to Ireland before they get here," I said.

"And not even breaking sweat," said Helena. "Oliver doesn't panic, he just makes instant decisions and acts. He'll be gathering up everything he needs to keep going somewhere outside the reach of British law, and then he'll head straight for the boat."

"Fabia, though – he can't just whisk her away in her nightgown."

"He won't give a damn about Fabia. She's just his court fool. No, he'll go alone, unhampered."

"Bugger that, he won't get away if I can stop him," said Harry, punching the air as he strode to the quay where the Lotte Lenya was moored. He jumped in, Gareth behind him. Before I could prevent her, Willow had followed, then Alex.

"Wait, Willow, you can't go."

"Yes I can."

"Then I'm coming with you."

"No, Mum... oh, you can't, no wait!"

I'd limped after them and was determined to climb down. "I'm not letting my daughter go chasing off after a madman." They had no option but to help me into the boat. I couldn't go back up if I wanted to, because Siân was clambering down behind me.

"I want to see that bastard brought down. Come on, Rhys!"

Then her younger son was jumping in too. Harry already had the engine running.

Helena was left standing on the quay, busy on her phone, probably calling the police again. She waved us on. Gareth had cast off and the Lotte Lenya was chugging forward into the darkness of the harbour.

I looked back to see the quay thronging with people, watching our departure. It must have been the entire population of Tregelli, come to witness the drama. A drama in which I could only play witness too. I clung to my hard seat, while the boat bounced out onto the dark churning waves, shaking my already agonised limbs.

Rhys was speaking to his mother. I might not understand the language, but I could interpret his distress and bewilderment, choked with tears.

"God knows," said Siân.

"I'm so sorry, Rhys," I said.

He blinked hard at me. "Will we get him?"

"Yes!" said Siân, snorting.

"I hope so," I said. I looked at Willow up at the front of the boat with Gareth.

"Willow!" I called, wanting her back with me, safe and sound, but she wasn't listening, or the wind carried my voice away. I looked at Alex, standing by the wheelhouse, staring out into the darkness ahead, where the boat's lights caught the spray and the surge of the ink-dark water. He had his mother back but was that enough to compensate for the damage his father had wrought?

Siân had moved to stand with Harry at the wheel, straining at the leash. If we found Oliver long gone when we reached the cove, I didn't like to think how she would react. She was an unexploded bomb with a primed fuse. The shore was a black mass rearing up against a dark sky. Pendiawel? The old legend had it wrong. It wasn't here that the Devil came ashore, it was at an inlet further along the coast.

Alex suddenly slammed his fist against the wheelhouse. "This is stupid! We'll never catch him. How fast does this thing go?"

Harry's shoulders rose in a shrug as he concentrated on the seas ahead. "Ten knots if I'm lucky."

"Our launch can do fifty."

"If he gets out of the cove. Let's see." The Lotte Lenya was slowing dramatically.

Gareth, leaning out over the prow, said "Kill the lights."

The glow of the navigation lights was snuffed out. The darkness around us began to give way to a monochrome scene, details picked out in varying shades of grey. There was a moon behind us, somewhere between drifting clouds, and its light caught the white foam on rocks at the mouth of a narrow inlet. I could make it out distinctly now. I couldn't see the quay under the overhanging cliff, but there was a dim golden glow deep in the darkness. Light on the steps in the tunnel. We bobbed up on a strong wave surging into the cove, saw the spray rise on the rocks as it hit and then, for a second, the faintest gleam of metal, catching the light from the tunnel, as the launch rose.

"It's still there!" hissed Alex. "Let's go in, ram it, before he can get going."

"Sorry, lad, but I'm not risking the Lotte Lenya in there, not in the dark, between those rocks."

We had drifted across the entrance of the inlet, nose in, an irritation perhaps, but not close enough to block Oliver's exit like the tractor at the gates. Our engine was virtually silent. Suddenly the light from the tunnel wavered, flickered, danced as the gate at its base was opened. It split in two. A torch was casting a moving circle of bright light on the concrete of the quay. Then the beam moved onto the launch. Something was being dropped into it, then another. Helena had been right. Oliver had coolly packed what he needed.

The torch beam flicked up suddenly as the sound of sirens blasted somewhere in the dark, echoing out to sea, impossible to place, but much closer than they had been before. At the gates of Cwrt y Frân maybe.

The torch beam lowered back to the launch, without any sign of panic. A cover was being neatly folded back, a grey ghost flapping in the dark.

"I've got to put the lights on or he'll be ramming us," said Harry, reaching for switches and we were suddenly imprisoned again in our own bubble of red, green and white light.

"Give him the spotlight then!" yelled Gareth from the prow.

"All right, all right."

A blaze of white light shot forward into the narrow cove, pinpointing Oliver in the launch as it bobbed in its moorings. Another figure, Veronica Erving, was struggling out from the steps, laden with luggage. She dropped it in alarm as the light caught her, raising her arm to shield her eyes, then stepped back into the mouth of the tunnel. Oliver straightened from his preparations to look our way. Still not a hint of panic. He merely reached down and casually raised something long and thin.

"The shotgun!" I said.

"We're too far out for a shotgun," said Harry, just as a shot rang out and Alex shouted "No, it's his…!"

"Rifle," he added, as Gareth sprang back, wringing his hand, gleaming red.

"Get down!" ordered Harry, roaring over the screams and pushing his sister down as she tried to rush forward.

Siân was snarling, "Let me get the bastard! Gareth, ti wedi brifo?"

"Fi'n iawn, Mam. Just a graze."

At the sound of the shot I'd lunged for Rhys, ignoring the shooting pain of movement, and pulled him down beside me. A second shot cracked and so did the spotlight, instantly killed.

A moment later, as we crouched low in terror, we heard the launch start up.

We heard Erving scream, "Wait! Oliver, wait!" Another scream and a splash.

"I've got another light," said Harry, swearing softly as he searched.

Gareth called, "Rhys, the flares."

Rhys sprang up, pushing me aside to get at a locker behind me. He wrestled a cannister open, grabbed a couple of yellow tubes, and chucked one to his brother.

Gareth's bloody hand snatched, missed, but Willow caught it before it rolled away and passed it to him. "Willow, get down!" I shouted, but she waved me quiet, then held Gareth's injured hand as he groped with the mechanism.

Harry had produced another light from somewhere. Its beam caught Erving, floundering in the water, grabbing at the rungs on the quay. Harry turned the beam to catch the launch as it glided towards the mouth of the inlet. Oliver was standing nonchalantly at the wheel, clearly recognisable now. He might have been planning an afternoon excursion.

"Get down!" I shouted again, but Oliver wasn't going to waste bullets on us. He was so confident he didn't even bother to look our way as Harry kicked our engine back to life and tried to head him off.

Alex leaned over the side and yelled "You bastard, Dad! I loved Gaynor! You killed our baby! I hope you burn in Hell!"

That made Oliver look our way at last, his jaw set. "You were always too soft, Alex," he called, his voice acid with contempt.

Then Alex's curse came true. Gareth fired the flare and balls of light shot across the waves into the launch, blazing like fireworks. Something must have caught because I saw sparks and flames leap up. I held my breath, waiting for fuel tanks to explode. They didn't. Instead, far out across the sea, I heard a growl, a pulse, a thud thud thud building up, coming closer. Lights in the sky.

I sat up to see better. In the launch Oliver was beating at the flames and they'd began to die down. Did it matter? He might outrun the Lotte Lenya but could he outrun a police helicopter? It was over, surely.

Suddenly the fire on the launch found new life. It went up like a torch, and the torch was Oliver. Flames were licking at his clothing. Even now, he didn't panic. He looked full at us for a split second, his lips set in a contemptuous smile, then he tipped himself backwards, into the sea. The launch, still burning, glided on without him.

"Where is he?"

"Is he dead?"

"No, the bastard's going to swim to shore."

"Don't let him get away!"

"He can't swim, he was burning."

Everyone was shouting at once, leaning out to peer into the waves.

"He won't swim away," I said, understanding him perfectly. "He'll drown himself, rather than lose. Always in command, to the end."

I could see Alex's fists clenching white. He knew I was right. Did he want his father to live or die? What a question for a boy to deal with.

No question for Siân, though. "Let him drown then! Let the crabs have him, like my Gaynor!"

"No!" I said. "Don't let him die. Don't let him choose his own fate. Find him. Save him. Force him to come to trial."

"I don't want a trial," said Siân. "I want justice for my girl. I want him dead, an eye for an eye."

"No, Siân. You want the truth. You want the world to know how your girl died, how she was the heroine, refusing to be afraid, how she stood up to him and wouldn't let him master her."

She faced me, snorting her fury, barely able to breathe, tears pouring down her cheeks. But her brother and Gareth had already taken action. It went against all a fisherman's instincts to let a man drown. Harry was edging the boat forward and Gareth, after a moment's hesitation, was standing by with a lifebelt, ready to throw.

The thudding of the helicopter was coming closer, deafening now, homing in on the bright lights of the drama. Helena would have told them exactly where to go.

I could see Willow shouting, even if I couldn't hear her. She was pointing to something in the water ahead. Gareth hurled the lifebelt, then jumped in after it.

"Willow, don't!" I screamed as she followed him. Too late. A school life-saving certificate was never intended for moments like this. I strained to see and there they were, caught in search lights, Gareth's and Willow's heads, arms waving out the waves, and a dark shape drooping between them. They had him.

But still, burned and half-drowned, Oliver Wyatt wasn't beaten. Suddenly there was a wild struggle, limbs thrashing, spray flying, and he was gone.

Willow was gone.

I screamed, throwing myself forward. Only Harry, grabbing me in a bear hug, stopped me hurtling over the side after my daughter.

"Willow! He's drowned my baby!"

"You can't do anything, girl!"

Siân was trying to hug me too, her face aghast. "Do something, Harry!"

Alex was poised on the gunwale, ready to dive in after them.

"Stop!" said Harry, pulling him back.

I saw Gareth's head, above the waves, his face brightly lit as he gulped a deep breath, then he was gone too. The helicopter was over us now, a loudspeaker booming at us, but I couldn't, wouldn't listen. My heart was pounding, my throat burning.

Then, in the white surging circle whipped up by the downrush of the whirling blades, a head popped up, then another and another.

Willow! Willow gasping, then laughing in triumph.

Gareth laughing with her.

Oliver, not laughing at all. For all his determination to be in charge, he had not succeeded in sinking like a stone. Oliver Wyatt was finished. Figures were dropping from the helicopter around him.

Harry let out a deep breath. "Right, let's bring our heroes in."

I wrapped my good arm around Willow as she clambered aboard. Teeth chattering, she smiled at me in triumph. We were both triumphant. We were survivors. We were undefeated. We were strong.

Of course we are, said Adam.

Dwed wrth mam i beidio becso. Fi'n iawn.

Printed in Great Britain
by Amazon